Julia's Violinist

Julia's Violinist

Anneli Purchase

ACQUILINE

Library and Archives Canada Cataloguing in Publication

Purchase, Anneli, 1947-

    Julia's violinist / Anneli Purchase.

ISBN 978-0-9878089-7-4 (pbk.)

    1. World War, 1939-1945--Czech Republic--
Sudetenland--Fiction.
I. Title

PS8631.U73J85 2013   C813'.6   C2013-900186-7

Violin in front cover photograph provided by
Scoggins & Scoggins Violin Shop, Inc.,
Salt Lake City, Utah

To my beloved sister Hanna,
who never had an unkind word for anyone
1934 - 2012

ACKNOWLEDGMENTS

The general conditions and events in Europe after WWI were described to me by my mother. My older sister Hanna filled in many of the gaps by dredging up what she could remember from those days long ago. I interviewed others who had experienced the years between the wars in Europe, usually elderly people with vivid memories, some of which they were happy to share, while others were too painful to speak of even 70 years later. I thank all of these people for helping me flesh out the background for this book.

My mother-in-law, Myrtle, my sister-in-law, Dawn, my sister Sonja, and my friends Ursula and Maggie have been very encouraging. Without their gentle nagging and harassment I might have given up on this novel. Thank you all.

My editor/designer and friend, Kathleen Price, and my critiquing/writing buddy and friend, Darlene Jones, have dedicated so much time and effort to this book that a mere thank you is not nearly enough for either of them.

In spite of having lost me to the computer, my husband, Gary, still encourages me to go on with my writing. For this I am truly grateful.

Map of western Czechoslovakia with borders as they were in 1945. At the end of World War II, three million Germans were living in Sudetenland, an area of 27,000 square kilometres.

TABLE OF CONTENTS

୧୨

PREFACE • 1

PART ONE
Julia • 3
Saaz/Neusattl, Czechoslovakia
Sternberg, Germany
1945 - 1946

PART TWO
Michael & Lukas • 59
Saaz/Neusattl, Czechoslovakia
1931 - 1932

PART THREE
Lukas • 137
Saaz, Czechoslovakia
Crimean Peninsula, Ukraine
1933 - 1944

PART FOUR
Karl • 169
Germany
1922 - 1946

PART FIVE
Canada • 261
1947 - 1973

PREFACE

སལ

The losers in a war are always deemed to have been wrong, evil aggressors, not worthy of a sympathetic ear. My mother was on the losing side during WWII. She told me many stories of her life in Saaz, now a part of the Czech Republic. She lost her home, her husband, and her way of life in the aftermath of war. Hearing the stories as a child, I didn't realize the enormity of the losses she suffered nor how widespread the atrocities were. Much later it became clear to me that these injustices were experienced by thousands of others like her, many of whom were not so fortunate, losing not only their homes, but also their families and their own lives. I wanted to tell a story that could easily have happened to any of my mother's fellow Sudetenlanders, a story of love, courage, and survival under the direst of circumstances.

When people of differing cultures are at war, they are capable of committing the most inhumane atrocities. This story does not attempt to take sides, to say that one was more vicious than the other. While there are many stories telling of the misdeeds of the German government and of Germans in general, this tells the story from the other side. I have tried to write it without prejudice.

Members of my family had mixed emotions about the writing of this book. Some were supportive, agreeing that the story needed to be told, while others were horrified, wondering why I would expose myself to the criticism that is sure to come. But I feel that this story is typical of so many that would otherwise never be revealed. For my mother, it had to be told.

On the cover image of this book lies a page taken from an old choirbook that my parents brought with them when they immigrated to Canada sixty years ago. When I was in my teens, my parents and I often gathered around the piano to sing as I played this song and several others from the songbook. That was a long time ago, but I can still hear their voices in my mind.

PART ONE

❦

Julia

Saaz, Czechoslovakia
Sternberg, Germany
1945-1946

1.

Men's voices, harsh and abrupt, sent a stab of fear through her. She peered cautiously up an alleyway towards the town square.

Julia knew she should keep moving, but her jangling nerves had immobilized her feet. *Oh, my God! It's Herr Keppler!* She stared, wide-eyed, as four uniformed men tied him to a lamppost and laughed at his terror. Their whips snapped and cracked in the air before slicing into his body. Julia pressed her hand over her mouth to stifle a shriek. She wanted to flee, and yet she knew she should help him. But what could she do? *Coward,* her inner voice hissed. *My girls,* she argued back. *I have to protect my girls.*

She covered her ears, but Herr Keppler's yelps of pain seared her heart. Frau Keppler dashed out into the street. In broken Czech, her hands pressed together as in prayer, she begged the men, "Please! For the love of God. Please let him go." A shot rang out. The woman lurched forward onto the cobblestones. Blood soaked her flowery apron.

In the alley, Julia gasped and shrank behind the corner of the building. She pressed her back against the brick wall, fingers splayed to hold herself steady. Her heart pounded and her legs shook uncontrollably. *We're next! Oh, dear God. My babies!*

A young man bolted across the far end of the side street. He had to be German. A Czech would have no need to look like a hunted animal. Slowly she realized the danger all around her. Things were much worse than she had imagined. She should have listened to Ingrid.

A few minutes earlier her sister-in-law had grabbed her arm. "No! Julia, don't." Ingrid's white face reflected the fear she felt. "What are you thinking? Those Czech ruffians don't need an excuse to grab you. They've been on a rampage for days. You'd think the war was still on."

Julia had seen how the stragglers from recently disbanded army factions, first the Russians and now the Czechs, roamed the streets at all hours, looking for anything to plunder. The rape and murder of women was everyday news; men were shot and hanged. It was as if, after centuries of evolution, the war had caused civilized ways to vanish overnight. But the war was over. Wasn't it? A month ago, already.

"I have to get some things from my house before it's too late. Watch the girls. I'll be as quick as I can." She had slipped out the door before Ingrid could stop her.

Again, sirens and loudspeakers blared through the streets of Saaz. "All German women and children report to the former SS barracks immediately. German homes are now the property of the Czech government." Julia felt as if she were sleepwalking through a nightmare. The crackling broadcast voice resumed issuing harsh commands. "All valuables, money, bankbooks, bonds, and jewellery are to be handed over to the Czech authorities at the barracks. Non-observance of this order will be punished by death."

Valuables? Did that mean all her precious mementos too? Hand them over? Death if she didn't? Only a week earlier, 5000 men had been driven out of town. Murdered, she'd heard. Yes, when the Czechs said "death to Germans," they meant it. *I just witnessed the proof!*

Julia kept to the side streets and walked at what she hoped was a normal pace. All the happy memories of her married life were linked to her house. She had to get the photo of her husband and his letters before they were lost forever to the mocking hands of strangers.

Weeks earlier, Ingrid had insisted Julia move into town. She, too, had lost her husband to the war. When her brother married Julia, the two women had formed a close bond. "It's too dangerous with all these madmen on the loose. A widow with two young daughters? A house on the edge of town? No. No. You have to come and stay with me."

Now Julia took a shortcut along the creek that flowed past her house. Her breath came in shallow gasps, stabbing needles in her lungs. Never before had she walked this path looking over her shoulder in fear. The war had, for the most part, bypassed the small town of Saaz. How strange to think that not so long ago she had herded ducks home on this same path. The little flock had foraged along the edge of the creek, but each evening they had always come home to the sound of her voice. It hardly seemed possible that life had once been that serene. The path still brought her home now, as it had the ducks, but the serenity was gone.

Distant shouts and rifle shots spurred her to fumble for the key in her pocket. With trembling hands she unlocked the heavy door and slipped into her house, unnoticed—she hoped. Former neighbours and friends might now be spies and informers in return for favours. These days it was best to trust no one.

She leaned against the locked door and surveyed the room. Her oak table and chairs reminded her of all the meals her family had eaten there. She struggled to concentrate. Besides the letters and the precious photo of her husband, what else should she take? In the linen closet, she found a sturdy pillowcase to use as a sack. The announcement had said to bring no more than twenty-five kilos of survival necessities. Extra clothes for the girls, soap, a few dishes maybe? It was so hard to choose. Food? But there was no food left here.

Julia spun around at the crashing sound in time to see the doorframe splinter. Two men in makeshift Czech uniforms kicked in the heavy door and barged into the house. Were they the ones who had whipped Herr Keppler? Her knees threatened to buckle.

"What are you doing here?" The men stepped towards her. "You were told to go to the barracks immediately."

Julia took a deep breath to calm herself. "I'm just doing as the announcement said, picking up the basic survival things." She tried her best to sound conciliatory. Her ability to speak Czech seemed to surprise them.

"That's good," the shorter of the two said. "We'll help you!" He strode to the open closet and yanked out stacks of neatly folded linens. "Maybe you have some money stashed away, huh?"

"Please. I have nothing. I'm a widow. I barely get by."

The man sneered at her. "Barely get by? Look at this closet full of linens. How many Czechs do you think have such nice things? German sow!" He tore at the tablecloths, sheets, and towels with angry jerks. A

piece of paper wafted gently down. Julia snatched at
it, but missed. As it settled on the floor, her husband's
handsome face looked up at her. She gasped as she
remembered taking this one special photo out of the
album and hiding it among the linens. There had been
so many break-ins and raids—houses ransacked for
valuables, but some treasures of only sentimental value
had been destroyed out of spite. She reached for the
photo, but a mud-caked boot stomped down on it almost
smashing her fingers. She recoiled. Her heart clenched
as the man ground his heel back and forth. She choked
back a sob. *No! No!*

"Widow, did you say? Good. He's one less German
then."

That was her only picture of him. Now all she had
left were his last precious words to her. She had hidden
the letters in her bedroom, but didn't dare try to get
them now. The brutes would take those too. *I'll have
nothing left of him. Nothing.* The man grabbed a white
damask tablecloth from the heap of linens on the floor,
propped one foot up on the upholstered chair, and
began to polish the top of his boot.

Julia's knees felt weak. She reached behind her for
support. The second Czech seemed only too willing to
help. He grasped her upper arms and pushed her down
onto the table. Its sharp edge cut into her lower back.
Gnarly fingers clawed into her hair and pulled her head
back so that her chin rose and she couldn't move for
the pain. He pressed himself onto her. His teeth bit into
her lips as he kissed her roughly. Julia could taste her
own blood. Her anger raged, but she was helpless to
fight back. When he reached under her dress and tore
away her underwear, she silently thanked God—if there

still was one up there—that she hadn't brought her daughters with her. The Czech's foul breath blew onto her face faster and faster. She choked back the urge to vomit.

Out of the corner of her eye, Julia saw the shorter Czech inspect the soles of his muddy boots. He chose a clean white sheet to wipe them and one last soft towel to shine the toes. Back and forth, back and forth, he buffed as he watched the pulsing action of Julia's assailant.

"Come on, Jurik. Finish up and let's get going. There's obviously not much here worth taking. We need to find another place with money or jewellery before the Russians come back and take it all."

The man buttoned his pants and gave Julia a shove. He stepped back and wiped his mouth with the back of his hand. "That's what you German sows are good for. Whores!" He sneered and showed a mouthful of bad teeth. With a backwards glance, he waggled his tongue at Julia, as his partner with the newly shined boots dragged him out of the house.

Julia slid, trembling, to the floor and sobbed. Moments later, she heard the sound of boots kicking at a neighbour's door. Her body tensed and she knew she could not waste another second. She scrambled to straighten her dress, grabbed a few things, including her husband's letters and his ruined photo, and hurried back to her daughters.

The moment Julia arrived, Ingrid pulled her in through the door and locked it behind her. "I heard a shot right after you left. I was frantic. I wanted to come after you, but the girls...."

"No, no! Just as well you stayed inside." The pillowcase, bulging with various items, clattered to the floor. Julia's eyes were pressed closed, but tears leaked out.

"Those bastards! Look at your poor lips," Ingrid hissed. "Did they...?

Julia trembled and nodded, her face wet with tears. "Where are the girls?" she whispered.

Ingrid pointed with her chin to the living room while she steered Julia towards the bathroom. She brought in a pitcher of water. "Here, clean yourself up quickly. I'll see to the girls." Julia, usually so strong, was falling apart. Ingrid knew she had no choice but to gather her strength and take charge.

"Sofie! Steffie! Come to Auntie Ingrid. I have to talk to you." The girls left their paper dolls on the floor and came into the kitchen. Julia's daughters, aged eleven and nine, were almost twins in appearance. Both had gray eyes with flecks of jade, braided dark brown hair, pale skin, and fine features. Their delicately drawn eyebrows formed worry furrows as the sisters approached their aunt. They reminded her so much of their father when he was little. *God rest his soul.* The girls looked fragile and innocent and far too young to face the brutality that had invaded their lives. Ingrid couldn't imagine what kind of god would unleash the monsters that now roamed the towns. Having no children of her own, she wanted to do whatever she could to protect her nieces.

"Yes, Auntie?" they said together.

"This is a very serious time for us all. I don't want to frighten you, but you heard the announcement that we all have to go to the barracks?"

"Ye-e-s ... but why?" Sofie asked. She was the older of the two and had to know there was no logical reason for civilians to go there.

"Listen. We may never be able to come back to our homes and so wherever we are, we must stay together. It's most important that you always do as you are told immediately and don't ask questions. Just do it. Do you understand?" The girls' faces reflected the worry and fear she had just instilled in them. Ingrid berated herself for sounding so harsh. She simply wasn't good at mothering. Her own chin began to quiver as she realized how tactless she'd been. She turned about looking for Julia, needing her to do this. But it wouldn't do to have the girls running to her now. No, she would have to do this herself. For their own good, the girls had to take her seriously. She put her hands on Sofie's shoulders and gave her a shake. "Do you understand?" Sofie nodded. Tears rolled down her cheeks. Steffie, too, cried and clung to Ingrid's leg. "Do you understand?"

"Yes, Auntie Ingrid," the girls said in little more than a whisper.

"Where's Mutti?" Steffie looked around the room anxiously.

"She's washing up."

At that moment, Julia appeared at the living room doorway. Both girls ran to their mother and clung to her.

Julia gritted her teeth against the pain as the girls hugged her. "Everything will be all right," she managed to say. Ingrid had never seen her sister-in-law so fragile.

"Yes." Ingrid prayed that her voice sounded stronger and more confident than she felt. "Everything will be all right. We're all together and we'll be fine."

Ingrid had seen the terror in the streets during the previous weeks as tension built between the Czech- and German-speaking populations of Saaz, a city in the border territory known as Sudetenland. It was a part of Austria-Hungary when Julia and Ingrid were born, but when WWI ended in 1918 everything changed for them. The region was given to the Czechs although it was home to over 3,000,000 German-speaking people who made up ninety percent of the area's population.

Schools and all government agencies that had until then been operated in the German language, were henceforth conducted in the Czech language under Czech laws. Little wonder, Ingrid thought, that we welcomed Hitler when he reclaimed it for us in 1938.

During the war, Julia and Ingrid had heard of terrible atrocities committed on Hitler's orders. Now that the Germans had lost, Ingrid's terror grew as she saw the violence increase every day—Czechs taking revenge for Nazi outrages on their civilians by killing, torturing, and expelling Germans.

She'd watched as all able-bodied German men were herded from their town of Saaz—most of them killed, she'd heard. Stories from some who had escaped told of terrible cruelty. Many of the men suffered for days, crowded into outbuildings in the heat, craving a sip of water or a breath of air, only to be taken out and shot. Others, ordered to fight each other, were shot if they didn't beat their fellow Germans hard enough. With most of the men gone, the women were now helpless.

The swelling and bruising on Julia's lips were already more pronounced. Her upper arms had turned a deep reddish-blue. Ingrid could imagine the scenario. She had seen women with bruises like these when they came to the pharmacy where she worked, asking for any medication that might act as a spermicide. She'd had little available to offer them. She had nothing to offer Julia now. She only hoped the children didn't notice the bruises and ask too many questions—and that Julia would be spared a pregnancy.

"Come now." Ingrid tried to rally everyone. "I put a few things together in a sack. Blankets, a bit of food, a tin cup, a pot. It's so hard to know what to take."

"I know. I went through the same thing at home." Julia's chin quivered again.

Ingrid gave Julia a quick squeeze on the shoulder. "Come. We'll watch out for each other."

Sofie's head tilted to the side as she looked at her mother and her aunt. Ingrid could almost see the questions forming on her tongue and spoke to distract her. "Girls, do you have the bundles that I made for you? We have to go now. It's safer to co-operate."

Ingrid took one last look around. Every picture and household item had a story that kept alive memories of her aged father who died last year and her husband who fell soon afterwards on the Russian front. Her brother, too, would never return from the war, leaving Julia a widow and their daughters without a father. Czechs or Russians would take over her house and wipe out the last traces of her family's life together. The same fate awaited Julia and thousands of others if the Czechs really did what they said they were going to do—expel the Germans and take possession of all their belongings.

The betrayal and treachery of the townspeople infuriated her. These were the same Czechs who were once her friends and customers. The same people who had borrowed a cup of sugar from her not so long ago.

The same ones who came to her at the pharmacy for advice. War made people do hateful things—people who knew right from wrong—and she had helped so many of them. *How dare they treat us like this? Barbarians!* A grunt of outrage escaped her.

"Why did you make that noise, Auntie Ingrid?" Steffie asked.

"What noise? Oh! That." She had forgotten that the girls were standing there waiting for her. "Are you ready then, Julia? Girls? Ready to go? Now remember, do not let go of our hands. Steffie, you go with your mother. Sofie, you take my hand. Julia, you and I can each manage a big bag. Girls, you each carry one of the smaller ones." Two women, two little girls. What chance did they have?

"We have to keep together." Julia was putting on a brave face, but Ingrid could almost smell her fear.

"That's right, Julia. Now don't you worry. We'll be fine if we stick together." *Dear God, if only I could believe my own words.*

2.

Heidi waded through the current of foot traffic and craned her neck for a glimpse of Julia among the hundreds of women and children flowing like a slow-moving river towards the barracks. Mothers clutched babies tightly and gripped toddlers by the hand. Except for the smallest children, every person lugged their allowed twenty-five kilos in a satchel, suitcase, or cloth bag. Their faces contorted in grief and bewilderment, some sobbed openly; many cried silently. Others walked as if in a trance. Tears blended with the cold drizzle that wet their cheeks and seeped into their clothes. Who knew what horrors they had witnessed in the last weeks? Who knew what ugliness lay ahead for them?

Only days before, Jan had said, "Heidi, you're going to hear terrible things about the Czechs."

"You mean it's true?" How did he know? Was he one of them? One of those bastards who were taking out their lust for revenge on innocent civilians?

"Yes, I'm afraid it is." He put his arms around her and held her close as her knees began to buckle. "Here. Sit down, sweetheart. I'm so sorry." He sat beside her and tried to take her hand, but Heidi pushed him away roughly.

Jan stared at her, his mouth open in surprise. "Heidi! You don't think I had anything to do with it?"

Heidi shrugged. "I don't know what to think."

"Look. I can understand them wanting revenge. You know as well as I do, Hitler was a bastard—the things he did to the Czech people."

"Yes, it was terrible for the Czechs, but still...." She clenched her fists. "This retaliation is madness. The war is supposed to be over. Surely things will get better now?"

"I wouldn't count on it. The hatred won't end that quickly," Jan said.

"I can't believe what's happening."

Jan opened his mouth, then hesitated. "To the devil! You're going to hear about it anyway." He let out a big sigh and looked at the ceiling as if searching for help from above.

"What?"

"Last week, when the Czech militia cleared the town of German men, they marched a few thousand of them to the barracks at Postelberg. They shot them, hanged them, beat them to death. Miroslav told me." Heidi clapped her hands over her ears and tried to get up. She couldn't listen to this. But Jan held her back. "Heidi, darling, you don't think I was part of this?"

"Did you stop it? Did you even try?"

Jan paled. "How can you say that? How can you think it?" he whispered. "I wanted to. You must know that. But what could I do? It would be suicide to try to interfere."

"Oh God, I'm sorry. I'm.... Oh Jan, it's so awful. The war was bad enough, but this? It's madness."

"It's only the beginning. It will get worse. I've heard that they plan to get rid of the women and children too."

"Oh, my God!" Heidi shrieked. "They're going to kill us? Can't you stop them?"

"No, no, no. Sh-h-h ... I'm sorry, Heidi." Jan hugged her and tried to calm her sobs. "I meant they are planning to send them away to Germany—well, across the new border." He stroked her hair. "Hush. No one's going to hurt you—or your family. But I'm glad your brothers took their families into Germany when they did. Your father will be all right. He's too old to be a threat. The old men and the very young boys are being spared; women and children sent away."

"My mother? My sisters? Their children? You can't mean it, Jan. It can't be true. It's too horrible to be true." She clung to him. "And what about us? Does that mean they will send me away from you? Oh, Jan! This can't be happening." She sobbed into her handkerchief.

"Don't worry. German women who are married to Czechs will be allowed to stay. And of course you will stay." Jan held Heidi by the shoulders and looked straight into her eyes. He took a deep breath. "Won't you?"

Heidi's face clouded. "Jan? How could you doubt it?" She threw her arms around him. "Of course I'm staying with you." She realized the depth of her love for Jan—to stay with him after all this. He was a Czech, but he was nothing like the crazed animals on this hate-fuelled rampage. She had to remind herself of that. He is a good man, she told herself. A good man. "But my family...." She broke down sobbing again.

Still threading her way through the masses trudging towards the barracks, Heidi searched for Julia's group.

There they were. Thank God! She pushed ahead faster, then thought better of it and slowed her pace. Czech militia, with eyes that seemed able to bore through walls, patrolled everywhere. Best not to attract their attention.

"Julia," she hissed softly. "Psst! Over here!" Although Julia spotted her and slowed down, it seemed an eternity before the distance between them closed. Heidi linked her sister's arm with her own, pulling it close towards her in a makeshift hug. Julia winced. "What's wrong?" Heidi looked at her face more closely, saw her bruised lips and blotched cheeks. "Good heavens! Julia! What happened to you?"

"Sh-h-h." Julia gave Heidi a signal with a quick shake of her head. "The children," she whispered. "I'm fine. Don't worry."

"Jesus!" Heidi muttered under her breath. Her own sister? God damn them! But what could she do? Damn them! What if she was making a mistake after all, staying behind? No. She and Jan had been friends since they were in their teens. She loved and trusted him completely. He was not like *those* Czechs.

Heidi squeezed Julia's hand. "I'll go back to Elisabeth's house and find her. Mother is there and I'm sure she must be terribly worried about having to leave Father. I'll bring them over this way if I can. It's best to stay together."

"That's what Ingrid said too."

"Walk as slowly as you dare so we can catch up to you." *Wait till I tell Jan what happened to Julia.* But even as she seethed with anger, and as angry as Jan would no doubt be, she knew it was not his fault and he was powerless to intervene. Even if he could, it would be dangerous for him to be seen sympathizing with "the enemy." The militia would be watching him. They would watch all Czechs married to German women.

Heidi! There you are." Elisabeth took her by the arm as she entered the house. "Mother won't come with me. She doesn't want to leave Father."

"You need to go with the girls, Katerina." Heidi's father put his arm around his wife. "You could be bludgeoned to death or shot if you disobey the order," he said. "And besides, Julia and the grandchildren need you."

"That's right." Heidi decided that she needed to be firm with her mother. "I've just seen Julia, Mother. She'll be looking for us to catch up to her. Here, let me take your bag." She would have to find a moment later on to prepare her mother for Julia's bruises, but right now, she had to get her moving.

"Where's your bag, Heidi?" Her mother looked towards the entrance for Heidi's pack.

In all the turmoil, Heidi had not dared tell her parents that she was staying. "I can't go with you." Heidi squeezed out the words. She felt dizzy and realized that she had been holding her breath. She gulped for air.

Three shocked faces stared at her in the silence of Elisabeth's living room. "What!?" Her mother grabbed at Heidi's arm. "What do you mean?" The clock ticked loudly. Their time together was running out, possibly forever.

"Heidi?" Her father's eyebrows furrowed. "What are you talking about? Of course you're coming with us."

"Well ... that is ... Jan told me German women who are married to Czechs are allowed to stay with their husbands. I can only go as far as the barracks gates."

"Heidi, you can't stay. You ... you just can't. You must come with us." Katerina pulled Heidi into an embrace. "Please, don't do this."

"I'm so sorry, Mother." Heidi felt her eyes filling with tears and blinked several times fighting for control. Her stomach lurched and burned with worry over the anguish she was causing her parents. She hadn't even thought about how she would deal with missing them herself.

"Are you sure you want to stay here with these animals, Heidi?" Thomas asked.

"No. I don't. But I love Jan. I can't leave him. He's not like the ones who are raping and killing and making trouble. He'll take care of me. I can't leave him. You understand, don't you?"

Heidi saw her own pain reflected in her father's eyes. It wasn't fair to have to choose like this. She felt as if her heart were being squeezed and bruised.

Thomas put his arms around her and patted her back. "Yes, I do understand. Jan is a good man. It's just that at times like this it's hard to remember the Czechs aren't all bad." He hugged her again tightly, then held her at arm's length to search her face. "You're sure?" Tears filled her father's pleading eyes and she thought her heart would break.

Heidi nodded. "I'm sure," she whispered.

She knew that if the situation had not been so urgent, her father would have argued more. Instead, he sighed. "I see you've made up your mind. Keep safe, my sweet."

His voice trembled and threatened to break. "I pray that when all this is over we can be together again."

Heidi pressed her lips together and nodded. She looked at the floor and quickly brushed the tears away. "Now, we have to hurry and catch up with Julia. You wait here, Father. I'll come right back afterwards." She knew that the only way she could regain control of her emotions and keep the pain at bay was through action. "The Czechs will probably gather up all the remaining men separately," she said. "When I come back I'll stay with you until then."

She turned to hug her sister. "Take care of yourself, Elisabeth. I pray that Andreas will find you after the troops are allowed to come home." Her tight throat closed and the words squeaked out. "I'll have to leave all of you at the gates so it's just as well we say goodbye now." Heidi took a deep breath. She picked up her mother's bag and took her gently by the arm. "Mother, remember you have to stay well so you can help look after Elisabeth and Julia and the children." She hugged her mother tightly and tried to choke back the pain of parting.

Oh, for the days of her childhood when it was her mother who reassured Heidi with hugs. If only they could all go back to a time before the war, before the hate, before the reprisals and atrocities. It was all too ugly to bear. She wanted her mother's hug to take the pain away.

Katerina's shoulders quaked, her face wet with tears. Thomas wrapped his arms around his wife. Heidi heard him whisper, "I'll find you, Katya. I promise." She'd never thought of her parents as old, but today they looked fragile and shrunken with fear and misery.

Her throat ached from trying not to cry. Seeing them look so vulnerable almost broke her resolve. Thomas's voice trembled when he spoke. "No matter what it takes, I'll find you. Don't worry about me. Just take care of yourself and our family."

"Now go," he said to his wife and daughters, "before the Czechs come to speed the stragglers on their way. They would relish that." He nudged Katerina and Elisabeth gently towards the door.

"I'll be back as soon as I can, Father." Heidi saw him turn his head quickly. He was not normally a man who showed so much emotion and he would not want to appear weak.

Minutes later, not far ahead of her, Heidi saw Julia looking back, searching the lines for them. When Heidi caught up to them, she chose to stay with her family until they neared the barracks and the long line of people slowed. Up ahead loomed the old army facilities looking barren and neglected. A sense of foreboding sent a shudder of goosebumps rippling over her skin. Guilt and shame over abandoning her mother and sisters to their fate gnawed at her conscience. She should be going with them. But that would mean leaving Jan behind forever and she simply couldn't do that. Julia no longer had a husband—a casualty of the war—and Elisabeth's husband was still a POW somewhere. Each of the sisters had been dealt serious blows, but Heidi was lucky. She had allied herself with what became the so-called enemy. Whether out of guilt, or love, or both, she offered what little consolation she could give. "If they move you from the barracks, I'll try to find out where they're taking you and help you any way I can.

Take care. I love you all." She choked out the last words and fled. She didn't dare look back.

The brooding sky that had been dropping sprinkles of rain for most of the morning opened up at last, soaking streets already muddy from the previous night's rain. The downpour seemed to be the crowning touch from above to ensure their misery.

Julia watched with envy as her sister disappeared into the crowd. Heidi was lucky. She had her husband. She'd keep her home. "Oh, God," Julia moaned. "To have my husband back. What I wouldn't give for that." She closed her eyes and willed the past to be real and with them still. They had been in their prime, happily married, working together to build a good life for their children. Then war came and everything changed. She missed his laughing face, his strong arms around her—missed him terribly. And now, as if losing him wasn't enough, she was to lose her home and all her belongings too. At least she had her daughters. Panic jolted through her body. Her daughters? Where were they? She gasped with relief when she realized they were holding onto her coat. She had to keep close watch over them. She couldn't bear it if something happened to them. She dared not let down her guard.

"Mutti, when will we be there?" Steffie asked.

"Soon, Steffie. Just a little bit farther."

"But that's what you said the last time I asked you."

"Which was about two minutes ago." Her nerves were stretched to the limit and she was exhausted, but it wasn't fair to be impatient with her daughters. Julia took a breath and tried to smooth over the rebuke.

"Look, over there, you can see it. That big building. That's where we're going."

"You mean the one with all those tiny little windows? Are we going to live there?"

"For a while." Julia shuddered involuntarily.

"How long?"

"I don't know how long. We'll take it one day at a time. Try not to drag the pillowcase in the mud, sweetie. I know you're tired, but we're almost there."

3.

Czech officials at the gate collected their house keys and bankbooks. Boxes overflowed with confiscated valuables.

Julia leaned over to whisper to Ingrid, "I'm so glad I burned his letters before we left your house."

"Oh, my God, yes! Can you imagine the fun they would have reading them if you'd had to hand them over? It was the only thing you could do."

Defeated and demoralized, Julia and her family allowed themselves to be nudged and shoved along towards the old army barracks. Many of the women in the crowd looked familiar. Frau Altmann stood nearby with her younger sons, Theo and Herbert.

"Ingrid? Doesn't Frau Altmann have another son?"

"Yes, Johann. But I don't see him." Ingrid hesitated and then gasped. "Oh, Lord. He would have been about fifteen. He must have been rounded up last week in that horrible massacre."

Julia's grip on Steffie's hand tightened. No wonder Frau Altmann looked so haggard. She seemed years older than the last time she'd seen her, only a couple of weeks ago. Julia wondered about herself. What did other people think when they saw her? Did she too look that much worse, especially after the outrage she'd been forced to endure that morning?

She caught a glimpse of Frau Gebhart's stress-lined face. The woman clutched her wailing newborn close to her body. The toddler at her side laboured to drag a satchel. Julia glanced down at Sofie and Steffie, each putting on a brave face, carrying their bags without complaint.

A pang of fear for them shot through her. God only knew what awaited them. Her daughters must also be worried, being too young to understand the reasons for these strange events. "You're doing a great job, girls. I'm so proud of you. We'll be able to rest soon."

Inside the fenced compound, several huge buildings loomed over either side of the parade grounds. The German army had at one time organized and trained at this facility. Thousands of women and children now crowded the large barren rooms. Outbuildings, garages, and stables were crammed with people. All around her, Julia saw faces reflecting fear and despair.

"Where are we all going to sleep?" Elisabeth surveyed their assigned room. "No beds, no tables, no chairs. Nothing but an empty hall."

"Far from empty, Elisabeth. There must be more than a hundred people in this room alone." Julia jostled her way through the crowd, finally claiming a small space in the far corner.

"Let's get these wet coats off," Katerina said, "or we'll all catch colds." Julia helped her shake them out.

"I guess we'll just lie down on the floor to rest?" Ingrid searched Julia's face for agreement. "I see other people doing that. For the night we can cover up with the two blankets we brought and use the driest coats as extra blankets if we need to."

Julia looked at the floorboards smeared with the muck from hundreds of shoes. *Good God! Lie down in that?* "We'll have to use one of the blankets to lie on. It's unthinkable to lie down in this filth.

"I wonder what we should do about water. And a toilet?" she mumbled to no one in particular. As the initial shock of the day's events wore off, the wretchedness of the new reality settled in.

As if reading her thoughts, loudspeakers boomed out instructions and little by little their questions were answered, although not necessarily in ways that made them happy. "Water is available from the pump in the courtyard and will be rationed. Two latrines are located at the end of the parade ground. You will be assigned to work parties to dig more latrines in the morning. No food will be provided until three days from today at the earliest."

"I'll take the big pot and go for water." Julia rummaged in the pillowcase for it. "Keep an eye on the girls."

The former parade ground was a sea of mud softened by the rain and worked over by the passage of hundreds of feet sucking in and out of the muck. Julia steeled herself against the idea of being up to her ankles in grime. The length of the water lineup added to her despair. As she waited, the misty air gnawed at her throat. She had noticed earlier in the day that it hurt to swallow. She couldn't get sick now. Not with everyone depending on her.

An hour later she reached the front of the line. It took only seconds to fill the pot. She worked her way back through the masses and the mud, wincing at every bump that caused even a drop of the precious water to slop out.

Inside the barracks each room she passed was tightly packed with women and children. Entering the second-floor room where her family awaited her, she wrinkled her nose at the warm, sour stench of anxious perspiration.

Many of the women lay on the floor clasping their children to them. Others sat up as if anticipating the signal to return home. Babies cried piteously. How many of them would die without the necessities? Julia stepped over and around women weeping with exhaustion and dread. The same emotions crowded her own soul, but she fought them back whenever they rose in her like waves of nausea. She concentrated on the task of the moment. It was too overwhelming to think about tomorrow, or next week, or next month.

She set the pot down on the floor by her family. "Let's be careful not to spill any. Ingrid, did you say you packed a cup? We'll dip it into the pot and each person can have a sip to start with. Then if anyone needs more we can have a second sip and so on."

As she passed the cup to her mother, Julia noticed her red, puffy eyes and the tear tracks on her cheeks. "What's happened, Mother?" Julia whispered.

"Worried about your father. After last week's slaughter of so many of our men—what's to become of us all? What if...?" Katerina's brow furrowed and her lower lip trembled.

"Sh-sh-sh-sh, Mother." Julia spoke to her mother quietly not to upset the children. "You have to believe that he'll be fine. Heidi said she would stay with him. I'm sure she'll do her best to see that he's not mistreated. Now, don't cry. It will all work out. You'll see." Her mother pressed her lips together tightly, squeezed her eyes shut, and bobbed her head three quick little nods. Julia hoped she was right. She had no idea how she could take back her words or bear her mother's heartbreak if she was wrong.

"Mutti, I have to go peepee," Steffie said.

"Me too," Sofie added.

The adults looked at each other and shook their heads slightly. Katerina took a deep breath and seemed to be gathering control of her emotions. "I brought another pot," she said. "Why don't we call this the chamber pot and then we can take it outside in the morning?"

"Good idea, Mother." Julia was relieved to see her mother take the initiative and keep busy. It would help to keep her focused.

Elisabeth and Ingrid agreed. "We'll sit with our backs turned and block the view so each person can have a little bit of privacy. And after that we can all try to get some sleep."

It was June, but they shivered in their damp clothes as evening approached. Meager light filtered in through the small grimy windows of the outside wall. The family arranged the water pot, the chamber pot, and their few belongings while they could still see. Then they snuggled together for warmth.

When Julia let out a long sigh, Elisabeth whispered, "I know. It's hard to believe this is really happening."

"I was just thinking how our world has turned completely upside down." Julia kept her voice low. She heard the soft breathing of her children and wished they could sleep through all the hardships that were sure to come. "Remember the lovely Sundays we used to have? Soccer games and then a big dinner of potato dumplings and pork?"

"And what a table we prepared, with all of you children at home," Katerina added. "So much work. So much cooking. So many dishes to wash." She clicked her tongue. "But you girls always helped."

"I didn't think about it back then, but it was fun to be together, everyone pitching in," Elisabeth said.

Ingrid, not being part of the immediate Sommer family, had only listened, but now she added her thoughts. "Our family was much smaller, but it must have been warm and cozy to have so many brothers and sisters."

"Ten of us," Julia said. "Three boys and seven girls."

"Good thing it wasn't the other way around," Katerina added. "At least I had some help in the kitchen."

"The boys were good for entertaining us later on." Julia's voice became wistful. "Wouldn't it be nice to have Roland playing his violin for us tonight?"

"Yes, and Konnie playing his trumpet and Walter beating on that little drum he made himself," said Elisabeth.

The women sighed softly almost in unison. "Those days are gone." Katerina sniffed quietly.

Julia placed a gentle hand on her mother's shoulder. "But we were so lucky to have had a happy home. Maybe someday, when this is all over, we'll be happy again."

Tired as she was, Julia couldn't sleep. The whole building was a mass of misery. Groans and wails and sobs and shouts reached her ears no matter how she tried to cover her head to drown them out. With the deepening darkness, the noises became muted as exhaustion and sleep took over. In spite of the hard floor, Julia too drifted off to sleep at last.

She had no idea how long she had been asleep when her eyes flashed open. She strained her ears. Male voices speaking Czech, heavy boots tramping across the wooden floors. Was it real or just an echo of her experience at her house this morning? There it was again, the unmistakable sound of boots in the downstairs hallway. Terror gripped her. Every muscle in her body tightened. She nudged Elisabeth and Ingrid and whispered to them. "Don't make any noise, but do you hear what I hear?" They listened intently as the footsteps faded towards the farther end of the barracks.

Moments later they shrank together at the sound of fearful shrieks. Men shouted orders in Czech. Women screamed and cried out. Smacks, thuds, and slaps. Julia felt an icy lump of fear in the pit of her stomach. Her mother was lying very still, but even in the darkness, Julia could tell from her shallow, quiet breathing that she was awake. She was glad Sofie and Steffie did not awaken. The orgy of violence downstairs seemed to go on forever. Would it never stop? At last the loudest noises faded. Her family had escaped tonight. Julia wondered how long their luck would hold.

For two weeks the nightly rapes by Czech militia and their friends continued. Maybe God would consider Jurik's assault on her as payment for her whole family and they would be spared. She thought of her older sister Susanna who was not so lucky.

A month earlier, when Russian tanks had rolled into Saaz, her sister had told Julia of her fears. A Czech neighbour had told Susanna with a satisfied smile, "The Russians are raping any German women they can find, especially ones like you who have husbands and sons who fought against them in the war."

Although she was older than Julia by ten years, Susanna was much more timid in nature. After her husband and oldest son had fallen in the war, she lost courage altogether. When news of the first atrocities reached Susanna, she robbed the Russians of their pleasure. Like hundreds of other local women, she hanged herself instead, leaving her young teenage son under the care of her husband's family. Julia hadn't followed her sister's example. It wasn't her nature to give up without a fight. And how could she expect her little girls to face these brutalities without her protection? At thirteen Susanna's remaining son was not as fragile as Julia's girls. But Sofie and Steffie were still very young, and girls were more vulnerable to harm. No, she had no choice but to face whatever came along and fight to keep her children safe.

In the water lineup, Frau Faber, a former neighbour, stood next to her. She reached for Julia. "Ach, Julia. Isn't it terrible?" The elderly woman's arms were little more than sticks. Julia looked at her own finely toned forearm as Frau Faber's claw-like hand gripped it. "Are you all right? How is it in your barracks at night?"

"I hear noises downstairs. People are getting hurt."

"In our barracks, it's terrifying." Frau Faber shook her head as if in disbelief. "The Czechs shine flashlights into the room and pull the women up from their sleeping places. 'You, you, you, and you,' they say." Her voice dropped to a whisper as two guards strolled past and her claw tightened on Julia's arm. "And the women, mostly the young ones, have to go with them. Many of them are raped right there on the spot. Maybe you heard the screams."

"Yes. We heard."

"On the first night some of them tried to resist, but now they go along and hope to survive it. Some don't come back."

"I'm sure it will all be over soon and everything will go back to normal." Julia didn't believe her own words, but it helped—a little—to pretend.

"Believe me, Julia; we saw it with our own eyes. Some of the poor young girls were raped over and over right in front of us and there was nothing we could do."

Julia shuddered. "I believe you, Frau Faber. I do." *Shut up! Shut up! Shut up!* If only she could make Frau Faber stop talking. Jurik's bad teeth and waggling tongue flashed through her mind again. She felt nauseated, the taste of his bad breath lingering in her mouth. "Our barracks are near the end of the row and we're upstairs, so I hope we'll be all right. But will it ever end?" And would Frau Faber's blathering ever end? Julia clenched her teeth, resisted clamping her hands over her ears, and prayed they would get to the front of the line so she could get her water and escape.

"Well, it may end soon. I've heard that forced labour groups have been sent out to different locations, so maybe it won't be too much longer in this hell. Julia, are you all right? You look awful."

"Thanks, Frau Faber. I guess none of us is looking her best today."

"Please God, we'll look back on this someday and wonder how we survived," Frau Faber said. "But seriously, Julia. Are you sick? Your face is flushed and yet your arms have goosebumps."

"I have a sore throat that should have been better by now, but you know it's not like we have clean beds and decent food and water to help us get better. My Sofie has it too and I'm really worried about her."

Frau Faber let out a snort of disgust. "That thin slop they bring in is hardly fit to feed a pig and not enough to keep a sparrow alive. I can only pray that we are all assigned a decent workplace. Ah, here we are, almost at the front of the line now. You take care of yourself, Julia dear."

"Good luck to you too, Frau Faber." *Thank God that's over. I thought she'd never shut up.*

When Julia returned with her pot of water, she told her mother, Elisabeth, and Ingrid some of her conversation with Frau Faber.

"I think I should sleep at the front of our group," Katerina said, "and you girls and the little ones lie behind me. If any of those animals come up here at night, all they will see is an old woman and a bunch of bodies with their coats pulled up over their heads."

"Thanks, Mother. It may help a bit, but who knows?" It was brave of her mother to make the offer, but from what she'd heard, the nightly visitors didn't care if their victims were young or old. They'd rape anyone. Julia knew it was all about revenge.

Her sore throat, fever, and chills continued for ten days. Sofie was over her sore throat sooner. Weakened by her illness, Julia allowed herself to be persuaded to relax and let Elisabeth and Ingrid stand in the water line and empty the chamber pot for the family. She had done almost everything so far. Yes, she would take a rest. Just for a little while.

Weeks went by. Conditions were still grim but the women had gradually been able to clean the floors by sharing a broom they had scrounged. Personal hygiene was an ongoing challenge because of the water rationing. They learned to use every drop wisely.

They worked at keeping their spirits up with games and stories. Steffie and Sofie scratched squares on a scrap of wood and used light and dark pebbles for playing checkers.

"Mutti?" Steffie looked up after losing another game of checkers. "Tell us the story about when you went swimming."

"You want to hear that story again?"

"Yes. It's scary," Steffie said, "but I like it."

"All right. Let's see. I was about your age, Steffie—nine years old. The Eger River went by not too far from our house in Neusattl where I lived with your uncles and aunts and Oma and Opa."

Steffie looked over at Katerina. "That's you. Right, Oma?"

Katerina nodded and smiled. "And it's a good thing I didn't know what was going on in that river."

"Your Aunt Heidi, Aunt Brigitte, and Uncle Konnie and I went to the river to dip our feet."

"But you dipped more than your feet, right?" Steffie giggled and glanced at her grandmother who winked back at her.

Julia nodded. "You remember I told you how Uncle Roland had tied a big rope between two trees on either side of the river."

"Because he was older and bigger and could walk across to the other side."

"That's right. So he made a sort of rope bridge for us to hold onto when we were in the water because most of us couldn't swim. Still can't," she added. "On that day it was hot, but it was also early in the summer and the snow had melted from the hills and made the river high and fast."

"How high?"

"Oh, it was up to here." Julia put a hand to the bottom of Steffie's ribcage.

"That's deep."

"When you can't swim and the river is rushing past very quickly, it's deep," Julia agreed.

"And you followed Auntie Brigitte and Uncle Konnie."

"Yes, I wanted to go where they were going, so I walked into the river step by step holding onto the rope with both hands. The water was lovely and cool and I felt very grown up because I was able to go so deep. With the rope I felt safe."

"But something happened, right?"

"Something happened, all right. I slipped on one of the rocks on the river bottom. I held the rope tightly but my feet went out from under me."

"Did you scream?"

"I think they heard me all the way to Saaz."

Steffie pressed her hands together and laughed. "Did your head go under?"

"Yes, it did, just for a second. But the problem was that I couldn't stand up because the river was flowing from my head to my feet and it kept lifting me up. It was like lying in a bed made of water, holding onto the headboard."

"What did you do?"

"Screamed. And screamed. And screamed some more."

Steffie put her hands over her ears as if hearing her mother's cries. "Then Uncle Konnie came."

"He tried to save me, but it wasn't so easy for him."

"Why not? He was bigger than you."

"Yes, but I was so terrified. I wouldn't let go of the rope. He had to take the rope in one hand while he was still holding me, and lift it over my head. Then I could hold the rope in front of me and try to stand up. But my legs were shaking so much I could hardly walk."

"Uncle Konnie held you up and brought you to dry land."

"All the way back to the riverbank, I said, with my teeth chattering, 'D-d-don't let me g-g-go, K-k-k-konnie.'"

Steffie laughed. "You're so funny when you talk like that, Mutti." She hugged her mother. "I'm really glad Uncle Konnie saved you."

"You wouldn't be here if he hadn't." Julia smiled as she watched the girls' reactions. They never tired of hearing her stories. If it helped to pass the time, and it made them feel close, she would think of all sorts of little stories and memories to keep them entertained. Keeping the family stories alive kept them grounded in a time of fear and uncertainty. The main thing was to survive confinement in the barracks and keep their minds diverted from hunger, thirst, and fear.

In the water lineup two weeks later, Julia spoke to Frau Faber again. "You were right about the forced labour parties. We've been assigned to the brewery."

"Just in time," Frau Faber said. "So many people are dying. Mostly babies and old people. I've been lucky. Still hanging on."

"I hope they'll feed us better at the brewery."

"It can't be worse than the food here."

"True," Julia said, "things can only get better." She prayed she would not regret wishing for change.

4.

October 1945 - May 1946

The brewery was their salvation. After weeks in the barracks, Julia was thankful to have the one small room they were given to accommodate her family. Even sharing them, the beds were a huge improvement over sleeping on the floor.

"Mutti, look! We've got blankets. Each bed has a blanket." Sofie was beaming.

"Yes, we're very lucky. You and Steffie will sleep with me and that will help to keep us warm as the nights grow colder." More importantly, Julia could keep a hand on each as they slept and be assured they were safe.

The German men had been reunited with their families at the brewery. When Julia's father arrived, they nearly crushed him with hugs. Katerina cried and cried until Thomas asked her what was wrong. "Nothing," she said, between little gasps for air. "I was just afraid I'd never see you again."

Julia, Elisabeth, and Ingrid worked side by side in the production line filling and capping beer bottles all day. Because of her age, Katerina was allowed household duties in the lodging. "This is so much better than the barracks." Julia raised her voice above the clinking of the bottles. "Mother can keep an eye on the little ones. In a way it's almost a blessing that the children can't go outside to play. Inside, I know they're safe. As safe as they can be for now."

"A big improvement over the barracks," Elisabeth agreed.

In the evening Julia watched as the girls entertained themselves, drawing and writing. She smiled at Katerina and said, "Remember how you taught us at home, Mother?"

"Was Oma a teacher?" Sofie asked.

"No, but after we came home from the Czech school, she taught us to read and write in German."

"It wouldn't do to forget our own language," Katerina said. "And now, Sofie and Steffie, we'll do the same thing. We'll play school and you'll see how it was for your mother to learn at home. It'll be fun and give you something to do."

"And don't forget to make them do some arithmetic too." Julia turned to her daughters. "The adults have to work in the brewery, so the children have to work too. Oma's school will be your work. Make sure you do your best, the same as in real school."

Food was scarce, but the Czech manager of the brewery provided what little he could for the workers. He also allowed them to take a bottle of beer each day which they shared with the children. Any kind of nutrition was precious.

Over the fall and winter, Heidi had made short, discreet visits, sneaking in bits of bread and potatoes for them. She had provided pencils and paper, a few books, and scissors for the girls to make paper dolls. Then one spring day she appeared in the capping line. She put her fingers to her lips as Julia was about to call out her name in joy.

"Hush! I can only stay a few minutes. A sympathetic overseer let me in, but I have to be quick. I heard that they're moving you all out to Germany in a few days. You'll go back to the barracks tomorrow and soon they'll put you on a train. After that I won't see you again."

"Oh my God, what will happen to us now?" A million uncertainties whirled around in Julia's head. "I won't be able to see you again?" she mumbled. "Ever?" She felt the blood draining from her face. Heidi reached out to take her arm and moved closer to her sister.

"I feel sick about this, Julia." She choked back a sob. "But who knows? Maybe when you get to the other side of the border, you'll be able to start a new life." She smiled—such a forced smile. Julia wondered if she would have had the strength to smile if their positions were reversed. "So listen. Day after tomorrow at three o'clock, I'll walk by on the road outside the barracks. I'm not sure which building you'll be in, but I'll look for you if you can get to a window. I won't be able to wave to you or they'll lock me up too. I just want to say goodbye."

"I'll watch for you. Heidi, I can't thank you enough for the help you've given us. All the food and little things to keep the children happy. I ... I just can't believe I won't see you again." Her brow furrowed. She swallowed hard, trying not to cry.

She threw her arms around Heidi. The sisters did their best to muffle their sobs. "I love you so much," they told each other.

Julia dug in her apron pocket for her handkerchief. "Go now," she whispered, "before you get into trouble." Her dear, sweet Heidi. Would they ever sit and have tea together, as they did in years gone by, and talk about old boyfriends or all the scrapes they got each other in and out of? If only we all survive.... Julia had a terrible feeling she'd never see her sister again.

Back in the barracks two days later, Julia packed their few belongings in preparation for moving out at a moment's notice. She guessed it was nearly three o'clock and loitered near the small window that overlooked the street. In the distance she could see a woman walking slowly along the sidewalk, arms folded across her chest. As she came closer, she stole frequent glances at the upper level windows. Julia pressed her face against the window as the woman approached. Yes, it was Heidi. Julia looked over her shoulder to make sure no guards happened to be nearby before blowing her younger sister a kiss.

"Take care, Heidi," she whispered. Julia blinked hard and wiped her eyes. She didn't want to blur the last glimpse of her sister. Below the window on the street, Heidi did not respond. Julia knew she couldn't. There were Czechs on the sidewalk and the street. But, keeping her arms crossed, Heidi turned her head briefly to look up at Julia. Then she raised one finger and wiggled it back and forth to wave goodbye.

5.

May 1946

Apprehension filled the barracks. Guards bustled about, lists in one hand, guns in the other. Julia had spent the night shifting from one uncomfortable position to another. After having a bed at the brewery for almost a year, the hard floor of the barracks felt like an assault to her body.

"Good Lord, my bones are aching today," Katerina grumbled. Julia wished she could spare her mother such hardships. She knew how her own body ached and she was thirty years younger. She limbered up by going downstairs to stand in line at the water pump. If they were to be moved out today, Julia wanted to be sure they all had a good drink of water before the journey. She had the pot for now and a small jar she filled with water to take along with them. She hoped it would be enough. It had to be.

"Where do you think they're sending us?" Elisabeth's hands trembled. They hadn't stopped shaking since their arrival in the barracks a year ago.

Julia placed her hand over Elisabeth's and patted it reassuringly. "Try not to worry. We'll be together. We'll be all right, wherever they send us."

"I'm glad we're together," Elisabeth said. "Makes it easier, wondering about what's happened to Andreas."

"At least you still have hope that he'll come back." Julia forged on, not wanting to think about her dead husband. "From what Heidi said, we're to be taken to the German side of the border, but then what?"

"I wonder which town they'll send us to. More barracks? And how will we find food?" Ingrid asked. "It's outrageous to have no say about our own future."

For Julia, the thought of leaving Saaz where she had lived all her life was mind numbing. The regimes may have changed, but the Saaz area was always Julia's home. Her family had lived here for centuries. *How can it be that we're being sent away?*

Julia thought about her older brothers and sisters—wondered where they had ended up. She knew that Roland, Konnie, and Brigitte had taken their families and moved north inside the German border just before the war ended. *I wonder if we'll ever see them again.*

The unknown filled her with fear. These days everything filled her with fear. If her children knew how terrified she was.... No! She couldn't let them see her weak and afraid. She had to be strong for them. She thought of her husband's words, "Your inner strength that I love so much will see you through." He had told her she was strong enough to deal with anything that came her way. She would do her best to live up to his ideal of her. Yes, she felt better already.

The grating crackle of the loudspeaker broke into her thoughts. "All persons, gather belongings and report to the marshalling area immediately."

Julia took a deep breath. She was ready. She led her family downstairs and out to the parade ground.

"Form lines and proceed to the gate." The loudspeakers continued to blast orders.

Like docile sheep they plodded along, two or three abreast. Near the railway tracks, the line slowed to a crawl as each person and all their belongings were searched. Julia stopped in her tracks. Another search! Heidi's generous donation of jewellery which she had sewn into the lining of her father's jacket might still be discovered. *Dear God. There would be hell to pay if they found it. Why hadn't she made him leave it behind?*

Most people had nothing of value left, but a few had acquired small items from friends or Czech relatives during their winter of forced labour. Rings and money were immediately confiscated. Cutlery or anything that might be considered a weapon was taken away. As Julia's group reached the checkpoint, the line split into several branches so that a number of people could be searched at the same time. In the split Ingrid and Elisabeth were separated from the rest of the family.

An official seated behind a table motioned for Julia to come forward. She set her bag on the table to be inspected and held onto her daughters' hands.

Julia studied the man as he felt around in the sack. Tufts of dark hair stuck out from under his cap. Wire-rimmed glasses perched on a hawkish nose, magnifying his amber eyes. He pursed his thin lips and scanned Julia from her ankles to her breasts, and there his eyes stopped. "So," he said softly, rubbing his chin, "it would appear that you have no contraband in the bag. In this case we must search more diligently in other more personal hiding places." Julia felt bile rising in her throat. Her brain clamoured for a way to prevent the man from groping her. She took a quick step towards him and spoke politely using the dialect and vocabulary that could easily pass for that of an educated native Czech.

"Sir, I assume that you are not personally responsible for what is going on here and that you are a respectable family man yourself. I'm sure you would expect your own wife and children to be treated with the dignity they deserve."

The official's eyes widened as he heard Julia speak. He sat up straight in his chair. "You are quite right. We are not the animals that most of you Germans take us for. Pass quickly. Your parents too."

"Thank you." Julia nodded to the official and turned to her parents, telling them in German to come along with her quickly. *Quickly! Before he changes his mind.* Julia resisted grabbing her father and pulling him along. She let out a long breath as he passed by the checkpoint unmolested. The hidden jewellery was safe. With any luck, it could buy them food.

On the other side of the checkpoint, Julia turned to the sound of Ingrid's rising voice. "But the rest of our family is right over there. Please, we have to be on the same train with them." Ingrid's brows were furrowed with fear and she cast about as if looking for a way out.

"You will all be on the same train ... as long as you behave," the guard told her.

Elisabeth reached over to Ingrid. Julia saw her tug at Ingrid's arm and nod her head as if to say, "It'll be all right."

Over her shoulders Julia saw Ingrid and Elisabeth being shoved to a railcar farther to her left. With her bundle of belongings under her arm, Julia's grip on her daughters' hands tightened. "Stay close by me. Stay close."

The empty railcars normally used to transport pigs and cattle were boarded up except for space near the top to allow for some ventilation. Julia stepped up on the ramp with her family. She wanted to bolt and run, but there was nowhere to go. As she was nudged into the warm darkness she would have liked to stop for a moment to let her eyes adjust and to filter that first breath of dung-filled air, but the throng behind her pressed forward. She stumbled and headed instinctively for the place on the far wall with the biggest airspace where a board was broken at the top of the wall. As more and more people squeezed on board, the air in the railcar became stifling. Julia could feel what she assumed was straw and animal waste underfoot. No sooner had her eyes adjusted to the half light, than they began to water from the powerful stench that rose from the floor. She kept a firm hold on her daughters' hands, lest she lose them as they jostled for space. Sofie and Steffie clung to her with eyes closed and noses pressed into her skirt. Katrina and Thomas shuffled along beside them as if dazed.

"Why don't we claim this little space here against the wall and clear off the floor as much as we can with our feet?" Julia said to her parents. "Then, if we have room, we can put out the blanket and sit down. We're going to be here quite a while."

Katrina laughed hysterically as she scraped the manure sideways with her shoes. "Mother, please!" Julia whispered. "Don't upset the children."

Thomas raised his chin in a nod to Julia and put his arm around his quivering wife. "Now Katya, don't worry. I'm here and everything will work out, you'll see. At least we'll soon be leaving the Czechs behind." As her hysteria eased, Katerina alternately gasped for air and sobbed.

These past months her mother had aged ten years, her lined face and sagging cheeks testimony to the months of near starvation and lack of sleep. Thomas's once sturdy frame was little more than a skeleton in a suit. His bald head was pale. His clear grey eyes had lost their sparkle. The handlebar moustache hid the downturn in his mouth which had always been so quick to smile. But what was there to smile about these days?

They staked out a small space for themselves, packed in next to other families on three sides, but with their backs against the wall. More and more Julia looked for security of a wall at her back. They huddled together as the huge doors slid shut with a grating rumble. In spite of the heat, a frosty shower of goosebumps covered Julia and she shuddered at the sound of the bar being slammed into place. Her chest felt tight and heavy, as if an unseen hand had piled stones onto it. She gasped for breath, but no amount of oxygen could fill the need. For the sake of her daughters she fought the claustrophobia that threatened her composure. *Count to ten ... slowly. Do it again ... slowly*, she told herself. It must have been almost an hour before they felt the first jerks of motion as the train left the station. As the railcar picked up speed, Julia blessed the faint breeze that began to blow through the airspaces.

In time it became clear that there were holes in the floor at either end of the car. These served as latrines. They had long since given up hope for any privacy. It was irrelevant anyway, since in most cases necessity took precedence.

They leaned on each other, alternately talking and dozing. No one commented on the foul air anymore.

They had become inured to the smell as it permeated their clothing, hair, and skin.

Through the ventilation spaces at the top of the railcar walls, they glimpsed the changing sky and flashes of trees and rocky cliffs. They guessed the time by the colour of the sky.

The next day, as the first streaks of morning light filtered through the air spaces, people began to stir, stretching arms and legs into any available space. "Mutti." Sofie tapped her mother's arm. "I'm really thirsty," she whispered.

"I know, sweetie. We all are. But there's no water left. I hope we'll be there soon."

"Where?"

Julia suppressed a sad, tired laugh. "I don't know. I think it will be somewhere in Germany. I hope so anyway. We'll get some food there too. Try to sleep a bit more, Sofie. It will make the time go by faster."

"I'll try, Mutti."

By noon, in spite of the faint breeze coming through the air spaces, people complained about the heat. "My God! How is a person supposed to breathe in here?" one woman said.

"Move over and give me some room," another cried, panic in her voice. "My baby. Oh God! My baby! He's not breathing. My baby, my baby. Oh, my poor baby!" Clutching the infant, she looked around, mouth distorted in pain, wild eyes filled with tears.

An old woman put her arm around the young mother. "There, there. You did your best for the little one. He's gone to be with our Lord now."

"Old crone. Such a stupid thing to say," Julia muttered to herself.

The sobs eventually quieted and changed into mournful keening that seemed to come from somewhere deep inside the young mother.

"You'll have other children someday in a better time. Don't you worry now," the older woman said.

"Humph!" Julia allowed a snort of indignation to escape her. *What a load of manure. You can't replace one child with another. Every single one of them is precious and unique.*

"Ow! Mutti, that hurts." Steffie said.

"Oh, Steffie, sweetie. I'm sorry." Julia forced her hand to relax its grip on her daughter, but did not let go. Nothing, nothing was going to take her girls away. Not the Czechs, not death, nothing.

Julia cried silently for the poor mother, for the baby, and for her own children who were not safe from harm either.

"I think we're slowing down," someone said, and a hush fell over the car. "Maybe we're here."

The rocking motion of the train eased as the thumping and clacking rhythm slowed. The train crawled ahead until, with a last squeal of metal, it clunked to a stop.

The heavy door trundled open. Everyone threw a hand over their eyes against the stab of daylight. "Stay on the train!" a stern voice shouted in Czech. Militia men were everywhere. Their ordeal was not over yet.

"Have your water containers ready and they will be filled," one of the militia said.

"Quick, Mother, Father, let's work our way to the front. We have to get some water. Looks like it will be a long time before we get wherever we are going," Julia said. She rummaged through the pack to get out the jar and the pot and a cup for each of the girls.

When their turn came, the woman who filled their pot muttered, "Such pigs you are. You even smell like them. Pfui!"

And whose fault is that? Julia closed her mind to the shame and humiliation in order to get the water she needed for herself and her children. Under other circumstances she would have fought back—her command of the language was such that she could have given the woman a tongue-lashing—but at the moment she had no choice but to endure the cruel comments.

The family stumbled back to their filthy blanket and sat down. Each of them had a drink and Julia was careful to save some for later. She leaned back against the railcar wall with an arm over each child's shoulders. Pulling them close, she put her head back and closed her eyes. She was glad for the dimmer light when the doors closed again so she could allow her tears to flow.

The train squealed to a final stop on the morning of the third day. Julia listened for clues to their whereabouts. She couldn't hear a word of Czech. The cattle car doors slid open. She squinted into the square of white sunlight that filled the doorway. When her eyes adjusted, she saw a crowd of people by the train. Julia cringed at the pity and disgust she saw on the faces staring up at them.

Soldiers moved among the crowd, but this time they were Americans. Sofie and Steffie gaped open-mouthed, shamelessly pointing their fingers.

"Mutti! Look how dark that man's face is," Steffie said.

"Hush, Steffie. He comes from a different country. Mind your manners and don't point."

As the refugees burst into the fresh air, thirstily breathing it in, the reception committee stepped back, their noses wrinkled in disgust. Soldiers threw candies towards them and children scrambled to pick them up. Sofie and Steffie lurched forward, but Julia held them back.

"Mutti!?" they both exclaimed. "Let go! We want to get some candy."

"No! We will not be crawling on the ground to pick up scraps thrown to us. We are not animals and we are not beggars."

"Aw-w! Mutti, ple-e-ease."

"Do you want to look like crows picking up garbage at the roadside?" As Julia looked at their stricken faces, she doubted they would ever forget this moment. "We'll all get back to normal one day soon and you'll have lots of candies. But not these candies that have been thrown to us in the dirt."

"My dear woman," said a friendly German official who was meeting the train, "the American soldiers are under orders not to *give* Germans anything, but they know that if they drop something on the ground, anyone can pick it up."

"I understand." Julia tightened her grip on the children and stood by her decision. She was exhausted, humiliated, and beaten down, but she raised her chin defiantly.

Julia searched the drawn faces of the others disembarking from the cattle cars. "Have you seen any sign of Elisabeth or Ingrid?" she asked her parents.

"No. They may have ended up in another town," Thomas said. "Remember when we heard the clunking and banging noises that sounded like cars being unhitched? I think they redirected some of the cars to other places. It makes sense. There are too many of us here as it is."

"That must be it. We have to try to find out where they were sent."

The local citizens helped Katerina and Thomas up into one of several waiting farm wagons, along with others who were too old, too sick, or too young to walk to Sternberg.

"We'll see you there." Julia handed her bag up to her father. "Shouldn't take us long."

Julia and her daughters were used to walking long distances and the ten kilometres should have been manageable. But after many months on a starvation diet and then weakened further during the last three days' journey in the cattle car, it was all they could do to drag themselves to the refugee camp.

The white castle, with its dark baroque-style corner towers, was to be their new home until housing could be found in nearby Koenigshofen. Built almost three hundred years earlier, Sternberg castle would have made a romantic postcard photo, but that was where the charm ended. It was in sad disrepair—an austere, cold place that sent a chill through Julia even on this warm spring day.

Settling in took several days; getting the stench of animal dung off their bodies and out of their clothes took longer. Gradually, donations of basic necessities arrived from the townspeople and the Red Cross.

"It feels so good to be able to wash," Julia said.

Her mother rinsed out a rag she was using as a washcloth. "I almost feel human again," she said.

"I've got that clothesline put up for you, Katya." Thomas looked proud as he pointed to the creation made of old rope.

"That's good. Isn't it amazing how some of the most basic items are so precious?" Katerina shook her head.

"And now that we have a washtub, I'll do some of our clothes next," Julia said. "Soap and water. Almost as precious as food."

"I even found a few clothespins." Thomas held up a coarse cloth bag.

Julia and her family stood at the food table in the courtyard. "Here you are," a local woman said. She filled their pots with potato soup and identified herself as Frau Mueller.

"Many thanks, Frau Mueller," Julia said. "We appreciate this very much."

"We do what we can, but you know we are all going through hard times."

It was obvious to Julia, as she noted the woman's clear skin and bright eyes, that her benefactor had no idea what hard times were. Her skirt and blouse too, were of good quality. She thought about the beautiful clothes she'd had to leave behind. Someone else was wearing them now. At the moment she would have been in heaven just to be able to wear clean clothes. The woman had no appreciation for what she had, Julia thought bitterly. But no amount of telling would make Frau Mueller understand that, so she simply answered, "Of course we are." She took her bowl of potato soup from Frau Mueller and sat on the bench beside her children trying not to think about the ham that Frau Mueller would probably have with her supper.

After the first week of receiving food donations from the townspeople, they began to forage for food in other ways, offering their services in exchange for whatever was available. Julia joined others who were able to work in the nearby fields. The farmers provided a meal for them at the end of each day. She saved as much food as she could to bring back for her daughters and her parents. It wasn't enough to live on, she often said, but enough to keep from dying.

One day Thomas came into their lodgings and dropped a piece of meat on the table. "Meat!?" Katerina exclaimed. "Meat?" Her eyes were huge.

"Where did you get this?" Julia asked.

"From Koenigshofen. An old horse died, and the townspeople portioned out the meat to give to the refugees."

"But what are those white things in it?" Sofie asked.

"Never mind, Sofie," her grandmother said. "It's meat. Real meat. I'll scrape those maggots away and make a stew. We'll use the new potatoes that Julia brought home. It will taste just fine."

"That's right, Mother. We can make it last for several meals if we're careful."

That summer of 1946, Julia chopped weeds between the rows of potatoes. Though the fields were not her own, she felt comfortable working in them, taking in the fresh air and healing her psyche with the soothing sound of gentle birdsong. The rich smell of the earth rose up as she cut into it with the hoe. She stooped to pull out weeds and savoured the texture of the soil between her fingers. It was almost like home.

Thank God for the farm work. Thank God? What was she thinking? Why should she thank God for anything? She supposed she should be thankful to be alive and that her daughters were unharmed, but—her husband, her home? How did she end up a widow so young, a refugee among her own people? Her life had become a journey through peaks and valleys of emotion.

In her mind she escaped to a happier time. How comforting were the memories of those days when all was right with the world, when she was in love with Michael.

PART TWO

Michael & Lukas

Saaz/Neusattl, Czechoslovakia
1931-1932

6.

Michael felt out of place among the group of singers gathered in the Neusattl community hall. At 23 he was the youngest person there. Unlike many of them, he came for the music rather than the social perks. He checked the tuning of his violin and looked to Max the choirmaster for direction. At Max's nod Michael began, and after a few bars of introduction, the choir began to sing.

Today something was different. Michael continued to play, but turned slowly to scan the rows of singers, searching for the new voice that had so attracted him.

He'd been to several practices and hadn't heard it before. A couple of new faces peered out from the back row. He watched discreetly as he continued to play. A mousy woman he hadn't seen before stopped to wipe her nose with a handkerchief. It wasn't her then, since he still heard the rich tones. Farther along the same row, the second new face contributed to the hymn. Her wavy chestnut hair gleamed in the sunshine.

He positioned himself to get a better look. Her trim athletic figure was rounded in the right places. She was not especially tall and he liked that. Tall women made him feel inadequate. Her shy smile suggested that she was approachable.

As he accompanied the village choir in several more hymns, he frequently allowed his eyes to wander in her direction. From time to time he closed his eyes and let his ears spy on her as she sang the traditional German songs, her voice so full, yet gentle. He imagined he played his violin for her and she sang for him alone.

Someone requested a tune from the past about the workday coming to a close. It was a fitting way to end the choir practice, Michael thought, and he did his best to add special instrumental flair to what was one of his old favourites too. Afterwards clusters of singers stood around on the grassy area near the community hall, chatting before heading home again. Michael hurried to put his violin away. He stood on his tiptoes to scan the group of singers, but somehow that pretty girl had already slipped away.

He craned his neck this way and that. "Are you looking for someone?" a stout middle-aged woman asked him.

"The young lady from the back row. Dark hair, mellow voice?"

"Oh, you must mean Julia. Yes, what a voice she has." The woman looked around. "I don't see her."

"That's too bad. I was hoping to meet her." *Julia.* "Very pretty name." *Very pretty girl.*

"You'll meet her next week. She just joined the choir and I'm sure she'll be back. Her family is very musical. They're all talented. And smart. But that's not surprising—they're a good family." The woman took a quick breath and continued, as if happy to have someone to chat with. "Did you know that her father was the mayor of our little town of Neusattl? Three times they elected him."

"No, I didn't know that, but I'm not from here. I live in Saaz." Normally he would have tried to find ways of easing out of a conversation with a matronly woman he didn't know, but his interest was piqued by her references to Julia and her family.

"Her father is very well-liked. Such a kind and friendly man. I'm surprised you never met him. He was the stationmaster of our town."

"The line doesn't go from Saaz to here, so I always ride my bicycle or walk."

The stout woman patted Michael's arm lightly and laughed. "What am I thinking? This would have been well before your time anyway. He hasn't been in either position since the war ended in 1918." She shook her head at her own lapse. "How foolish of me. Where did the last thirteen years go?"

"I was ten when the war ended."

"Oh my, I'm probably boring you. Don't let me hold you up with my prattling."

Michael had hoped to hear more about Julia. "It's been nice chatting with you," he said, "but I should be going. I have a long ride home ahead of me."

The following week on choir day, Michael shaved more carefully than usual. He flashed a toothy smile at the mirror, and stepped back pondering the effect it might have on Julia. His smile had worked for him in the past to charm the ladies and he was counting on it this afternoon. All week he'd thought about Julia, his mind working on the best opening lines for conversation with her. "What a lovely voice you have?" he'd say. No. That wouldn't work. She'd say, "Thank you," and that would be the end of it. Maybe, "Hello, my name is Michael."

And then what? Darn it all. He had to think of something smart. He needed to make a good impression. This time he couldn't let her slip away.

He ran a comb through his wavy, almost black hair, threw the comb down and flopped onto the bed, reaching under it to grab his shoes. He had to hurry. All this dawdling in front of the mirror, lost in fantasy over yet another girl.

Mustn't forget the most important thing. Michael opened the brown case. The delicate instrument lay cushioned in a velvet-lined depression. Lifting it out gently, he checked that he had an extra string in the flip-up compartment. He pushed the violin snugly back into its space before securing the bow and snapping the latches shut.

Downstairs in the bakery, his father was preparing the next day's dough. "I'm off to play for the choir, Papa. I know it's not much pay, but I enjoy the music."

"I know you do, boy." Rolf Hiebert slapped the flour from his hands and wiped them on his apron. "You go on and have a good time. But speaking of pay, you'll soon have to start spending more time helping me out. It's getting more and more difficult to make ends meet."

"Can we talk about it later?" Michael hovered in the doorway shifting his weight from one foot to the other. "I have to hurry now. I'm late already."

"Sure, sure. But when you get home, we'll talk. Time is running out."

7.

Michael pedaled with his right knee sticking out at an awkward angle to accommodate the violin case. He knew it looked clumsy, but with the bicycle he could cut the travel time by two-thirds and it would save him a long walk home later. It occurred to him that he should rig up a way to tie the violin case to his back next time, or tie it down inside a rucksack he could wear on his back. For today this would have to do. He pedaled furiously to make up for the time spent preening. In his haste he saw the pothole too late. He slammed on his brake, sending the bicycle into a skid. The front tire rammed into the hole and Michael was airborne. The violin case bounced twice and then skittered along the road adding a few more scratches to its tough covering. Michael scrambled to get up out of the dust and inspected the hole in his pantleg and his jacket sleeve shredded at the elbow.

"Oh, that's fine!" he muttered. "Just fine!" He gave the bicycle a kick and immediately looked around to see if anyone was in sight. Fortunately the road was empty of travelers. He brushed himself off, retrieved his violin, and quickly checked inside to make sure it wasn't damaged. The bicycle was a bit mangled, but he hopped on, hoping it was still functional. When the front wheel dragged, he noticed the flat tire. "Damn! Oh, dammit all. Now I'm going to be late for sure." He began walking his bicycle and then realized how illogical that was since he would have to walk it back again after the practice. He found a sturdy tree, leaned the bicycle against it, and took off running towards Neusattl.

The Community Hall was sweltering in the summer, so practices were held outside on the park grounds. As he approached the hall, half jogging, half walking, Michael saw the choir members already assembled. Someone pointed towards him and all heads turned his way.

"Everything all right?" Max asked.

Michael nodded. "Bicycle troubles," he managed to say between gasps for air.

"So I see." Max pointed from Michael's knee to his elbow. "It's good that the violin survived. I hope your arm is in better shape than your jacket."

"Yes, thanks. It'll be fine." Michael brushed himself off once more and straightened his jacket. "Let's get started then, shall we?" He glanced around and, not seeing Julia, wasn't sure whether to be disappointed or relieved.

Choir practice had been the highlight of his week, but thoughts of Julia there had shifted his enthusiasm from the music to her. Michael found the outdoor setting especially pleasant. He imagined the strains of his violin traveling on the light breeze of the open air, mingling with the buzzing of insects and the twittering of songbirds carrying messages of love to Julia. Max's instructions to the choir brought him out of his romantic daydreaming, but almost instantly he was thinking of Julia again.

He had hoped to talk to her before the practice. Even with his clothes torn and dirty, and knowing she wouldn't give him a second look, he was crestfallen because of her absence. The group prepared to sing. Dutifully he began to play. Somehow it now seemed like just another job.

It was not until the first song was well underway that he noticed Julia slip into the back row and join the singing. Several of the older members looked his way when his violin playing became noticeably sweeter. His happiness poured out through the strings. *Why not?* he thought. Life was grand.

As the practice ended, he wasted no time reaching Julia to ask if she would mind waiting for a moment while he put his violin away.

"My name is Michael Hiebert. I'm from Saaz."

"Yes, I know," Julia said. "Max was saying how lucky we are to have you for instrumental support."

"So you know all about me then." *Oh, that was a stupid thing to say.*

"Well, not all about you." She twisted the edge of her dress in her fingers. "Only that you were willing to come and put up with our singing."

"I'm enjoying the singing very much." Her gold and green hazel eyes were drawing him in like magnets. "You have a lovely voice." *And a lovely figure.*

"Thank you. That's very kind of you to say so." She averted her eyes and the toe of her shoe played with a tuft of grass.

"Please excuse my torn clothes. I had a little accident with my bicycle on the way here." Michael brushed ineffectively at the threads hanging from his jacket elbow.

"Oh, dear. Are you all right?" She frowned slightly as she reached for his arm. "I hope your elbow is in better shape than your jacket."

"I'm fine, thanks." *Especially if you keep holding my arm like that.* He almost forgot to breathe. "I just don't *look* so fine today, but I wonder if you'd mind if I walked along with you on your way home?"

"That'll suit me as long as you'll agree to borrow my bicycle to get you home."

8.

Michael was barely aware of the road. With each push of the pedals, his mind sang, "Julia, Julia, Julia." She was all he could think about—her shy laugh and gentle sense of humour, her bright smile. She had kept him fascinated and entertained as they strolled along the footpath.

At the alley that led to her house, she had stopped. "No sense getting my family's tongues wagging. They like to tease. Wait here and I'll get my bicycle."

He had stayed there waiting for her, although he would have liked to follow her right into her house, right into her bedroom. Delicious thought! The things he would have done. He saw himself pulling her clothes off, kissing her as he fought with her buttons. Oh, to hell with the buttons, rip the blouse off, push her down on the bed, lift her skirt, slide his hands up those soft thighs inviting him into a warmer place. Now, as he wheeled into the backyard of the bakery, he shook his head to clear it of the fantasy.

Tomorrow was time enough to retrieve his broken down bicycle. He parked Julia's against the wall and climbed the stairs. The sliver of light under the door told him that his father was home, most likely spending another evening alone.

Michael was an only child. He might have had a sister, but his mother and the unborn child had died in childbirth twelve years ago. Outward signs of his father's grief over the loss of his wife and child had gradually subsided, but Michael suspected that he had simply buried his feelings.

At fifty Rolf Hiebert was still a handsome man in spite of the beginnings of a pot belly. Michael was aware that several local women would have been happy to snare a baker for a husband and be guaranteed bread on their table, yet Rolf had never shown interest in finding another wife.

Michael pushed open the door and kicked off his shoes. "Papa? I'm home."

"In here, in the living room. Come sit for a while." Rolf slouched in an overstuffed chair nursing a glass of slivovitz, the distilled plum liqueur that was so precious these days. He ran a hand through his thick, dark brown hair. His grizzled temples gave him a distinguished look. "Have a little shot with me." He waved his arm towards the bottle on the small coffee table in front of him. "What the hell happened to your clothes? You okay?" He sat up straighter.

"Just a spill on the bicycle. I'll be fine after I wash up." He poured a pitcher of water into the basin around the corner from the living room.

"All the more reason you need that drink."

"No, thanks." Michael dried his hands.

"Come. I insist. Pour yourself a slivovitz. We have to make a toast." Rolf's eyebrows were furrowed.

A sinking feeling came over Michael. "What are we celebrating?"

"Prost!" The happy clink of the glasses was at odds with the look on Rolf's face. Michael wondered what pronouncement was about to follow.

"Here's to you taking over the bakery, Michael. It's time." His father lowered his glass. "Ach, don't look so distraught. I'll still be there to help you, but it's more than I can manage alone. If the bakery is to stay afloat at all, it will need all of your energy and what's left of mine."

Michael sat on the sofa across from his father and leaned forward, hands on his knees. "Did something happen?" He felt a twinge of concern. His father had always run the bakery, leaving his son to enjoy the single life. As long as the baking was done, Rolf had not pressured Michael to stay home.

"No, nothing happened. Not really. Only the same thumping in my heart that I often have." Rolf waved at the air in front of him as if to swish the problem away. "But business has been down for a few months now and if something happens to me, I want to be sure you'll manage."

"It's been almost two years since the stock market crash, and people are still having a hard time. They may have had to give up meat, but they can't do without bread." Michael tried to sound positive.

"Yes, yes. They still buy bread, but the problem is that they buy it at Rosenberg's, down the street. He's lowered his prices again. I can't compete." Rolf raised his arms in the air and let them drop onto the armrests of the old chair. "Goddamn Jews and their ways."

Michael was shocked. His father was always so fair-minded. He must really be concerned to be talking about the Jews like this. Other businesses struggled because of competition from Jewish businessmen, but this was the first time it had affected their bakery.

"We need a gimmick," Michael said. He thought a moment. "How about, 'Buy a loaf of rye bread and get one bun free'? People love getting something for free."

Rolf thought a moment. "It's worth a try, although it goes against my philosophy. I've never had to advertise. Always sold a good product. Humph! Never thought I'd have to beg people to buy my bread." He refilled Michael's glass.

"I've noticed some signs in other store windows 'Don't buy from Jews,' but somehow it doesn't seem right to single them out like that."

"I can see that you're very naïve, Michael. If our positions were reversed, do you think the Jews would hesitate to put up signs saying, 'Don't buy from Germans'?"

It hadn't occurred to Michael that Jews might not all operate under the rules of fairness as they did. If his father had concerns, then there must be something to it.

"Well, I'm not going to put a sign like that in my bakery window," Rolf said. "It's bad enough watching what goes on in the streets."

"What do you mean?"

"Just this afternoon, right after closing, I came upstairs to make tea and I heard a commotion in the street. I looked out and there were three young German fellows. They were perhaps a few years younger than you. Goddamn hooligans were bullying Herr Rubin and all he was doing was going for a walk."

"Bullying, how?"

"They circled him. Poked him with sticks. Called him a dirty Jew. Made him piss on the sidewalk."

"And?"

"And what?" Rolf growled. "He pissed in the street while they taunted him. He's an old man! What do you expect him to do? Take on the three bullies?"

"Of course not, Papa. That's terrible. But he's a Jew, after all."

"Michael! Don't ever let me hear you talk like that. Yes, he's a Jew, but he's a human being first. No one deserves to be treated like that. Those cowardly ruffians. They feel strong when there are several of them together."

Michael didn't know what to think. His father complained about the Jews and defended them at the same time. "Are you sure they were Germans?"

"Oh, they were Germans, all right. I'm ashamed to say it. But this is what worries me. These boys are so full of hate and misguided idealism. I yelled at them, but they shook their fists at me. Called me a Jew-lover. Said I'd be next."

"My God! What's going on with everyone?" He thought for a moment. "I wouldn't be surprised if we were working up to a war. I've heard that in Germany the Hitler Youth Groups are being encouraged to march and praise Hitler blindly."

"He's grooming them for something, no doubt."

"The good thing is that the Czechs don't allow the Hitler Youth and we don't have them here in Sudetenland."

"The *only* good thing about the Czechs, as far as I can see." Rolf snorted. "Meanwhile, we have to keep a low political profile and get our bakery working better or we'll be bought out by the Rosenbergs. It happened to the Webers with their clothing store." Rolf sipped his slivovitz. "And this is what will happen to us if we're not careful. So you need to make a commitment to our bakery now, Michael. It's going to be yours sooner than you think. No more chasing girls. I'm not well and I want to make sure you'll be able to hang on to the bakery."

"Don't talk like that, Papa. We'll find a way to manage. I'll help out more. I promise."

That night Michael dreamed he was in the bakery surrounded by mountains of bread dough rising and rising until it threatened to fill the room. Outside the bakery window he saw Julia arm in arm with another man—one of his friends. She gave him a little wave as they laughed and strolled by. He tried to reach her, but the dough was everywhere. He worked furiously to cut and roll and shape the dough, but no matter how hard he worked there was always more dough. It continued to rise until it occupied every space in the room. Michael bolted upright in bed and gasped for air. His heart was racing and he was filled with dread for his future.

9.

"Ju-u-u-lia!" After two hours of choir practice, the singers spread out in all directions, heading towards home. The sun cast a late afternoon warmth across the land, its last effort before it would slowly sink behind the hills. Julia had just turned onto the trail that threaded its way through the fields to her home. Bright red poppies dotted the yellowing grass and sky blue cornflowers lined the edge of the path. Clusters of white and yellow daisies added their colours to the palette. She turned when she heard the familiar voice calling her name again. "Julia. Wait up!"

His violin case bumped a rhythm against his thigh as he came running up to her, slightly out of breath. "Of all the flowers in this field, I hope the prettiest one will yield, and let me walk her home."

"Michael! What a poet you are."

He beamed and caught her around the waist with his free arm. Julia felt a warm glow rise up her neck. She started to pull away ever so slightly—but hesitated. No, she didn't really want to disengage his arm completely. Still, what if someone were to see them? What would her parents think? Michael didn't appear to be aware of her inner struggles with etiquette. He let his hand drift back down to his side, casually brushing the curves at the back of her skirt.

"Wasn't that a wonderful time? I love our choir practices. You sing like a bird, Julia," he chattered on as he adjusted his pace to match hers.

"A bird?" she teased. "That could be good or bad. I hope you don't mean a crow?"

Taking her hand, he stopped and looked at her. "No, not a crow." He chuckled. "I don't really know what kind of bird, but it's not a sparrow or one of those birds with a thin high-pitched call." He put a finger on his upper lip, squinted his eyes, and furrowed his brow. "It's a much more mellow kind of bird. Perhaps a nightingale that has just been tasting honey. Yes, a nightingale. That's the one." Julia watched Michael's animated face as it changed from thoughtfulness to puzzlement, to smug amusement and satisfaction. She was thrilled to be the center of his world and to be compared to a melodious bird. She loved animals, especially birds. How did he know just what to say to make her feel so good?

She felt her face heating up and tried to shift the attention from herself. "Well, it's easy to sing along with your violin playing." Seeing his smile and the tilt of his head, she pushed on. "And I love how you can make it sound bright and sunny for the happy songs and then make it almost cry for the melancholy ones. You really are talented you know."

"That's sweet of you to say so, but then you are sweet."

"Oh, Michael, you're such a flatterer. But seriously now, tell me how did you learn to play like that?" She searched his dark eyes waiting for his answer.

Michael took her hand and looked into the distance as they walked on. "When I was a young boy, my father played the violin late in the evenings. I lay in bed listening to my mother singing as he played. She had a clear, rich voice. When it melded with the violin's song, it was as if they were making musical love. Of course I didn't think of it that way when I was little, but it was always a very emotional time. I couldn't wait to learn to play the violin like my father."

"You certainly learned it well!"

"I love playing. And wasn't I lucky to find a girl who sings like a nightingale to accompany me?" He smiled and nudged her.

Leaning over still more, he purred, "Shall we find out if the nightingale has been tasting honey? One little kiss will tell the story."

"Michael!"

He hadn't expected the playful shove and, caught off balance, tripped backwards into the potato field next to the path.

"Aw-w-w, Ju-u-lia! One little kiss!" With a quick look back, Julia could see that he hurried to dust himself off and catch up to her, but she was already well down the path. Another second and she would be out of his sight in the narrow back lane that led to her parents' house.

Julia floated through the door. "Oh, there you are, Julia," her mother called from the kitchen.

Did his hand really brush my skirt right there or was it my imagination?

"How was choir practice?"

Did he do it on purpose? "Hmm...? Oh, good. We sang a lot of my favourite songs. Not only the church songs this time." *He likes me!*

"Was your violinist there?" Julia felt heat rising in her face. She knew she must be blushing, sure that her mother had been able to read her thoughts. Images of Michael and his tousled dark hair crowded every corner of her mind.

"Ah ... um ... yes, he was there." She wished now that she hadn't mentioned him to her mother. She hadn't realized how much she had talked about him after choir practices.

And that kiss—almost! He likes me! Maybe I should have let him kiss me. I know Heidi would have. I don't want him to think I'm a prude. But if I'd let him he might have thought I was too easy. Or does he already think that? Does he think I'm cheap that he could take such a liberty when we've only known each other for two months? Back and forth she played the event until she felt confused and a little foolish to have spent so much time thinking about it.

The important thing was that he liked her. This talented young man who played the violin as if it were an extension of his soul—he liked her. She supposed he must be experienced and she should be careful. After all, he was four years older than she was. But she was no longer a child either.

Almost nineteen she had been working at the metal fastener factory in nearby Saaz for three years already. Still living under her parents' roof, she often forgot that she was old enough to start her own family if the right person came along.

"Julia? Julia? Girl! Aren't you going to answer me?" Her mother's voice had a sharp edge.

"What's that? Did you say something, Mother?"

Katerina sighed. "I asked if you talked to him today?"

"Oh, I ah ... yes, well, no ... just a little bit."

"I swear your head is in the clouds. Put your apron on, girl, and come help me slice this rye bread and sausage for supper. And stop that daydreaming."

As Julia tied her apron on, she looked at her mother and felt sheepish for all the thoughts that had gone through her head moments earlier. Katerina was shaking her head in disbelief as she cut slices of the hard homemade bread, but Julia saw that her lips were twitching as if trying not to smile.

10.

Thomas grunted as he pried at the heel of his polished black leather shoe with the big toe of his other foot. With a flip the second shoe clunked to the floor beside the first. It had been years since he had gone to work at his old job of stationmaster, but he couldn't leave the habit of dressing up to go out.

Katerina stuck her head around the corner. "You're home at last."

"Yes. At last." He sighed. "I think by tomorrow evening we should have the new table and benches finished. Roland can do the varnishing himself." He heaved another big sigh as he lowered himself into his rocker in the far corner of the large kitchen. He tapped out the contents of his pipe.

"I hope you're using the ashtray for that pipe, Thomas. I don't want that mess on my floors."

"Yes, yes, yes," he grumbled affectionately and sat back to relax. "How did your day go, Katya?"

"Not so bad, considering I didn't have five minutes to sit down all day. But never mind. I'm sure you're tired yourself."

"Yes, it's a bit of a walk from Roland's house. Did you save me some supper?"

"Of course! What do you think!? I would let the children eat it all? They had plenty of potato dumplings with gravy and your plate is over here with a fine piece of pork to go with your dumplings. A working man has to have something substantial after a hard day."

Thomas winked. "That's my girl, Katya." He set aside his pipe, and pushed himself up out of the rocker.

Katerina pulled out a kitchen chair and sat across from Thomas at the massive wooden table. "I'm worried about Julia. She hasn't been herself lately. She's been so distracted."

"Oh? What do you think is on her mind?" Thomas cut his pork slice more slowly. His quiet grey eyes rested for a moment on his wife's plump face as he wondered what was coming.

"Boys!"

"Oh, well," Thomas mumbled as he chewed. "Why shouldn't she be thinking of boys? After all, she's eighteen, almost nineteen." She should have been married by now, but he knew he would hate to see her go.

"Yes, yes, but this time it's one boy." Katerina stabbed the table with her finger. "Always the same one."

Thomas lowered his fork. "Do you think it's serious? Who is it?"

"It's that baker's boy, Michael."

"Humph! I wouldn't worry about it then." Thomas tucked into his supper again. "At least he has a profession and a business to take over. Julia would be well looked after."

"I don't know." Katerina spoke half to herself. "All he does is play the violin. Not a lot of baking going on, if you ask me. Julia seems to be crazy about him. It's a good thing she's shy, but still, that boy shows up everywhere she goes—choir practice, soccer games, town square.

He even escorts her home from Saaz if I ask her to run an errand after work. And he doesn't even live here. He lives in Saaz."

"Now, now, Katya. Don't tie yourself into a knot." Thomas gave a quiet belch. "That was a wonderful dinner, by the way. If Julia cooks like you do, she'll make Michael a good wife."

"Thomas! She's only eighteen! What are you thinking of?"

"Well, to tell you the truth, I was thinking of how pretty you were—"

"Were!?"

"And still are, of course. How pretty you were at sixteen when I married you."

Thomas smiled under his handlebar moustache as Katerina picked up his empty plate and marched into the kitchen with a "Humph!"

He looked around the empty table. It seemed lonely tonight to be the only one sitting there. At one time twelve sat down to dinner, but his five oldest children had married and left home, and the younger five had already eaten. "You know, Katya, I was just thinking how lucky we are that the children all found work as they grew up. So many people are without jobs and going hungry."

"That's all supposed to change if Hitler's promises come true. 'Jobs for everyone,' he says. I heard Frau Kassel talking about it after church last Sunday."

"That's all well and good if he comes to power and can make it happen. Too late for me though. I'm too old to get another job now."

"But Thomas, you know it wasn't just you. As long as the Czechs rule, they'll get the good jobs and we Sudeten Germans will get the leftovers."

"I was good at my job too." He went on as if he hadn't heard her, nursing the old hurts again. "But even then— what was I, forty when the war ended? I was too old to start learning Czech. Horrible language anyway! I could have kept that job. It was a good one. But those damn Czechs. They knew that most of us wouldn't qualify under their new laws where only Czech is spoken on the jobs. It's all right for the young ones who learned Czech quickly, but I just couldn't do it. I feel I've let you down, Katya."

"Now don't start that again. You know we are doing just fine. You have your little pension, and the few animals and the garden provide our food. It's good that the children help out when they can."

"I hate to take anything from them. They have their own children to feed now."

"But Thomas, it all works out. Roland is glad of your help with the furniture. The children all appreciate when you help them."

"Yes, I suppose...."

Oh, for the days of his youth. They still belonged to the Kaiser and Austria Hungary back then. Life was normal. The man went to work and got paid. The wife kept house and raised the children. Both worked hard and had a happy life. That happy life was disappearing since the Empire dissolved at the end of the war in 1918.

He remembered his grandfather telling him stories of his Sudeten-German ancestors who had lived here since the 13th century. And now? The allies had given the Sudeten German area to the Czechs who began to settle there in greater numbers. Jobs went to Czechs. Germans were dismissed. He worried that their German way of life was disappearing. He worried for his children's future.

"Thomas?" Katerina waved her fingers in front of Thomas' face. "Are you all right?"

"Huh? Oh, I was lost in thought. Why don't you make us a cup of tea and come sit with me. Tell me what else Frau Kassel said. I haven't decided yet if I like this Hitler fellow."

11.

Julia, Elisabeth, and Heidi strolled around Neusattl's town square. The early evening sun painted a golden hue on the buildings around the market place.

"I love this time of day," Julia said. "All the colours turn rich and warm and the air is the perfect temperature on my skin." She felt attractive in her white blouse and flowered skirt. All three sisters had taken pains to look their best before going out for a walk together.

"I love this time of day too," said Heidi, "because Michael and his friends are sure to show up." She burst out giggling when the men appeared at that moment. "And there they are!" She held her hands palms upwards as if she had conjured up the men.

With the nudges and laughter of youthful bravado, four young men swaggered up Kirchenstrasse.

"Hey, Julia!" called Michael. "You remember Jan and Andreas from last Sunday's soccer game."

"Yes, I do!" Heidi blurted out, pushing herself in front of her sisters. Julia gave her head a little shake as she watched Heidi toss her hair to the side and tilt her head. She did everything but bat her eyelashes at Jan. Heidi had a self-confidence that Julia envied. Her sister was fine-boned and petite and full of enthusiasm, but at times Julia was embarrassed by her boldness.

"Julia, I'd like you to meet Lukas. I told him you had pretty sisters and he insisted on coming along."

"Pleased to meet you, Lukas," Julia murmured. Lukas's handshake was warm and firm. She didn't want to let go lest her trembling became noticeable. For a moment the rest of the world disappeared and she was aware only of Lukas. Thankfully he had the presence of mind to let go of her hand. When she glanced over at Michael and caught his dark scowl, Julia immediately dropped her head and looked at the ground. *Good grief! I'm getting to be just like Heidi.*

Lukas was slim, but muscular and several centimetres taller than Michael. His straight, white teeth sparkled. Looking up at his blue-grey eyes and dark lashes, Julia was mesmerized. If anyone spoke to her, she didn't hear them.

"Why don't we go for a little walk down the lane to the pond?" Michael said, claiming Julia's hand the second it dropped from Lukas's grasp. "I saw some ducks there a few days ago."

As Michael pulled Julia closer and began walking, Lukas fell into step on the opposite side of her. Michael fumed and snorted. He gripped Julia's hand tighter and picked up the pace. The others were well ahead of them up the lane. "Where's Brigitte tonight? I thought Lukas might meet her."

"Catching up on some sewing."

"Maybe she'll come out next time," Michael said.

"Maybe. Tell me, Lukas, how do you know Michael?"

"We live in the same neighbourhood of Saaz and we've known each other all through school. Michael told me that the prettiest girls live here in Neusattl, so we rode our bicycles over. I think he's right and it's a lovely way to spend an evening."

"But what about the daytime? What do you do all day?" Julia was surprised at her own assertiveness.

"I work in the metal fastener factory in Saaz."

"No! So do I!"

"Look at the ducks, Julia!" Michael said. "Isn't that a teal? My father used to hunt them. They're quite good to eat."

Julia gasped. "But they're so small, and so pretty. Why would he kill such beautiful birds?"

Michael rubbed his forehead and grimaced. His jaw muscles clenched and unclenched. "Every animal is beautiful in its own way, but we all have to eat. Oh, never mind. I wish I'd never mentioned the ducks."

"No, you're right." She realized then that she hadn't given much thought to Michael's feelings. "I've killed many a chicken myself. But there's something so precious about being beautiful, wild, and free. It seems a shame to kill them."

"Real life is not always what we would wish." Michael kicked at a pebble on the path.

They walked along in silence for several steps. Julia squirmed to think that she was the cause of the awkwardness between them. Michael's face was a tight mask. He seemed barely able to hold his anger in check. She stole a quick peek at Lukas. He leaned his head to one side as if he were pondering something. "No," he said, "you're quite right, Michael. Life is not always what we would wish, but at least in the case of people, we can take actions to help steer things our way."

Michael's chin rose. "Yes, and it looks like I'll have to be wary of yours."

Julia walked faster, pulling on Michael's hand. "Let's catch up with Heidi and Elisabeth. They're already on their way back to the square and I promised Mother I'd keep an eye on them."

"And who will keep an eye on you?" Lukas asked with a wink.

"I will!" Michael glowered, his face as black as a thundercloud.

The rows of hop plants towered above them. Julia waited for Michael to snag the vines using a long pole with a hook. Then she carefully picked the prickly hop cones and let them drop into a large basket that stood nearby. Picking hops for the famous Saaz beer was an annual social event; a way to spend a few days on a working picnic while earning an extra bit of money.

"Oh-h-h-h, phooey!" Julia shook her hands. "Those darned hop lice. I hate the way they squish in my hands."

"But you're wearing gloves."

"Still, they managed to get inside."

Michael took her gloves off, brushed her hands free of lice, and then kept her hands in his. "You're very brave."

"What do you mean?"

"Most girls would have given up on the job rather than risk handfuls of squashed bugs." He pulled her through the tall thick row of hop plants, out of sight of the rest of the pickers. "What's this in your hair?"

"What?" Julia reached for her hair, but Michael took her hand and put it down by her side and behind her back. Still holding that hand, he pulled her closer. Her heart pounded. She inhaled his lemony aftershave. It was so manly and intoxicating, although being so close to him made her feel self-conscious and insecure. He was so handsome. Was she pretty enough for him? What if she had the wrong idea? Maybe he really was looking for one of those crawly things in her hair. She didn't want bugs in her hair.

"Let me have a look. I think it might be one of those hop crawlers. I'll get it if it's there." He inspected the top of her head. She felt hot all over as he touched her hair. Tingles raced up and down her body. She stood perfectly still, not even breathing for a moment.

"Do you see it? Can you get it off?" she said into his chest.

"Hmm ... just a minute ... I think it might be on the other side." He laid his cheek on her head and then turned to nibble her ear.

"Michael!" The tickle that rushed from her ear to the pit of her stomach surprised her. She tried to pull away, but Michael's grip tightened.

"No! Wait! I've almost got it. I have to check the other side once more." He touched her hair so carefully, fingers lingering. She basked in the sensuality of it.

"And?"

"And, I think you're all clear." He kissed her.

Julia opened her mouth to speak only to feel Michael's tongue probe inside. Another flush of heat washed over her body. Should she give in or pull away? Her knees felt weak and she let down the barriers to enjoy the kiss.

Voices. Her eyes widened. Was someone watching them? She pulled away.

"Where did those two lovebirds go?" It was Heidi. Why did she have to show up now of all times?

Then Julia recognized Jan's voice. "I have a feeling Michael is reaping his harvest behind that row of hops." A moment later she heard Heidi's squeal of delight, giggling, and the sound of kissing and moaning. They were certainly enjoying themselves. Julia wished she could let herself relax like that, but she felt unsure of how far to let Michael go and whether she would be able to stop him or herself.

"We'd better get back to work," Julia said as she straightened her sweater. "Thanks for checking my hair." She looked down at the ground and smiled.

Michael shook his head. "Julia, if only you would submit. Isn't that what women are supposed to do?"

She laughed. "Submit?" That word wasn't in her dictionary. At least not in her current edition. "You'd like that, wouldn't you, Michael?" She gave him a peck on the cheek and slipped back into the rows to continue picking.

The skies were clear and the autumn air was cool when the neighbouring towns of Neusattl and Saaz faced off at a Sunday soccer match in the Saaz community fairgrounds. On a wooden bench at the edge of the playing field, Julia and her sisters huddled together for warmth. They shouted and cheered for their brothers and cousins, who made up a substantial part of the small-town team, but Jan and Andreas on the Saaz lineup were the attraction for Heidi and Elisabeth.

Heidi nudged Julia, grabbed her elbow with one hand, and patted it rapidly with the other. "Isn't that your fellow? I know you haven't seen him for weeks, but I'm pretty sure it was him."

"What? Who?" asked Julia.

"The violinist! Who else?"

"Well, I thought you might mean Lu—"

"Lukas the looker! He's handsome and I think he was interested in you. We really should go back to the square sometime soon. We could see Jan and Andreas again too." Heidi babbled on happily about Jan's beautiful eyes and what he had said to her last time they met. She never seemed to tire of talking about Jan. "I was talking to Jan at half time and they'd like to meet Elisabeth and me in the square next week. I told them I'd let them know after the game."

"So, where did you say you thought you saw him?"

"Who?"

Julia glared at her.

"Oh, you mean Michael. He's right over ... he *was* right there a minute ago."

Julia put her head beside Heidi's and tried to follow the direction of her outstretched hand. "I don't see him there. It was probably someone who looked a bit like him." Julia's shoulders sagged. "Oh!" She shrieked and gave a little jump. She spun her head around and came face to face with Michael who had bent down to tap her shoulder.

"How are you?" he asked.

"Oh ... ah ... fine, I guess. I'm surprised to see you. It's been quite a while and you don't come to choir practices anymore."

"My father has put his foot down and insists it's time for me to learn more about the baking business than just how to knead a bit of dough."

"I wondered why I hadn't seen you."

"Will you walk with me a bit now, Julia, before the game ends?" Michael offered his hand to help her up. His deep brown eyes looked hopeful and inviting.

He was terribly handsome, Julia thought, with his straight nose, firm chin and freshly shaved face. His dark wavy hair was in need of a cut but it made him look a bit roguish and exciting the way it curled around his ear and over his collar. So different from the usual short haircuts. She admired the way he dared to wear his hair longer than was considered proper. She wished she could find that kind of courage and assert herself more.

Within minutes they were walking arm in arm and talking the way they had in the summer. Julia no longer blushed when Michael's hand wandered to her backside, as long as they were out of sight of the soccer fans. Today she wasn't worried about prying eyes. She knew that all attention was on the game.

"Julia, I don't know what you've done to me, but I can't stop thinking about you."

"What are you talking about? I haven't seen you for ages?"

"I told you I couldn't get away from this baking business. Up before dawn to get the dough mixed and rising, baking all morning, cleaning up, and taking care of the shop the rest of the time."

"But after that?"

"After that I fall into bed like a dead man for a few hours just so I can get up soon and do it all over again." He gave a short, sad chuckle. "But somewhere in between I have Julia on my mind." He was quiet for a moment and suddenly burst out laughing.

"What? What?!" Julia stopped to face him.

"Never mind. I shouldn't have laughed."

She put her hand on his arm. "But you have, so now you have to tell me what's so funny."

"Promise me you won't take it the wrong way or be offended?"

Julia nodded. "I promise. Just tell me what's so funny."

"All right then. As I said, I can't stop thinking about you." He hesitated.

"Yes, go on."

"When I'm working in the bakery, kneading the dough, I'm thinking, 'Julia, Julia,' knead, knead, and before I know it I'm making bread and buns shaped like your beautiful body parts."

She punched his upper arm playfully. "Oh-h-h!"

"You see, this baking business has its plus side. I find I quite enjoy touching and patting breast-shaped buns and loaves of bread shaped like bum cheeks."

"Michael! You're so naughty. Does your father know what you do?"

He grinned. "No, but I must say that sales have been up lately." He stopped abruptly and took her in his arms. His fingers spread gently through her thick, wavy hair and pulled her head towards his. She didn't resist and allowed him to kiss her. A warm and gentle, but demanding kiss; his lips were soft and hard at the same time. Heat surged through her. Julia had not expected to feel so weak. It would be hard for her to walk away right now, with her knees feeling like gelatine. But it seemed that Michael was not about to let her escape so easily anyway. He kept a firm grip around her waist while his lips wandered to the tip of her nose, her cheeks, her eyelids. When he ran his tongue down the side of her neck to her collarbone, she no longer thought of resisting. A shudder of pleasure tickled her skin. Julia found herself returning kisses and pulling Michael closer, although that was hardly possible. Her weak knees could go to the devil, she thought. Through the pounding pulse in her ears, Michael's whispers sent waves of delight through her. "Julia, Julia. I love you so much, Julia."

"Julia! Julia!" Heidi panted as she came running up to them. "I've been looking for you!" She looked over her shoulder. "Quickly! Mother will be coming this way in another minute. Tidy your hair!"

"I'd better go," Michael said, and he was gone before Julia finished straightening her clothes.

"Thanks, Heidi," Julia mumbled. She pulled her jacket around her more tightly feeling the afternoon chill now that she was no longer in Michael's warm embrace.

"Your face is all red," Heidi teased. But then she became serious. "Let's run back to meet Mother. We'll say we've been going for a brisk walk to warm up after sitting on those cool soccer benches too long."

Julia gave her sister a hug. "You're a dear!"

"I know you'd cover for me too if I met Jan some time."

"You know I would."

Julia lay in bed that night, alternately remembering and blushing. Again she felt his fingers massaging the back of her head, soft lips exploring her face, a strong arm pulling her in at the waist towards that hot, hard maleness that she had no experience with and yet understood instinctively. And that tongue sliding down her neck to her collarbone. Where else might it have wandered, given the opportunity? She sighed. Over and over she replayed the scene, until she finally began to drift off with her lover's face lingering. Drowsy with sleep Julia struggled to see it more clearly in the half-dream. Blue-grey eyes, dark lashes and straight, white teeth didn't seem to fit into the dream, but she couldn't shake off the image. The tall figure pulled her closer, whispering, "Julia, Julia. I love you so much."

"I love you too, Lukas," a voice inside her head murmured.

12.

A cold wind had sprung up since he left the soccer field. Michael looked forward to the warmth of the bakery. Shoulders hunched, he clasped his jacket lapels together at the neck. As he hustled home, his mind whirled in a muddle of emotions. Julia had allowed him to kiss her. The kiss in the hops rows some weeks earlier hadn't really counted. He knew he had stolen that one. But today he could feel that Julia wanted it too. Weeks of wishing and daydreaming had finally become reality. He wanted more, of course, but with Julia the kiss had been hard-won. His fingers tingled with the memory of her silky hair. Her cheeks, cold from the autumn air, had burned his lips. Her eyelashes had tickled his cheeks—he had delighted in the closeness of her. She'd been his willing captive for a few seconds. If only her mother hadn't come along, oh, the things he could have done. He knew Julia would have given in to him with only a little more persuasion.

Michael tore his thoughts away from Julia and picked up the pace. He was already late getting the dough mixed for Monday morning. His father must be getting anxious about it and the last thing Michael wanted was to cause him more stress.

Only two days ago, he had watched his father's lips take on a bluish-grey tinge and his face turn as ashen as the rye flour he was working into the dough. When he insisted that his father sit down and rest, Rolf actually did just that. That was when Michael knew it was serious.

"You should see a doctor," he had told him.

Rolf let out a big sigh. "I've been."

"And?"

"I didn't want you to worry. There's nothing they can do. It's just a bit of angina."

"What does that mean?"

"Nothing serious. Nothing at all." Rolf batted at the air. Michael searched his father's face for any clue that he was brushing him off. Seeing none he had washed his hands and gone to the table to finish kneading the recently abandoned clump of rye dough.

His thoughts wandered as he worked. Was his father putting a brave face on his illness? What if he was sicker than he admitted? What if he died? His hands stopped pushing the dough around as he considered that unbearable thought. He would be left alone. Completely alone. He did have his Aunt Karin, but he didn't see much of her. She and his father had not been close for years—some rift that neither talked about and he had long ago stopped wondering about.

His Aunt Karin wouldn't be much comfort if his father died. He cut the dough and rolled it into loaves on the floured board, pondering the possibility of a bleak future. Operating the bakery alone would end his freedom to be out and about. How would he ever see Julia?

Michael knew he was fortunate to have the bakery since he had no other business skills or training, but still he was not prepared to lose his father. Fearing the yoke settling on him, he had made a point of going out to the soccer game in hopes of seeing Julia. And she had been there today, bless her sweet heart.

Just as well her mother had come along though, or God only knows what might have happened. He would have found some outbuilding for them to hide behind, and oh, Lord, there'd be hell to pay afterwards. At least Katerina's threatened arrival reminded him that he had to get home. He'd forgotten all about the bakery and his responsibilities.

Here he was now only a little bit late. He pushed open the back door and looked around the bakery. Empty. That was odd. Why hadn't his father started work yet? Guilt flooded his mind as it had so many times before. Despite his father's nonchalance regarding his health, Michael had a niggling feeling that he wasn't as well as he pretended to be.

"I'm home!" His voice echoed in the silence. It was too quiet. With growing trepidation, Michael took the stairs two at a time. "Papa! Papa? Where are you?"

The door to the upstairs suite stood wide open. Rolf Hiebert had not even made it across the room to the sofa. He lay on his side, clutching his chest, eyes wide open, staring at the floor. Michael sank to his knees. He rolled his father over onto his back and tried to sit him up.

"Papa! Are you all right? Papa! Papa? Please! Say something." Cradling and rocking his father in his arms, he sobbed, "Oh, no, no, no!" A wailing moan filled the room.

The black horse-drawn coach turned in through the cemetery gates. Aside from Aunt Karin, Michael had no relatives at the immediate gravesite. Several of his friends, including Lukas, Jan, and Andreas, stood nearby for moral support. But the chilly morning air had not deterred other mourners from attending. Beyond the area close to the freshly dug grave, the cemetery was crowded with townspeople who had enjoyed Rolf's bread for years. Men in dark suits and women in black dresses and shawls stood shoulder to shoulder on the damp gravel pathways between the graves. As the hearse arrived, Michael was aware of snatches of muted conversation.

"... a kind man."

"... always laughing."

"... should have married again."

"Plenty of women interested ..."

"God rest his soul."

He was pleased that his father had been so well liked, and battled wave after wave of emotion, not the least of which was guilt. So many times he could have been there to help his father. As Rolf Hiebert's body was lowered into the ground, Michael silently promised him that he would make the bakery thrive—if not this one, in these hard times, then another one, another time.

With tear-filled eyes, Aunt Karin squeezed his hand. "I'm so sorry, Michael. He was a good man. I'm going to miss my little brother terribly." She stopped to dab at her eyes with her handkerchief and took quick breath. "I should never have let our feud go on so long. It was...." She shook her head. "Ach, Michael, such a silly argument and so many years ago. I wish I'd made the effort to mend things." She sobbed and hung her head.

After a moment she took a deep breath and stood up straight. She looked Michael in the eyes. "But it's worse for you. He was your father. You'll find it hard to go on without him, but we'll sit down and talk business very soon. The bakery must go on and you won't be able to do it alone."

"I have to try, Aunt Karin."

"Yes, of course. Your father would want that." She crumpled her handkerchief between dabs at her face. "You're coming to my house for the reception, so we can talk a bit when everyone is gone. Now you need to be with your friends." With a nod of her head she indicated Lukas, Jan, and Andreas, who stood nearby waiting.

Lukas shook Michael's hand and gave him a quick embrace. A couple of soft slaps on the shoulder conveyed feelings that Michael found impossible to speak out loud. He simply nodded and looked at the ground without speaking. The huge knot in his throat ached as he fought to contain his emotion.

"Sorry," Lukas whispered hoarsely. Jan and Andreas followed suit, each shuffling from one foot to the other.

"We're really sorry for your loss, Michael," they said, shaking his hand.

He took a deep breath and swallowed the lump in his throat. "Thanks." The bottom had just dropped out of his world and he was a hollow man; a dull pain filled his head—the rest was emptiness.

Dry alder leaves scooted along the sidewalk as Karin and Michael walked to her house together. A small group of Rolf's close friends and neighbours followed them from the cemetery. Karin prepared tea to go with the pastries that Michael had brought from the bakery earlier. Solemn respects were paid and bittersweet memories of their baker were relived for a suitable length of time.

Karin closed the door behind the last guest. "Thank God, that's over." She let out a long breath and collapsed onto the sofa.

"Yes, it was good of them to come, but it's a relief to get the duty part over with and just be with family," Michael said.

"And I want to be there for you, Michael. I should have made amends with your father. Perhaps I can make up for it now." Karin poured herself a glass of water. "We have a lot of things to deal with," she continued. "I hope you don't think I was insensitive and callous to bring up business at the cemetery."

"No, no. Not at all."

"I didn't survive on my own this long by being soft and mild-natured." Widowed after a brief marriage to an abusive husband, Karin had managed to get by on the savings she had put aside. Frugal management of her small sewing business had become second nature to her.

"I'd like to help you get on your feet," she said. "We can't feel sorry for ourselves too long because your father is gone. If you are to survive, you must get to work and make plans for the business immediately. The house and bakery are yours now, but the challenge will be to hang onto them. Other bakeries in town would love to take advantage of this situation."

"Yes, I know. Papa mentioned that just the other day. He was worried because they were underselling us."

His aunt nodded knowingly. "I was wondering about that. You will have to come up with ideas to improve sales. Encourage them to buy *your* bread and cakes. Give them a good reason not to shop at the bakery down the street."

"I've been thinking about this a bit already and I have a few ideas."

"Good! And another thing—you need to get some help to run the bakery. It's too much for one person. I'm too old to be of much use to you in baking, but I can help you sell at the front counter. Meanwhile, we must advertise for a capable baker's assistant for you."

The day after the funeral, Aunt Karin showed up at the door with a "Help wanted" sign.

"Let's get this sign placed in the window and get you back in business. Now what do you want me to do? Mix dough for bread or bake cakes?"

"But I thought you said—"

"I know what I said. Never mind that. Now where do you keep the aprons?"

With Karin's help, Michael survived the next few days. He interviewed several women who responded to his aunt's sign, finally deciding on Marlies. She looked as if she heartily enjoyed the wonderful breads and pastries that she said she was able to bake. With her round, happy face and pleasant manner, she had a way of putting him at ease almost immediately. She would be perfect for baking as well as handling the sales. A week later Michael knew that Marlies was the best thing that could have happened to him under the circumstances. Twenty-nine and single she was available for working the early hours. She had a way with dough, patting it lovingly into shape, almost apologizing to it for having to bake it. The dough, gently treated as it was, rose into light and tender bread. The townspeople flocked to the "new" bakery, first out of curiosity, but later, for the excellent bread and pastries.

Michael put his earlier ideas to work, offering a free bun with every loaf of bread. Pieces of cake were cut just a little larger than those of the bakery down the street. Although he was barely breaking even, word spread that Michael's was the place to go and, for the time being at least, the bakery was surviving.

But for the baker himself, the workday hours were long. Guilt pushed Michael out of bed in the morning and goaded him into putting in hours that he knew he should have offered his father while he was alive. His remorse fueled a determination to make sure his bread was an excellent product. He had no time to see his friends, no time to visit Julia, no time to take days off from his work. Yet he had too much time to think.

What was Julia doing these days? Was she wondering why he didn't come to Neusattl anymore? Was she still singing in the choir on Sunday evenings? Had she found someone else? He would love to be taking her for walks, but the weather was too cold for that, and of course it was dark so early now that meeting her in the evening was impossible. His world shrank. He passed the days mechanically.

13.

Week followed week of grey skies and cold. In spite of the chilly weather, Julia pedaled her bicycle the seven kilometres to Bechert's metal fastener factory in Saaz. She was one of many young women who started out with simple sorting jobs; so many screws in a box, so many boxes in a carton, each sorted by type and size. Records were kept and submitted to the office daily. Julia's neat handwriting and accuracy made her the natural choice to complete the daily report for her department.

"Ah, there you are, Julia," the tall man said with a smile. "The weekend is coming up and Sunday is All Saints' Day. The boss wants things finished up early. Do you have the report ready?"

Julia felt a rush of fluttering nerves. "Lukas! What are you doing here? Where's Herbert? He usually takes the report to the office." Her hand involuntarily checked her hair. "I thought you worked in the metal fastener factory."

"So I do, and here I am."

"But I mean, I-I assumed that you were in the manufacturing part. This is such a huge place; I never expected to see you."

"I didn't expect to see you either, until today. Franz asked me to collect the reports. Said you're the person to see in packaging." He took the report from her and glanced at it. Julia wondered why the paper didn't catch fire when their fingers touched. "I can see you don't belong here if you can do calculations like this. Most of the girls don't have that kind of schooling."

Julia looked at the floor to hide her embarrassment. "Thank you," she mumbled. She was annoyed with herself for allowing her discomposure to show. Lukas was certainly suave and composed, but then he'd had the advantage of knowing she would be there.

"Well, must run. It's been very nice to see you," Lukas said. "Now that I know where you are, perhaps I'll see you again sometime."

"I'll be here." Julia laughed softly. "Where else?"

Julia watched the trim, muscular man leave. What would it be like to have those strong arms around her? Little tickles rushed through her as she imagined him holding her. She was still staring at the door when someone called her name.

"Should I go on packaging then? Or are we to stop for the day?" Julia snapped out of her momentary daze and felt her face getting hot until she remembered that Hilda couldn't read her thoughts.

"Hilda, it's not as if I'm your boss."

"I know, but you're so organized. You always know what to do next." Hilda stood there gaping, slack-jawed. Heaviness in the jowls and neck gave her a porcine look, but she had her assets in her big breasts and shapely legs. She seemed to be very conscious of her blonde hair—Julia was sure the colour came out of a bottle—flipping it to the side and taking a tress of it as if to inspect it for split ends.

"Well, then, don't start any new boxes. Why not just put the ones we've done on the shelves and tidy things up? Get Herbert to bring the stepladder for you."

"Herbert? That idiot!" Hilda snorted. "Him and his blue face. I wish he'd get rid of those hectograph pencils he carries in his shirt pocket. Stands around all day checking to see if they're sharp," she whined in her nasally voice. "You ever watched him?" Hilda mistook Julia's roll of the eyes as encouragement and ploughed on. "He's in a world of his own—checks one pencil after another, wets his finger with his tongue, touches the tip of the pencil, puts it back in his pocket. 'This one's sharp. This one's *not* sharp.' For sure we know *he's* not too sharp. And you know how the blue dye comes off those pencils? He's got it all over his shirt, never mind his fingers, tongue, lips, and chin." She shuddered.

"Yes, Hilda, I know, but he means well." *And you're so perfect.*

With a gasp for air after her tirade, Hilda lifted her nose a little higher. "I'll go find him," she said through tightly pursed lips.

Julia tidied her small corner desk and organized her paperwork. Then she went to the shelving area in the back room for one last look to make sure everything was put away neatly. As she neared the doorway she heard Hilda's heavy steps on the ladder.

"I'll hold the ladder steady for you, Hildy." Herbert sounded eager to help.

"Hold it tight. I have to climb to the top shelf with these boxes and I only have one hand to hang onto the ladder."

"I've got it, Hildy." Julia came around the corner just then. Unaware of her presence, Herbert stared in awe at Hilda's breasts. As the blonde climbed to the third rung, his eyes followed her ample hips swaying back and forth. Casually he bent over slightly in order to peer up Hilda's dress.

"Herbert!" Hilda snapped. "Hold the ladder!"

"Yes, yes, Hildy. I'm holding it."

"Pretty blonde," he babbled through purple spittle that settled on his chin. He reached for Hilda's leg.

"Herbert! Shame on you!" Julia snapped. "You could make Hilda fall. For heaven's sake, keep your hands to yourself. And go wash your face."

Herbert's hand shot back to his side and the ladder wobbled. Head lowered, with his lower lip stuck out, he looked at the floor. "Don't tell the boss, Julia, please?"

"Now why would I want to do that?"

"Some people would tell." He turned his head slightly and let his eyes drift in Hilda's direction.

"All right," said Hilda. "We won't say anything as long as you remember to keep your hands to yourself from now on."

"Yes, Hildy. I'm sorry."

"And your eyes!" she added.

In the weeks that followed, Herbert kept out of Hilda's way and made every effort to be helpful to Julia. It still frightened him to think how close he had come to losing his job. His parents had allowed him to continue living at home when he grew up, but they insisted that he work and help pay expenses. If he had lost his job, he could have been out on the street, and he knew where that would end. He would have to beg for his food. Begging was against the law. He had heard frightening stories about the Czech police putting beggars in jail and beating their feet. No, he thought, he had better follow the rules. He needed to keep this very important job.

"He's coming, Julia," Herbert chirped. "He's coming!" Herbert held his arms straight down by his sides, but his hands fluttered back and forth in giant tremors.

"Yes, yes, Herbert. Calm down. Here you are. Give him the report."

"No, Julia. You go do it." He backed up a step. "I'll just watch!"

"What do you mean, you'll just watch?" Julia scowled.

"I-I mean, I'll just watch ... your desk! You know, to make sure nobody messes with it while you're ... you know ... busy."

"Oh, Herbert. Really! You're imagining things. There's nothing going on." But Julia turned that pink colour and Herbert knew he was right.

"You'll be wanting the report then, Lukas," Julia said.

"The report and...."

"And?"

"And you," Lukas mumbled. He looked so strong and handsome, still a bit bronzed from the late summer sun. Herbert watched Julia's reaction as Lukas smiled at her and reached for the report. The pink glow on Julia's neck turned a deeper red. She turned away from Lukas who grinned. Herbert wished he could be like Lukas. He wished he could impress Julia like that. He loved Julia.

"This one's sharp. This one's *not* sharp," Herbert muttered. He tried to look busy as he sneaked peeks at Lukas and Julia, but Lukas glared at him and Herbert could not maintain eye contact. With a hasty wipe of his drooling blue chin, he scuttled out of the room. From outside the doorway, Herbert continued to eavesdrop.

"Now Julia, what do you say to a cup of coffee after work today?" Herbert's mouth hung open as he listened.

"Me? Today?" Julia's words sounded choked.

"Of course, you. Of course, today."

"But I don't really know you. Maybe it's not a good idea."

"Uh-oh, he's going to feel bad," Herbert thought. "I knew she wouldn't go for it."

"What better way to find out about me? Come on.... Four o'clock, all right? Great."

As Lukas walked past him beside the door, Herbert beamed at him in adoration. *So that's how it's done.*

The warmth of Dettmeier's coffee shop wrapped Julia in a welcome blanket as she came in out of the cold. Her mouth watered at the sweet smells of cinnamon, pastries, and coffee that filled the room. It seemed like hours since her lunch of bread and cheese. She worried that her stomach would growl at the wrong moment. Lukas was already waiting for her. His hand on her waist gently steered her towards a corner table.

Lukas helped Julia out of her wool jacket and held the chair for her. He motioned for two coffees and asked what kind of pastry she would like. They decided on plum cake and then sat looking at each other in silence. Julia clasped and unclasped her hands while Lukas held his very still. After a moment, he put his large right hand over both of Julia's smaller ones. "Don't be nervous."

How did he manage to smile so easily?

"I don't bite," he said. "I just want to get to know you better."

"Sorry. I feel like a naïve, blushing schoolgirl." *Oh, dear, did I just say that out loud?*

"You're certainly not a schoolgirl anymore. You're a very lovely young lady."

Julia felt her face getting hot.

"And I know I'm not the only one who thinks that."

"Oh? Who else?" *Why did I say that? He's going to think I'm so vain.*

"Anyone I talk to at work says you're fun to work with, always pleasant, and very capable."

Julia wished she hadn't asked. She didn't know how to handle so much unexpected praise, or where to direct her eyes while she dealt with her embarrassment.

"You know, Julia, I think you could get a better job with your abilities."

"But I like what I do—"

"Yes, it's just that.... Listen. Old Frau Schneider, the manager's secretary, is finding the job too much for her and has asked to retire. She's not very neat or organized and you'd have no trouble doing a better job than she does."

"And you think—?"

"I think you could get that job if you just asked for it."

"You do? How do you know?"

"Franz and I chat quite often when I bring in the reports and he's always saying how neat and accurate yours are."

"Really? Did he really say that?" One thing about Lukas, he sure knew how to make a girl feel good.

"He's impressed with your work."

"I suppose I could give it a try." *But if I fail, I'll feel really stupid.* "You really think I should?"

"Yes, I do. But that's not why I asked you to come for coffee."

"No? Then why?"

Lukas squeezed Julia's hand one more time before he let it go as the coffee and plum cake arrived. Once the waitress had left, he leaned forward again.

"Julia, is it so hard to see that I think you're wonderful? Ever since that time, long ago now, when I showed up at the square hoping to meet one of your sisters—"

"That was awkward," Julia interrupted with a little laugh. "Three of us walking."

"Yes, if ever there was a rose between two thorns. Ever since then, I've been hoping to see you again. I never got lucky, except here at work."

Julia peered over her coffee cup at Lukas. She knew that by now her face was flushed red. It was so stressful, trying to make a good impression. Time to turn the tables. "So here we are, Lukas. Why don't you tell me about yourself?"

"Me? Well, let's see. I'm everything a girl could want—tall, dark, and handsome." He grinned. "Oh, and smart and hard-working. Do you need more?"

She nodded.

"Fine, then. I'm ... whatever you want me to be. What would you want me to be, Julia?" His blue-grey eyes were soft now as he waited for her response.

"Above all I would want you to be yourself. To me it's important that a man be truthful and sincere. After that, everything else is a bonus."

"In that case, I'm perfect for you." His sat back confidently and folded his arms across his chest. "But tell me more about yourself. What do you like to do?"

Julia squirmed. She didn't like to talk about herself, but Lukas did not take his eyes from her face as he waited for her to begin.

"All right then. Let me think. I like flowers, the garden, birds—all animals, really."

"I didn't realize that you loved nature so much."

"No wonder. You only know me from working inside in an office. Not much nature there."

"True."

"I like to imagine that the animals can talk." Julia felt her face getting hot again as Lukas's smile broadened. "I can't believe I just said that. I meant that I believe animals have feelings and communicate with us more than we realize. If we only listened more closely."

"That's interesting."

"You don't think it's silly?" If he did, he was being very kind about it.

"Not at all. My horse lets me know when it's hungry. My dog is very smart. Sometimes I think he can talk. Certainly he understands a lot."

"You have a dog?" *That's a good sign. He likes animals too.* "What kind?"

"A shepherd. Alsatian. His name is Astor."

"A very noble name."

"He's a noble dog. You should come and meet him sometime. If you would like to, that is."

"Maybe sometime ... that would be nice." She pushed her empty cup and plate aside. "That was delicious plum cake. Thanks, Lukas. I'd better get going home now before it gets too dark." Lukas put money on the table and jumped up to help her with her jacket.

"I'll ride along beside you to make sure you get home safely."

"But it's really out of your way."

"Not that much. I'm living at my Aunt Theresa's house just outside of town here.

"Are your parents not alive then?"

"My mother died two years ago, and my father sold the family home. He lives with my older sister. She looks after him. Better than I could."

They pedaled along, side by side in the dusk, first along the cobbled streets of Saaz and soon along a narrow country road that led to Neusattl and Julia's parents' house.

"The time passed so quickly," Lukas said. "Let's do this again soon."

"What? Pedal home? I do it every day."

"Smarty! You know what I mean, Julia. Let's meet for cake and coffee again soon."

"But what about Michael?" As she said his name, she realized that she hadn't given him a thought until now. Guilt washed over her. She'd betrayed him.

"What about him?"

"I think he's serious about seeing me except he doesn't have much time since his father died and he's had to take over the bakery. I shouldn't have gone with you."

"Look, Julia. I'm sorry about his father, but if Michael is serious he should be making sure no one steals his girl. I am serious and if he isn't around to look after you ... well I am."

14.

Icy winds spun whorls of dry snowflakes around them. Julia set a brisk pace, the snow crunching a steady rhythm under her boots. The commute that had taken fifteen minutes on her bicycle now took almost an hour on foot.

"You sure move fast." Konrad hustled to keep up with his sister. He worked in the brewery in Saaz and often accompanied her to town.

"If I slow down, I start to feel the cold, so fast is better."

"I suppose we're in for plenty more of this cold weather as we get near Christmas." Konrad pulled up his collar against the wind. "Margaret is hoping it will snow more so the children will have a beautiful, white Christmas this year. God knows it won't be much of a holiday for them in any other way."

"What do you mean, Konnie? Is something wrong?"

"Oh, no. Nothing serious. I only meant that there won't be many presents this year. You know we're handing over part of my pay to Mother and Father to help out, just as you and Roland are doing."

"I guess I hadn't thought about how much harder it is for you and Roland with your families. And I hadn't thought about how few presents there will be for the children. Maybe I could help you out a bit?"

"It's sweet of you to offer, Julia. We aren't doing that badly, but there won't be luxuries this year."

"Speaking of Christmas, you know there is a concert in Saaz next Saturday and our choir is joining with the Saaz choir to sing a few carols. Are you and Margaret planning to go?"

"I'd love to, but the children are too young to walk that far."

"You could leave them with Mother and Father overnight and pick them up the next day."

"Why is it so important to you that we come to this concert? Are you planning to meet your baker friend? Need a chaperone?"

"No, of course not." She knew she must be blushing, but as she glanced up at her brother, he was looking at the road. Good thing. If he had noticed her embarrassment he would have teased her unmercifully. "But it would be nice to know for sure that I had someone to walk home with after the concert." If she didn't have someone to escort her to and from Saaz, her parents would probably not allow her to go. She hadn't seen Michael in a long time, but she assumed that work and the miserable weather were responsible for that.

"I'll see what I can do," Konrad promised. "Here we are. Have a good day. You'll make your own way home after work, you said?"

"Yes, thanks, Konnie." She gave him a quick hug. "You have a good day too."

Julia entered the cold building and shivered as she made her way to Herr Ostermann's office. Once inside that room, she felt more comfortable. Not only was it warmer here than in the packaging department downstairs, but the office looked friendlier and tidier since she had taken over. Herr Ostermann had even commented on this. He smiled as he entered the room moments later, humming to himself as he hung up his coat on a hook behind the door.

The day passed quickly as Julia prepared a letter Herr Ostermann had dictated earlier and answered other correspondence that had arrived late the day before. She had her mother to thank for this job.

She'd been too young to understand the politics, but not too young to understand her father's despair that sad day in 1918 when Sudetenland was given to the Czechs.

"I've had to give up my post as stationmaster," her father had said in a quavering voice. "I could keep it if I were fluent in Czech, but I'm too old to start learning it now."

Julia almost cried too as she watched his shoulders shaking. He had bent forward to hide his face in his hands as he let himself drop into his rocking chair and sob quietly. Her mother rubbed his shoulders and put her arms around him. "The older children will help us out," Katerina said.

"Will we have to learn Czech, Mother?" Julia had asked.

"I'm afraid so, Julia. All the classes in our German school will be taught in Czech now, but it'll be easy for you. You're still young."

"But won't I learn to read in German then?"

"Oh, yes. We'll make sure of that at home." And so, Julia was well prepared for life in this bordering territory, whichever language was called for.

Saturday morning Julia took her green hand-knitted woollen dress out of the closet. She rummaged through her small wardrobe looking for a scarf to give the dress a festive look. Dark green or the red? Dark green. And her ivory pin. She hoped the greens would set off her hazel eyes and immediately scolded herself for being so vain, but she felt tingly with anticipation. Content with her choice, she hooked the dress on its hanger on the top of the closet door for later. She pulled her good black shoes from the bottom of the closet and went in search of a rag to shine them.

The heat thrown by the kitchen stove seemed extra friendly this morning. Katerina hummed a Christmas carol as she stirred the porridge. Julia loved the happy bustle of the kitchen at this time of year. The humming stopped abruptly as her mother handed the wooden spoon to Elisabeth. "Here. See that it doesn't burn. I just remembered that I have to get that striezel dough braided and set to rise again or it won't be done by tonight. Heidi, are those hazelnuts shelled and chopped yet? I'm going to need them soon for the cookies. Thomas! Breakfast is almost ready. Wash up and come sit at the table. What are you looking for, Julia?"

She smiled to herself, thinking that her mother was like a sergeant-major, but under her guidance, things ran smoothly in the household. *I hope I'm as efficient in my own home someday.*

"A rag for my shoes."

"In the porch under the stool. Are you all ready for the choir performance tonight then?"

"As ready as we'll ever be. We've been practicing for weeks."

"Will your violinist be there?" Katerina asked.

"Mother! He's not *my* violinist. But, no, I don't think so. I don't know really. I haven't seen him for a few weeks and he said he would be very busy with the bakery now until the Christmas rush is over." *Still, I wish ... I hope I'll see Michael there.*

"You know Konnie is bringing the children over so you can go to the concert with him and Margaret. You make sure you come back with them afterwards so you aren't walking home alone after dark."

"Yes, Mother. I know."

"That's fine, now go heat up some water so you can wash your hair. We'll do the chores without you today."

"Thanks, Mother. I love you." She hugged her mother.

"Oh, go on with you now. You go make yourself pretty."

The community hall was buzzing like the inside of a beehive when Julia, Konrad, and Margaret arrived. Many spectators were already seated on the rows of benches. A few stood near the walls, bobbing up and down on their toes, pointing here or there at possible choices for seating. A woman wearing a kerchief turned to wave at someone she knew and indicated empty bench space beside her. Konrad pulled Margaret along to a space near the middle while Julia hurried to the small room at the side and back of the stage. The rest of the choir was already assembled.

"Now remember," Max said, "there's no organ here so we'll have no accompaniment, but we expected that. Listen for your note and focus on it as we start each piece. If you start on the right note, the rest of the harmony will take care of itself. Watch me for the signals. And remember to smile. You'll do fine."

The stage lights dimmed and the crowd instinctively hushed. Dressed in a good suit, the moderator began his welcome speech. "Ladies and Gentlemen of Saaz and neighbouring communities, welcome to our Christmas concert."

As he spoke Julia looked out on row upon row of expectant faces reflected softly in the low lighting from the stage. She put her hand over her mouth to muffle the sound as she cleared her throat one last time to make sure she found her voice. Looking up at Max's face, she remembered to smile and watch for his signal.

The mellow voices seemed to cushion and carry the clear high ones like a flowing velvet ribbon. They wove in, out, and around the familiar melodies of age-old Christmas hymns. Julia shivered with the thrill of emotion that singing brought out in her. The beauty of harmony filled her with joy. She hoped the music pleased her audience as well.

The choir moved to the side of the stage to make room for a short nativity scene. Julia knew that the children must have worked for weeks to remember their lines, but inevitably, disaster struck. The third Wise Man had lost his shoe on the steps up to the stage and looked to young Joseph for help. Joseph hissed at him, unaware that the audience could hear each word distinctly, "Leave the shoe already! No! Leave it. Carry on." The third Wise Man hesitated and then lunged back to grab his shoe, but now Joseph forgot his next line. The first Wise Man promptly helped him out by loudly whispering his lines for him.

"What do you have there, O' Wise Man?" Josef repeated.

"My shoe—I mean—we bring gold, frankincense and myrrh," said the third Wise Man.

Julia saw shoulders shaking and hands over mouths as the audience members tried to suppress their laughter. When the scene ended, the warm applause had every little actor's face beaming.

As the room quieted down, a faraway note could be heard floating down from the ceiling, or the walls, or the stage. Heads swivelled looking for its origin. This note melted into another and another and Julia recognized the melody. As a child in an angel costume floated in from center stage, the violin softly continued to play in descending notes that seemed to guide the angel to Earth.

> From heaven above to Earth I come,
> To bear good news to every home.
> Glad tidings of great joy I bring,
> Whereof I now will say and sing.

Julia's heart pounded. *That's got to be Michael. No one else could play it like that.* The centuries-old Martin Luther hymn, the Christmas spirit, the notes that turned from melancholy to joyful—the emotion of the moment had her eyes brimming with tears. The concert ended soon afterward and people milled around.

For the moment Julia was content to delay facing the chill outside the community hall doors. She searched the crowd for Michael, but was drawn into the Saaz choir group who were intent on socializing. She responded to introductions mechanically, her mind on the haunting strains of the violin. "Very nice to meet you, Doris," she said, looking past the woman.

"Are you looking for someone?" Doris asked.

"I was just wondering where, ah … where … the violinist was. We couldn't see him from where we stood in the choir."

"Oh, no wonder. He was right behind our Saaz choir on the other side of the stage. Isn't he just the best player you've ever heard? Do you know Michael?" Doris prattled on.

"Yes, I've met him. He's an excellent violinist. Well, excuse me, I must find my brother who is walking me home."

Squeezing through the crowds, Julia was making little headway. No wonder. Someone had hold of her arm. She was still thinking of the violin music when she found herself looking into a tall man's eyes.

"Lukas! What are you doing here?" Her heart pounded faster and surges of happiness pulsed through her.

"I live here, remember? Did you think I wouldn't come to listen to my favourite singer?"

"You didn't mention that you were coming, so I thought…."

"You thought I didn't know about the concert? Or thought I wouldn't be interested? It's one of the nicest things happening around here these days. I wasn't going to miss it. And I didn't want to miss seeing and hearing you."

"Did you like the concert?"

"Very much. The singing was beautiful. And weren't the kids hilarious?" Lukas smiled. "Can I walk you home?"

"My brother and his wife are walking home with me, but thanks for the offer. It was nice to see you. I'd better go. I see them waiting for me."

"Maybe you can introduce me."

They wove through the crowd, Lukas holding Julia's hand as if that was the way they always walked. It was then that she saw Michael standing beside Konrad. Her heart thumped louder. *Oh, dear God!* She had forgotten all about Michael. What would he think? Julia tried unsuccessfully to ease her hand away. Why did these awkward situations always have to happen to her? She looked around for an escape, but Lukas gripped her hand possessively.

She realized then that she couldn't hide Lukas from Michael anyway. It wasn't her fault that he had come up and taken her by the hand. But it *was* her fault that she liked it, her conscience told her. And yet, did she really owe Michael anything? He hadn't been to see her for weeks. Still, Michael had a way of making her feel confused.

"I thought I might see you when you came to find Konrad. I see that you found Lukas instead." Michael's gaze rested on their locked hands.

"Actually, Lukas found me. That was very nice playing tonight, Michael. Everyone was wondering where that beautiful music was coming from."

"I had hoped to walk you home, but Konrad tells me that he and Margaret are doing the honours tonight. So I'll see you ... sometime." Michael looked so dejected that Julia wanted to hug and console him right there in front of everyone.

"I—"

"You don't need to explain anything, Julia. It's all right," Michael said quickly. "Have a nice evening all of you." Julia felt torn between running after him and staying in the thrilling grasp of Lukas's hand. Why did life always have to be such a drama? Why couldn't she simply have them both?

In seconds Michael had disappeared into the crowd. Filling in the awkward silence, Julia introduced Lukas to her brother and his wife.

"I guess we'd better get going," Konrad suggested after a few moments of polite conversation.

Lukas, still gripping Julia's hand, raised it to his lips and kissed it. "See you soon," he said with a happy grin.

15.

A cold wind rattled the grimy factory windows. Workers had put on sweaters under their aprons to ward off the chill. In the hall outside the machine shop, Lukas was showing a new apprentice where to take the finished bolts when Franz appeared.

"Lukas," he said, "what's this I hear about you and Miss Sommer?"

"I don't know." In spite of the cold, his face felt hot. Raising his voice, Lukas called, "You go on with those bolts, Georg. Down the hall, turn left, third door down." He looked back at Franz and mumbled, "What do you hear?"

"I see I'm right. Blushing, are we?" Franz nudged Lukas. "So, tell me. What's the latest?"

"Nothing to tell, Franz. I like her. She's a very nice girl."

"Nice girl?! She's a real catch for some lucky bugger. Why not you?"

"Well, she's been going out with the baker. You know, Rolf's son."

"Yes, didn't he die a couple of months ago—the old man, I mean?"

"That's right. Julia feels that she has to stand by Michael because he's feeling bad right now. That's what she says, anyway, and I don't want to be the insensitive cad who kicks a rival when he's down. At least, that's how Julia might look at it."

"Nonsense! Where women are concerned, they just want to be flattered and pursued. They don't care so much by whom, and the lucky bugger who scores first, wins." Franz stuck his barrel chest out a little farther than usual, as if to lend the authority of experience to his statement. "If I were you, I'd go after her. And quickly, young man, or you'll find she's been snapped up while you're wasting time trying to do the noble thing."

"You think so? You don't think I should wait until Michael gets over his father's death?"

"Boy, by then it could be too late. You mark my words. Get in there and get what you want or go without forever." He paused for a moment. "Listen. I'm going to be out of the office for about half an hour. It might be a good time to go and invite my secretary out to the dance this Saturday."

"Uh, yes, all right then. Thanks." Lukas saw Georg coming back down the hall. "I'll go and take care of that business right away."

"And don't take 'no' for an answer," Franz called out over his shoulder.

Lukas threw his shop apron aside and took the stairs two at a time without getting winded. Near the main office door he slowed his pace, gave his jacket a straightening tug, and took a deep breath. He had known about the dance—time and place—but he was unsure of how to approach Julia to persuade her away from Michael. He had planned to go slow, bide his time, but what if Franz was right and he waited too long? He put his shoulders back and shook out his hands to help himself relax. He would ask her. The worst that could happen was that she would say no.

Julia had been in his thoughts much more than he admitted to Franz. Something about her fresh clean look appealed to Lukas. He had gone out with his share of young women, but he found their lipstick and rouge annoying and messy on his face and his shirts. He hated the stiffness of the sticky lotions meant to keep their finger wave hairdos in place. Julia's hair was naturally rich in colour and texture and he couldn't wait to bury his face in her curls. He wanted to touch her and yet she seemed almost too precious compared to other women. The thought of holding her close sent a surge of desire through him as he approached her desk.

"Hello, Lukas! How are you? Is there something I can do for you?"

"As a matter of fact, there is. I need a young and pretty date for this weekend's dance and I would be honoured if you would be the one."

"Well, you certainly come straight to the point. I like that."

"And do you like the idea of coming to the dance with me?"

"I do, very much ... but...."

"Then that's a 'yes'?"

"I don't know, Lukas. I'm so confused. I know Michael thinks we're together, but ... he says he's swamped with the bakery and he can't see me as often as he would like."

"For you, I would make the time. Do you think it's fair of him to ask that you just sit and wait in case he can come around?"

"No, I guess not. But I feel bad for him. He's all alone except for his aunt."

"Well, don't forget he has Marlies now too. She's not a catch like you, but I'm sure her company is comforting to him. And they have to spend a lot of time together in that bakery."

"That's cruel of you to insinuate that—"

"Not at all, Julia. I think it's cruel of Michael to make you wait and wonder like this. Come to the dance with me. After all, it's only a dance. It'll be more fun than sitting at home waiting for Michael."

He crossed his fingers behind his back as he watched her take a breath and bite her lower lip. "All right ... I guess...."

He was quick to drive home his advantage. "Look Julia, you haven't made any promises, have you? Michael hasn't made any promises, has he? There you are. But I will make a promise. Come to the dance with me and I promise we'll have a good time. I'll be at your house at seven."

He spun around and left the room before she might change her mind or see his satisfied smile.

Lukas arrived at the Sommers' house a few minutes before seven on Saturday night.

"Come in, Lukas." Heidi and Elisabeth tittered. "Julia will be right down. Have you seen Jan and Andreas lately?"

"Not since last weekend's soccer game. If the weather is fine tomorrow, there's a good chance they'll be out for their usual Sunday stroll in Neusattl."

"I hope so," said Heidi.

"Ah, Julia," Lukas smiled widely as she glided down the stairs. "You look lovely. But then you always do." He caught a glimpse of the winks and smirks Heidi and Elisabeth exchanged as they ducked out of the room.

"Come into the living room to meet my parents before we go, Lukas." Julia took his hand.

"And how are you traveling to and from this dance, Lukas?" Thomas asked after the introductions. "It's not a bad walk in the summertime, but at this time of year and at night, it's something I'm concerned about."

"I've brought my horse and buggy, as well as extra blankets, so Julia should be comfortable and safe. I'll have her home right after the dance."

"That's fine then. Have a good time."

Lukas flicked the reins and clicked for the horse to start. "You look absolutely stunning, Julia. I'm going to have to beat the young men off with a stick."

"Thank you." Julia smiled and hugged her jacket around herself. "Brrr! I'm glad you brought the blankets. You've thought of everything, haven't you?"

"I've thought of nothing else but this evening. A shame we won't have many more opportunities to go to dances or any musical events."

"Why's that?"

"Oh, it's doomsday talk. I shouldn't have mentioned it." *Stupid of me.*

"But really, I want to know."

"Well, everything is wrong with our country right now. Hitler is becoming more powerful and I have a feeling he'll take over the government. It will be good for many people—more jobs, and hopefully we can become part of Germany—but I don't like the way things have been going behind the scenes."

"I don't know what you mean, 'behind the scenes.' And how does this affect our dances and musical events?"

"Part of Hitler's program is to stop frivolity and to focus on work. Music must be the kind that meets his approval—marching band music, military music, patriotic music. That's all very well, but what's to happen to our master composers and their music and our old traditional folk songs? Anyway, I don't want to spoil our evening. I only thought how lucky we are to be able to go to this dance and we should enjoy it while we can."

"How do you know these things? We've heard nothing like this."

"I've heard people talking at work, and I have a radio at home that I listen to ... quietly."

"Why 'quietly'?"

"Let's just say there are people who don't think like we do who would make trouble."

"We don't even have a radio. When we want music, one of my brothers plays the violin and another plays the trumpet, and my sisters and I sing."

"Very beautifully, I might add." He found it easy to compliment her because it was all true.

"I love to sing. It makes me happy."

"You make me happy, Julia. I know we'll have a good time tonight." *I still can't believe you're sitting here beside me.*

In the Saaz Community Hall, tables were set up along the walls, leaving a large dance floor in the center. Rosy-cheeked waitresses with the arms of weightlifters carried three or four mugs of locally brewed beer in each hand. The towering heads of foam spilled over as the serving women, dirndls swishing, wove their way to the tables. Music was playing somewhere behind the dance floor area; an accordion, a trumpet, and a violin.

"A violin! Oh, no! Michael is here?" Julia craned her neck to look and turned as red as the roses on her black dress.

"Julia, my dear, don't worry about it," Lukas said quietly. "He could have asked you out just as I did." *But he didn't.* "Anyway, he's busy playing, so let's just carry on and have a nice time." *Just my luck! Why did he have to be here tonight? Damn! At least he's stuck playing in the band. The evening might not be a total loss after all.*

"But what if he sees us? Of course he'll see us. Oh, Lukas, I knew this was a bad idea." Her voice sounded on the verge of nervous tears. He had to think of something in a hurry—anything to distract her.

"It will be all right. Trust me. Now why don't we get warmed up with this polka? Do you polka, Julia?"

"Do I polka? I love to polka!" But she looked over her shoulder again towards the band platform.

"Julia, we came to dance. Let's give it a try. Don't worry about Michael right now. Let's polka."

"All right. Just hang onto me if I get dizzy."

"I wouldn't dream of letting you go." He would have to act fast. She looked torn between wanting to dance and not wanting to be seen dancing. Lukas pulled her up onto the dance floor before she could change her mind. They hopped and spun and swung each other around. There was no time to wonder if Michael had spotted them in the crowd and by the time the dance was over, Julia admitted to Lukas that she was beyond caring if he did see her. Her words were like honey to a hungry bear and he hugged her close to him.

The waltz that followed gave them time to catch their breath. Her slight figure seemed so vulnerable in his arms. He had an overwhelming urge to protect her, to keep her forever and never let her go. They danced every dance—polkas, waltzes, and foxtrots—barely having time to sip their beer between numbers.

At intermission time, while Lukas was in the men's room, Michael appeared at their table. "Hello, Julia. I see you're enjoying yourself."

"Michael, I—"

"Never mind, Julia. You don't need to explain anything. It's me who should explain. I just haven't had time. It's too far. I'm tied to the bakery." He took a deep breath. "I can't expect you to understand or sit around waiting for me. You and Lukas have a good time. He's a decent fellow. I wish—" He paused, as Lukas approached, nodded to them both and walked away.

As Julia's chin began to quiver, Lukas leaned over to kiss her. "Everything will be fine. You'll see."

16.

The bell over the bakery door tinkled. "Hey, Michael," Jan called as he and Andreas pushed through the door. "We're heading over to Neusattl. You going to join us this time?"

"Can't. I have to get this bread dough going and the cakes made up for tomorrow morning."

"Aw, come on, Michael," Andreas argued. "You haven't come with us now for weeks. It's starting to feel like spring and the girls will be out and about, looking for lo-o-ove." He gave his eyebrows two quick lifts.

Only a few months ago, Michael would have answered those eyebrow lifts with a couple of his own. How many times had they gone girl-hunting together? It dawned on him that he was missing many outings with his friends. He felt like an old man already. And out of touch.

Michael shook his head. "You'll have to entertain the girls without me. Julia and I broke up."

"Oh, no. Sorry to hear that."

Michael shrugged, trying to look nonchalant. "It wasn't working, trying to run the bakery—the long hours—and then that long way to Neusattl. I could manage dealing with the distance if I didn't have the bakery, but I can't do both. You go on, and say hello to the Sommer girls for me."

When they left, the doorbell had a forlorn, dull tinkle. Michael looked out the bakery windows at the blue sky and felt a terrible longing to be free and outdoors. Free to ride his bicycle to Neusattl. Free to play his violin and serenade Julia. Free to seek her out at every opportunity.

Covered in a dusting of flour, Michael watched his friends ride off on their bicycles. His whole being ached to see Julia again, but it was hopeless. She was always with Lukas now. Since his father's death, he had no social life. He envied Jan and Andreas their freedom to go out walking with the girls, but he was tied to the bakery. His constant companion was now Marlies with whom he chatted for hours as they worked.

"Do you miss your skirt-chasing days, Michael?"

"What? Oh, certainly not. What do you care anyway, Marlies?" As soon as the words were out of his mouth, Michael regretted his tone. Marlies didn't deserve that. She had never been anything but kind to him, putting up with his dark moods while he nursed his hurts over Julia.

"I care. I once had a man I cared about." Her tone was quieter now. Defensive.

"What happened?" He made an effort to sound interested and to take away the sting of his earlier remark.

"Nothing happened. That's the problem. Nothing. A hot flame that fizzled out. He thought he was special. Thought he was Adonis. I guess that's what the problem was. He was always looking to see if he could find someone better. We'd be crossing a street and he wouldn't even hold my hand in case a single woman was around. He wanted to look like he was available all the time. I guess he was."

"Was?"

"Available. I just didn't know it."

"What happened?"

"Oh, he ended up with some floozie who gave him babies before he could figure out where they came from. Just as well it wasn't me. He never could keep his pants buttoned and I wasn't ready for motherhood then."

"I think you would make a good mother."

"Maybe, but he would have been a lousy father." Marlies finished forming the loaves and carried the huge baking sheet on her shoulder to the waiting oven. Closing the oven door quickly to conserve the heat, she turned around slapping her hands together to dust them off and bumped into Michael who had followed her to the oven.

"Oops! Sorry Michael."

"No need to be sorry." He put his arms around her and gave her a friendly hug. Marlies looked shocked, but a smile spread across her red face. "I just want you to know that I appreciate you and that I didn't mean to offend you.

She gave Michael a bear hug and said, "Don't worry. I always bounce back." She planted a kiss on his forehead. "Life goes on. For you too." Marlies was sweet. If only she were Julia.

As he sat in his apartment upstairs that night, Michael felt more alone than ever. His violin standing in the corner looked like the enemy now. He was playing it when he found Julia and he was playing it the night of the dance when he lost her. How had he let her slip through his fingers?

He would never forget the shock of seeing Julia there with Lukas. His first impulse was to run over to her, but the dance had started and he was stuck playing. He tried not to watch them, but couldn't help seeking her out over and over again. He had to admit Lukas certainly put on the charm. He held her closely and never allowed anyone to cut in. When he saw the adoring look Julia gave Lukas, Michael realized he had already lost her. And no wonder. He had really not made enough effort to stake his claim. At the break he had gone over to their table. He thought he might as well get it over with and let her go.

Walking home alone in the dark after the dance, Michael felt an emptiness that no amount of rationalization could erase. The ache in his throat threatened to stop him from breathing. In his quiet apartment above the bakery, Michael fell onto his bed fully clothed and sobbed as he hadn't done since his father died.

PART THREE

Lukas

Saaz, Czechoslovakia
Crimean Peninsula, Ukraine
1933-1944

17.

I hope your aunt and I will get along and be able to sort out who does what, now that I'm moving into her house." Julia fidgeted with her wedding ring.

"Aunt Theresa is going to love having you," Lukas assured her. "But really, it's our house, or will be. Remember she has willed it to me with the understanding that I will look after her."

"We'll both look after her."

The summer air gently brushed the cheeks of the newly married couple as they rode home from the wedding reception in Lukas's horse-drawn buggy. Julia squeezed her husband's hand. "It was a wonderful day, Lukas."

"And we'll have wonderful days for the rest of our lives together." Lukas planted a kiss on top of Julia's head as he pulled her close. "I'll always love you, my sweet."

Several weeks later Julia clung to Lukas on the back of his new BMW. "It's such a nuisance to have to wear this stupid skirt over my pants," Julia muttered. "And dangerous if it got tangled in the wheels." She tucked the skirt tighter about her.

"You know how tongues would wag if you were seen wearing pants." Lukas shrugged his shoulders. "I know it's silly, but never mind. You need pants for the riding lessons. As soon as we get out of town, you can slip off the skirt until it's time to go back."

At the soccer field, Lukas gave Julia a few basic instructions regarding gas, brakes, and the clutch, and off she went on her own. "This is so much fun," she shrieked as she putted past Lukas after a lap around the field. "I don't want to stop."

Feeling braver she opened up the throttle, roared around the field again, and then ventured onto the road for a short distance and back to the field. "I love it," she yelled to her beaming husband. She knew he had wanted the motorcycle for a long time. That he had let her ride it alone and enjoyed teaching her was a pleasant surprise for her.

"You're a quick learner," he said as she pulled up beside him. "Now hop on the back and we'll head home. It's getting dark, so don't bother with the skirt."

Julia snuggled into his back. "I won't make you go off the road if I hold onto you, will I?"

"Of course not."

"Does it matter where I hold you?" Julia imagined she could see Lukas smiling into the darkening sky.

"Try me, but be gentle. I'm made of marzipan."

"Hah! That, you definitely are not. You're all muscle," she purred into his neck. "And you're wobbling the motorcycle."

Minutes later Lukas parked the BMW. "It's a good thing we're home."

"Why? Were you having trouble driving?"

"You have a one-track mind, my dear. Let's see if you can help me with my driving once we get into the house. For starters, we'll have to get those ridiculous pants off you."

How are things working out in the new home, Julia?"

"Just fine, Mother. I expected Theresa to be a bit cool about making room for me, but she's not like that at all. I think she's actually happy to have female company for a change."

"How have you arranged the sleeping rooms? Who does the cooking?"

"She has her bedroom in the back, so often we forget she's even in the house. And at supper it's great. When Lukas and I come home from work, she has vegetables ready from the garden. All I have to do is pitch in and get the last few things ready. It really makes it easier for me. Did I tell you Lukas sold the horse and buggy? He talked about a motorcycle for weeks and at last he bought a BMW—his dream-bike."

"Men! They never really grow up. No matter, as long as he provides for you," Katerina said. "Lukas seems to be a fine man. Just make sure you keep him happy."

"Oh, I think I'm keeping him happy." Julia patted her belly with a big smile.

Katerina studied Julia's face carefully and suddenly her jaw dropped. "You're not?" she said. Julia beamed. "You are!"

August 1937

Julia watched as Lukas tinkered with the BMW's carburetor. Three-year-old Sofie played in the sandbox nearby while Julia rocked Steffie to sleep in the baby buggy. "Lukas, do you realize how lucky we are? We have food from our garden and our animals. We have jobs. Some of our neighbours are barely getting by."

"I know." Lukas stood up and wiped his forehead with the back of his hand, leaving a black smear of oil on it. "So many Germans lost their jobs after the war if they couldn't speak Czech."

"My father—case in point. He still wishes for the old days of Austria Hungary."

"No use wishing for the past. The Kaiser is long gone. But it wouldn't be a bad thing if we could be part of Germany. There must be about three million Germans here."

"Father told me that even though we outnumber the Czechs in this region we have no say in the government. Sometimes I worry that our good life won't last. We have our little girls to think of."

"Don't worry. They have us and Aunt Theresa to look after them." Lukas put down the screwdriver and wiped his hands with a gasoline-soaked rag.

"Yes, but I see more and more animosity between the Czechs and Germans. Remember last week when Sofie was playing in the front yard and one of the Czech boys from down the street started yelling at her?"

"Yes, that was disgusting. She's only a toddler."

"She had such a fright when the rock hit her on the head. So did I, the way she screamed. I'm afraid there is going to be more bloodshed in the coming months. What do you think, Lukas? Is it my imagination?"

He shrugged. "Feelings between Czechs and Germans are getting worse."

"I think so too. Yesterday, Frau Hruskova turned her back to me when I said good morning. We were always good neighbours. Why would she do that?"

"I think part of it is petty jealousy over our good lifestyle even though we aren't rich."

"But we don't flaunt it. And there are plenty of dirt poor Germans."

"Doesn't matter. There's a lot of anti-German propaganda on the radio, and haven't you noticed, more Germans in our Sudeten area are fed up with Czechs telling them what to do? You and I both had to do our schooling in Czech in our German schoolhouse. Maybe our generation doesn't want that for our children. I know I don't." He began to reach for Steffie's cheeks and was reminded by Julia's light slap on his hands that they stunk of gasoline. He gave Steffie a kiss instead.

"If the Czechs don't like us, why don't they let us go and be Germans as we want to be?"

"The Hitler supporters are calling for exactly that," Lukas said.

"I think they're right. Our ancestors have lived here for over 700 years. We have a right to rule ourselves. I don't know much about Hitler, but if he can overthrow the Czechs and stop them from taking over our daily life, I support him."

"The problem is, as you say, you don't know much about him. Neither does anyone else. When I hear some of these rumours about how fanatical he is ... I don't know. We need change, but we don't need a maniac at the helm."

Lukas hesitated a moment before going on. "I stopped at the bakery on the way home. I thought I'd grab a loaf of bread and say hello to Michael, but he wasn't there. Marlies was managing the bakery on her own and there was a 'For Sale' sign in the window."

"What? For Sale? That's odd. Michael swore he would make the bakery pay after his father died. Did Marlies say where he was?" She gave Lukas a quick sideways glance to see how he was interpreting her interest in Michael's welfare. She loved Lukas, but she hadn't been able to set aside all her feelings for Michael, even after all this time. But if Lukas suspected that she still cared for Michael at all, he showed no sign of it.

"She said he went to a meeting of the SPD—you know, the Socialist Party?" Julia nodded and Lukas continued. "That was three days ago and he hasn't come back. At first she didn't want to talk about it, but then she broke down and told me Michael had been afraid of how the Hitler movement was going and joined the SPD which is working against Hitler."

"Oh my God! Poor Marlies. He's been gone three days?"

Lukas nodded. "Not like him to drop out of sight without saying anything. He's more responsible than that."

"She must be sick with worry. Could he be hiding out somewhere? But three days without word?" Julia couldn't imagine how worried she'd be if Lukas suddenly disappeared from her life like that. She took his arm and looked closely at his face. "You wouldn't do that to me, would you?"

"Of course not. How could you think that?" He gave her a hug being careful not to touch her with his hands.

Moments later her mind was still on Michael's disappearance. "I just don't understand. Michael has always been sensible. Why would he join a party like that in the first place? Doesn't he see that with Hitler we could be part of Germany?"

"I think he does, but he's concerned about stories he's heard."

"Ah, you mean about the gypsies and Jews."

"Exactly. Hitler's supporters are ruthless with anyone who disagrees with them. I've heard that some SPD members have been shot or hanged and others were sent to concentration camps."

Julia's hands went to her face. "But you don't believe that, do you Lukas?" Images flashed through her mind. Michael slumping over as bullets from a firing squad slammed into his body. Michael's limp body next to others of his party, hanging from a beam like so many rag dolls.

"I'm not sure. There must be some truth to it or we wouldn't hear about it. But on the other hand, it would be good to be part of Germany—have our language back and jobs." Lukas waved his hands dismissively. "Those stories of cruelty are probably exaggerated."

Julia nodded in eager agreement. "They must be. I would hate for anything to happen to Michael. Just in case it's true about the hangings."

"Marlies said he was trying to arrange a way to leave the country. She told him if he goes, he has to go alone. She'll go back to her parents. They need her."

"Does she know if he found a way to leave or if he's been taken?"

"No."

In 1938 rumours of Hitler's activities were the topic of discussion all over Saaz. Julia had listened to them with growing hope. The latest reports told of Hitler reclaiming Sudetenland. Government offices and schools would once again use German and the laws would revert to German. The arrangements were to be finalized in the fall.

"Won't it be fantastic?" Julia said as she dusted the china cabinet.

"I just hope it will all go smoothly." Lukas took her hand. "I don't want to worry you, but Hitler has made threats of war if Czechoslovakia doesn't comply or if the big European powers don't support his bid for liberation. It's the same for Germans living inside Polish borders."

"Oh, dear! Do you think there will be trouble?" Julia clasped her hands over Lukas's. "I had assumed it would be a good thing. What if it doesn't go right? If there is a war.... I can't bear to think about it. Oh, Lukas, what are we going to do?"

He put an arm around her neck, pulled her close, and kissed the top of her head. "So far we are all right. Let's not worry about things we have no control over."

18.

September 1939

War! War? War. The terrible word was on everyone's lips. Julia's first thought was to find Lukas. She needed Lukas. As she pedaled furiously towards Bechert's to find her husband, she heard the word in every snatch of conversation that reached her ears. War was about to change their lives.

Julia threw her bicycle down outside the factory and ran to the department that Lukas managed. "Georg! Have you seen Lukas? Where's Lukas?" Georg turned from the pile of bolts in front of him and pointed down the hall just as Lukas appeared. "Lukas!" Julia shouted. "Did you hear?" Lukas looked white and shaken as he folded her into his arms.

"You're shivering, Julia."

"I'm still shaking from pedaling so fast, but I can't seem to stop. Did you hear?"

"Yes," he whispered, and pulled her closer. "Don't worry."

"You're not going, are you? Please say you're not." She felt as if vise grips had hold of her stomach. He couldn't leave her now, just when life was perfect. "Say you won't go, Lukas. Please, say it."

"Come, we'll ride home on the motorbike and we'll get your bicycle later."

The ride home seemed too short. Julia clung to Lukas so tightly that she could feel his heart beating. She dreaded the conversation she knew was coming.

"You know I have to go, don't you, Julia?"

She could feel tears trickling down her cheeks finding their way to her chin. "Why? Lukas!" She choked out his name. "You can't. What about the children? Your aunt? What about me? Don't you love me? How can you leave me now?"

"Sweetheart." His eyes brimmed with tears. "The Czechs will be trying their best to get us under their thumb again. I have to—"

"No, you don't have to. I don't want you to—"

"I have to do what I can to help stop them."

"If you really loved me you wouldn't go."

"It's for you and Sofie and Steffie that I'm volunteering to go, exactly because I love you all so much. What kind of a coward would I be if I didn't protect my family?"

Julia couldn't argue when he put it that way, but dammit, why did he have to choose now to be so noble? Their happy life would be torn apart. She loved him so much. Her children loved him, needed him. How could he do this to them? She wiped her wet cheeks with the backs of her hands and sank into the nearest chair.

"Oh, Lukas! How will I manage without you?" She knew that further entreaties would only add to his pain. She was sure he was hurting as much, well, almost as much, as she was.

"I'll be back before you have time to miss me. Meanwhile, you're a strong girl, Julia. I want you to remember that, if times get hard. That inner strength that I love so much in you will see you through. God willing, I'll come back to you."

"You still believe there's a God? How could He allow this to happen?" She flung out her arms indicating her crumbling world. She was incredulous at his naiveté.

"We aren't meant to question God. Please, Julia. We need to believe He will guide us."

"Oh, Lukas! There is no God. Why would God ask people to kill each other? How can you believe in God now?" She was amazed at his blind faith. They went to church, said the prayers, and sang the songs, but had never really had any serious discussion over their beliefs before.

"I have to believe in Him to see me through."

Julia clamped her teeth together tightly. She didn't want to take away Lukas's crutch if he was counting on God to see him through. She needed Lukas to come home safely. But every rational thought told her that God had forsaken her.

October 1941

Making mail pickups and deliveries for the factory was so much easier using the motorcycle than it had been with the bicycle. Julia often thought of the times before the war when Lukas had taught her to ride the BMW. In her mind she could still feel his warmth as she rode with her arms around his chest and her cheek nestled into the back of his neck. If only she could turn the clock back.

She had hardly seen Lukas since the war started two years ago. Twice he had come home for a week's leave. Twice the children had a reminder of who their father was. But last time five-year-old Steffie didn't even know him when he came home. She was not quite three when the war started; too young to continue to remember him through the empty, fatherless years.

"You're not my papa," she had said. "You're an army man."

Before the war, political changes were worrisome, but beyond their control, so why lose sleep over them? Now a general gloom hung over Europe, and still, the only thing that mattered to Julia and Lukas was that they loved each other and their two daughters. They had not caused the problems and yet they were asked to pay the price for fixing them. As the war raged on, it angered Julia that Lukas had been taken away from her just when they were so happy. As she lay in their marriage bed, it seemed too big and empty without him. *Our life was perfect. Why did he have to go and leave us? If only he wasn't so obsessed with doing the right thing.* She pounded the pillow with her fist. *Damn you, Lukas. We need you here. How could you leave me? I hate you, hate you, hate you.* She turned her face into her pillow and sobbed. *No, I don't.... Oh, Lukas, I love you. Please, please don't die.*

During the past four years, it had become Julia's habit after breakfast to listen for the war news before going to work. She hoped to hear reports that might give her an idea of where Lukas could be. In some crazy way, she thought she could minimize the loneliness and worry if she could mentally follow his regiment's progress.

A detailed report followed the usual fanfare of war propaganda. "And in the southeast regions, our divisions...." Transmission stopped. Julia slapped the top of the radio. The reporter's voice cut in and out. *Damn thing. Just when they're talking about Lukas's location.* Perhaps it was simply a matter of tightening one of the tubes in the back. She stood up to jiggle it, listening for rattles. She needed to fix it quickly before the report was over. Removing the back cover, she reached inside to feel the tubes. But as she touched the first one, a jolt of electricity buzzed across her forearms. Her hand muscles cramped and held onto the radio like clamps. Shocking pulses of electricity cycled again and again, each time searing a widening swath up her arms. She tried desperately to drop the radio. Her legs buckled and she fell. Julia lay on the floor, dazed and weak. She wondered why she was still alive. Then she saw the radio on the floor beside her. The fall had torn the cord from the wall, stopping the flow of electricity.

Theresa came running. "Did you hear that noise? Good Lord! Julia! What happened? Are you hurt?"

"Oh, my God! I'm so lucky! Stupid, but so lucky!"

Theresa was a heavy-set woman. She gave Julia the support of her strong arms and pulled her up from the floor. As Julia straightened her clothes, she checked her hands. They felt raw, but she didn't see any burn marks.

Theresa brought her a glass of water. Julia took a quick slurp. "Thanks. I'd better get going now or I'll be late for work."

"You're not going to work after this? Julia, really! You're in no shape to go to work today."

"I have to, Aunt Theresa. We need the money." With trembling hands, she gathered up the cloth bag containing her lunch and a few personal items. "Don't worry. I'll be fine. See you later." She gave Theresa a kiss on the cheek and went outside to start up Lukas's bike.

As she rode towards Bechert's at the far end of town, Julia was surprised to see the sun shining and to feel the morning air so fresh and wholesome. The world was carrying on as usual. She took a deep breath and tried to shake off the bad start to her morning. It was going to be a fine day after all.

Here and there people hurried to their jobs or to do their shopping errands. Across the street, a well-dressed woman strutted along, nose in the air, her spitz on a leash. Julia thought with regret of her own dog, Astor, the German shepherd who had been conscripted by the army for use in the war. She had heard that dogs carrying vital information between army units were targeted by the enemy and shot on sight. She didn't expect to see Astor again.

Old Herr Kinzl strolled on the sidewalk nearest Julia. He tipped his hat good morning to her. Julia nodded as she puttered by. She liked Herr Kinzl. He was such a dear, friendly man. She thought how lucky he was that he was too old to go fight and could stay with his family. She wondered how much longer she would have to be without Lukas. She could hardly remember his face. She had lived without him for almost four years already.

The barking, snarling spitz brought her out of her reverie. He tore across the street dragging his leash. Julia swerved to avoid hitting the charging dog. He snapped at her ankle. "Get away!" she yelled, and instinctively pulled her leg up. The motorcycle wobbled precariously. Julia felt a burst of adrenaline as her stomach clenched and the muscles of her recently burned forearms tightened on the handles. Herr Kinzl told her afterwards that she might have been all right if the dog's leash hadn't tangled in the wheel. The motorcycle skidded sideways across the cobbled street. Julia was airborne. The empty revving of the motor, the dog's high-pitched yelping, and her own shriek of terror played in her head like an out-of-tune orchestra. Her body scraped and bounced along the stones, and she tried in vain to keep her head from hitting the ground. Sprawled on the cobblestones in the early morning sunshine, Julia groaned as a dull pain enveloped her. She wasn't sure where she was hurt, but intense jabs of pain throbbed in her head.

From somewhere nearby she heard a woman's screams and incoherent screeching. "Mitzi! Ach, Mitzi! Are you hurt? Mitzi! Are you all right, Mitzi? Is Mitzi all right?"

Herr Kinzl, who was bent over Julia, snapped at the hysterical woman, "For heavens sake, Frau! Shame on you! Did you ever think to ask if the *woman* is hurt? After all, it's your Mitzi who caused this accident. And tell that damn dog to shut up."

"Accident!" The word echoed in Julia's head. Her daughters' faces flashed through her mind. *Oh, my babies! My babies!* Her brain seemed to be yelling the words. Her babies needed her. The thought spurred her to rally her strength. She tried to look at her arms and legs to check for broken bones or cuts, but a wave of nausea told her to slow down. Herr Kinzl's voice was there beside her. His arm went around her shoulders as she struggled to sit up.

"My nose doesn't feel right." She reached up to touch her face but Herr Kinzl's hand stopped hers.

"I think we'd best get the blood cleaned off first and then we'll see what the damage is. I believe I heard someone say they are bringing the doctor. Ah, here he comes now. He'll take good care of you."

Ingrid pushed her way through the gathering crowd, just as the doctor arrived. "Julia! Are you hurt? Oh, Lord! Look at your poor face. Do you feel like you broke any bones?"

"Ingrid! What are you doing here?" Julia wondered why her voice sounded so nasal, as if she had a bad cold. As she spoke each word sent stabs of pain through her head.

"The pharmacy is only down the block and I heard the dog yelping. Are you all right? You almost gave me heart failure."

"Yes, I'm fine, but I hurt all over, especially my head. Bad headache." Julia squinted up at Ingrid.

"Frau Brueckner," the doctor said to Ingrid, "would you be so good as to ride my bicycle over to the clinic and ask them to bring the horse and buggy for your sister-in-law? I don't think she should walk home like this. Stay right where you are," he said to Julia. She gave up her struggle to get up and half-listened to Herr Kinzl.

"Your motorcycle has suffered a few dents but rolls along well enough. If you want I can push it over to the pharmacy. You can make arrangements to have it brought home when you feel better."

"Thank you, Herr Kinzl. Thank you very much for your help. The dog...?"

"Don't you worry. He's fine. He'll need a new leash though."

"I'm coming home with you, Julia. You poor dear. I'll see to your cuts and scrapes." Ingrid patted her sister-in-law's arm. "It won't hurt for the pharmacy to be closed for a short while."

As the buggy pulled up to Julia's house, Theresa opened the door. Her face turned pale when she saw Julia. Ingrid hurried over and took Theresa's arm. "It's not as bad as it looks, Aunt Theresa. Don't get upset now."

"Oh, dear God," Theresa whispered as she sank down on the front step, fainting away before she could sit. Julia winced as she limped over to help Ingrid. It was no small feat to let the large woman down gently. The buggy driver brought out the first aid kit and smelling salts.

"Ooh! I'm fine," Theresa said as her head jerked up. "Just a bit dizzy for a second. What happened to you, Julia?" Theresa's voice was barely audible.

Ingrid and Julia struggled to help the big woman get up. "Don't worry, Aunt Theresa. It looks worse than it is," Julia told her. She thanked the buggy driver and hobbled into the house with Lukas's sister and his aunt.

Ingrid was putting a kettle of water on for tea when someone knocked on the door. Herbert was still pounding on the door when Julia opened it. "Julia? Is that you, Julia? What happened to your face?"

"I had a motorcycle accident on my way to work. But what are you doing here, Herbert?"

"Herr Ostermann told me to ride my bicycle over here and see what's keeping you."

"Please tell Herr Ostermann that I'll be at work tomorrow. I won't be able to ride the motorcycle for a while until I can have someone fix it though."

"Oh, Julia! I know all about motorcycles. I can fix it!"

"Would you, Herbert? That would be so sweet of you."

"I don't mind at all. You've always been good to me. I can fix it after work."

"It's behind the pharmacy. Thank you, Herbert."

"Bye, Julia." Herbert beamed as he wiped blue spittle from his chin. Apparently he still hadn't given up the habit of testing the sharpness of the hectograph pencils on his tongue.

Back in the kitchen, Julia saw Lukas's aunt sitting limply at the table. Her severe hairdo, pulled straight off her head into a bun at the back was in disarray, several white strands of it hanging limply to her shoulders.

"Aunt Theresa?" She jiggled Theresa's dangling arm. "Are you feeling all right?"

"Just a bit tired, my dear," she mumbled.

"Why don't you lie down on the sofa in the other room?"

"I suppose there's time before the girls come home from school. I don't want them to see me lying down. They'd worry. It's going to be enough of a shock when they see you all banged up."

"We'll have Julia all cleaned up long before the girls come home from school, Aunt Theresa," Ingrid said. "Are you feeling all right now?"

"Yes, fine. It was just a shock. What a day it has been. I didn't expect to be so weak and faint like that, but after all at sixty-eight a person can't expect to have perfect health. One has to put up with a few little problems. But never mind. What about you, Julia? How is your nose feeling? Is your headache going away yet?"

"No, I'm afraid it's a pretty bad one, but I'm sure by tomorrow it will be better. When I think of what Lukas may be going through right now, this is nothing by comparison. I hope he won't be too upset. He really loves that motorcycle."

"I'm sure he would be glad to know you are all right and not worry about the bike. For that matter he probably doesn't even think about the bike after so much time." Theresa sat with her head hanging down, apparently lost in thought. "Almost four years already. All that killing. For what?"

"I just pray that our men come back to us. We need them now more than ever." Julia felt herself beginning to slide into a depression of self-pity. She winced in pain as she stood up to pour more tea. Then she remembered Lukas saying how he admired her strength. She was determined to shake off the sombre mood. "We're going to get through it all," she said. "We just have to be strong. We women are tough when we need to be and we will survive. Remember that quote from Beethoven? It goes something like this: 'I will take fate by the throat; it will never bend me completely to its will.'"

"That's right, Julia," Ingrid said. "Now, I've boiled some extra water to clean your cuts and scrapes. It will sting a bit, so you might want to begin practising that Beethoven quote.

Four days later Julia was still stiff and sore. It was good of Franz to come by and tell her to take a few days off, but Julia knew there would be mounds of correspondence waiting for her.

She pushed open the door to the girls' room. "Sofie, Steffie, time to get up and get ready for school. Aunt Theresa will help you. I have to leave early because I have to walk to work for a few more days until the motorcycle is fixed."

"Mutti, will your nose always be blue and green now?" Steffie asked.

"Of course it won't, Steffie!" Sofie scolded her. "Don't you know anything? It's just a bruise. Right, Mutti?"

"Yes, it'll soon be the normal colour again. Does it look funny?"

"A little bit."

"No, it doesn't." Sofie nudged Steffie in the ribs with her elbow. "But Mutti, will it be straight again?"

"I hope so, Sofie, but right now it looks like it might be a little bit crooked."

"That's all right, Mutti. We love you anyway, even if your nose is crooked," Sofie said.

"Yeah." Steffie agreed as they both stretched their arms up for hugs.

19.

In January of 1944, the German army moved into yet another Ukrainian village. At the end of the row of houses, a woman in a black dress glanced over her shoulder at the advancing troops, swept a small boy up into her arms, and ran for her door. The Germans marched along the main street. When the bulk of the troops were well into the town center, the locals attacked from all sides. They threw rocks, sticks, bricks, slingshot projectiles—whatever they could find. German troops returned fire at snipers shooting from houses and in a short time the resistance was over.

A few old men and young boys slumped over rusty weapons that could hardly be called firearms. Many women were among the dead. Lukas thought of his own wife and children and felt ashamed. He was glad Julia would never know what kind of war he was asked to fight. When he saw the dead, the very young and the very old, he was sickened at having had a hand in their deaths.

In the encampment outside the town, Lukas sipped tea from his tin mug. He was so tired of the killing and butchery. He was a mellow soul. At least he had been, once. Now he wasn't sure he would recognize himself. The things he had seen. The things he had done—had had to do—killing soldiers who were sent to fight for their side, just as he was sent to fight for his. Young men, probably not so different from himself, with families at home? It didn't seem right. God's commandment said, "Thou shalt not kill." Did that mean except in the case of war? Lukas struggled to justify it, but his mind could not accept that slaughtering other human beings every day could ever be forgiven. And yet he felt powerless, caught up in the great machine that was the German army. If he laid down his rifle and refused to kill anymore, his own superiors would shoot him. He had to stay loyal to his troop for the sake of his own survival. For Julia.

His thoughts turned to her constantly. What wouldn't he give to be with Julia and the girls? How had this war come to be his life? He didn't hate these people. Why was he asked to kill them? But if he didn't kill them, they would kill him. Killing, killing, killing.

"Feldmann? Feldmann!"

"Yes. Here!"

"Mueller? Ehrhardt? Brenner?" The Lieutenant continued to call the roll. "Ten minutes. Meet outside the medical tent. Basic daypack equipment. We will patrol the area immediately to the south and maintain control of it. With any luck we can push ahead and give ourselves some breathing room."

Lukas had heard that German troops were struggling to hold their positions in villages to the north of them. One rumour said that the army was cut off at the isthmus on the north end of the Crimean peninsula and was being forced to retreat with nowhere to go.

Lukas was ready, rifle strap over his shoulder, grenade at his belt. At the medical tent, he waited with Mueller and Ehrhardt. "Mueller, do you think there's any truth to these stories of the Red Army cutting off our retreat?"

"Naw, that's horseshit."

"I almost wish, win or lose, that it would all be over."

"Don't talk like that, Feldmann. At least not so loud. That's traitor talk."

"It's just tired, disillusioned soldier talk."

All he could think of was home. Home. What a strange word that was. Home and Julia. He wondered what she was doing. Was she sick or healthy? Was she faithful to him? Of course she was. They had been so happy together. But that was over four years ago. Not four days, weeks, or months, but four *years*. Four eternities. His soul felt empty, hollow, vulnerable.

They marched south along the ruts of nearly frozen mud. At least the boots he wore still had some tread in the soles. He had taken them from a dead soldier of the Red Army in a skirmish a few weeks back. The poor fellow hardly looked old enough to leave his mother, yet there he lay, his milky brown eyes staring into space, shot through the neck. Lukas shook his head at the memory, wishing he could shake it out of his mind completely, but it would only be replaced by a hundred others. Limbs blown off, corpses contorted into impossible positions, the sickly sweet smell of spilled body fluids, faces smacked into the muck, bodies huddled together or lying across each other with vacant staring eyes. Someone's father, brother, husband, son. With each step of the day's march, Lukas spiralled farther down into a tunnel of despair. He had been such an enthusiastic volunteer for the army, to rid his people of Czech occupation; had told Julia not to worry, he'd be back soon; had believed it himself. It was a noble thing to do, the right thing to do, the *only* respectable thing for a man to do. He thought of Michael, avoiding the war with his funny politics. Whatever had happened to Michael? He snorted to himself as he walked along. Maybe Michael had the right idea—if he hadn't been captured by the S.S. and shot or hung, that is.

The troops stopped abruptly and Lukas nearly walked into Mueller. The road ahead passed at the foot of a gently sloping hill. "Spread out," the lieutenant called. "Secure the hill. Regroup at the top."

Lukas, Mueller, and the others started to climb. They kept low, dashing from one piece of cover to the next. Mueller was several feet ahead and to the left of him, about to gain the top of the hill where he would give the all clear. Lukas took a moment to catch his breath behind a tree stump and scan the hillside above him for the next piece of cover. There it was, an outcropping of rocks. He ran towards it, keeping low. Rifle tips appeared over the top of the rocks. Too late he realized he was running straight into an ambush. The force of the bullets propelled his body backwards and threw him onto his back. The world swam around him and bursts of gunfire faded as he slipped into unconsciousness.

Lukas woke to the sound of his own moaning. The stench of blood, urine, and excrement persisted in spite of the draft that blew through the tent. Men with a red cross on their uniforms worked on the wounded who lay on makeshift beds. Just a short time ago, he and Mueller had been speaking outside the medical tent—now he was lying inside it. He raised his head to look for familiar faces, half hoping not to find any, but there was Ehrhardt to his right with a bandage on his upper arm and shoulder.

"Feldmann? You awake?"

"Yeah, what happened?"

"Ambushed. Bastards got me in the shoulder. What about you?"

"I'm not sure," Lukas said. "I think there's something wrong with my guts." He reached down to his abdomen, and found a thick wad of bandages. Looking down under the thin blanket, he saw that they were stained and wet with an unnerving amount of seepage. "How long have we been here?"

"About twenty-four hours, I'd say."

"And I just woke up?"

"You've been in dreamland most of the time," Ehrhardt said. "The medics gave you quite a dose of morphine. I wasn't so lucky. They said they're in short supply of the stuff and they're only using it for—ah.... Sorry, I—"

"Never mind. I know I'm in rough shape." He drifted off again.

When he woke a second time he was shivering. "Ehrhardt, are you still there?"

"I'm here, boy—you've just had an eight hour nap!"

"Could you do something for me?"

"Anything, if I'm able."

"If your writing hand is still working, could you take down a letter for my wife?"

One of the medics brought a piece of paper and a pencil. Lukas tried not to think about the heat in his head or the pain in his guts that was difficult to ignore as he dictated.

"Jesus, Feldmann." Ehrhardt folded up the finished note. "I never liked writing letters, but this is one I hope I don't have to send."

"I know. I hope you don't have to, but ... oh God ... where's that medic? I need morphine...."

Sleep and release from pain came quickly with the medication. Deep in his subconscious mind, Lukas traveled home. The ducks waddled down the path to the creek. Sofie and Steffie fed the rabbits and chickens in the backyard. Julia looked up from her weeding.

"There you are, Lukas! Where have you been all this time? There's so much to do. You must have been at work. How was it? Are you tired? I'll go make us a cup of tea. But first look at these radishes—they're getting little round bodies already. Here, try one." She drifted away as if she were made of mist, beckoning to him. He hurried to follow but she stayed out of reach.

"Wait, Julia. Why do you keep pulling away?"

"I'm here, Lukas. Right here with you." She put her arms around him but he couldn't feel her. He hugged the air where she had been. "But why do you have all these bandages? What happened to you? Are you hurt?" She laid a feathery hand on his abdomen. "Don't worry," she crooned. "You'll feel better soon." She kissed him with misty cool but tender lips.

"I love you Julia. I'll always be with you."

20.

Julia tied the belt of her jacket snugly. A lightweight wool scarf protected her neck against the brisk morning air. She wondered if the crocuses and snowdrops along her walkway regretted having peeked out of the ground so early; their petals were tightly closed. Around the corner of the house she climbed onto the BMW and was about to start it up, when someone called her name.

"Frau Feldmann, one moment. May we speak to you please?"

"Yes?" She turned to face two uniformed men. Her heart pounded. A visit from officials was never a good thing.

"Perhaps you'd like to go inside?"

"I was just leaving for work. Is everything all right?"

"I'm afraid we have bad news for you. Our sincerest sympathies, Frau Feldmann," one of the men said as he handed her an envelope.

Julia forgot to breathe. With an effort, she swallowed the lump in her throat. Trembling hands picked at the flap. *Please God, don't let it be Lukas.* She had only begun to coax the card out of the envelope when she saw the black border—the standard form for a death notice. She sank down to sit on the cold front porch step and let her head sink to her knees. Then she realized that she hadn't read the name on the notice and a glimmer of hope flickered inside her. Pulling the card out farther, she scanned the notice and needed only to see the first two letters of Lukas's name before putting her hands to her ears to stop the terrible scream she felt building inside her head. Her keening wail brought Theresa to the door.

"Julia, what—? I thought you had gone to work. What is it?"

"Unfortunately it was our duty to inform Frau Feldmann of her husband's ultimate sacrifice for the Fatherland," one of the officials said.

Julia's head stayed on her knees but she lifted the hand with the letter for Theresa to take. Theresa glanced at the note, then sank down on the step and slipped her arm under Julia's. She thanked the men and gently lifted Julia.

"Come into the house, Julia. We can't stay out here and freeze."

Julia clung to Theresa numbly. Her body was someone else's, simply following instructions as Theresa helped her inside to the nearest chair at the dining table. Julia laid her head down on her folded arms and sobbed until her throat ached.

Theresa flipped the letter onto the table with a sigh. "What's this?" she said. "There's another note in here." Julia looked up and groped for the paper.

January 13, 1944

Dearest Julia,

In case I don't make it home, I want you to know I've never stopped thinking about you and our girls. I wish I could have been there for

them. I know Sofie and Steffie will grow up to
be fine young ladies just like their mother. Tell
them I love them. And you, my dearest, have
made me happy. The years we had were too
short, but I'll love you always.

Written at Lukas's request,
J. Ehrhardt

Theresa sat down at the table and pushed a shot
glass of slivovitz in front of Julia.

"Aunt Theresa, I'm so selfish. I'm sure you're hurting
too." She downed the slivovitz and held her glass out for
a refill, resting it on the table when her shaking hands
threatened to spill it. "Where did you get this?" she
asked, between sobs.

"I've had it under my bed for years, but I never
thought I would be bringing it out for an occasion such
as this. We'd best make a cup of tea to go with it. Julia,
dear, I'm so sorry. He was my nephew and I loved him
but I can't imagine your pain. I think it must be time to
dredge up that Beethoven quote of yours again."

Julia's shoulders shook as she tried to contain her
sobs. "Oh, Aunt Theresa! I loved him so much."

PART FOUR

Karl

Germany
1922-1946

21.

The boy's sobs, interspersed with shrieks of protest, echoed down the stairwell. With her apartment door open only a crack, Frau Gruber peered out into the musty hallway and up the stairs. She shook her head. "There she goes again."

"It's too cold. Please, Mutti! I want to stay."

"Shut up, I tell you. Goddammit! I wish you'd never been born. Just get the hell out of my life, you goddamned pest." A slapping sound punctuated each phrase.

"No-o-o-o-o!"

With thuds and knocks of bone on wood, the young boy's flailing body bounced off steps, wall, and railing, finally landing in a distorted mess on the ground floor. As the landlady watched, the pile of skinny bones that now lay almost on her doorstep started to pick itself up, but as if lacking resolve, collapsed again into a whimpering heap.

With a furtive glance up the stairs, Frau Gruber reached out and pulled the quaking boy into her apartment. He made no move to resist.

"Let me call Youth Services for you, Karl. They'll find you a good home." She stroked the back of his head. "This is too much. You could have broken your neck."

"N-no! Please don't call them, Frau Gruber. They'll take me away from Mutti." Tears tracked down his battered cheeks.

"But Karl! Look how she treats you."

"It's n-not what you think, Frau Gruber." He wiped his nose on his sleeve. A streak of blood stained the thin, torn shirtsleeve. "She l-loves me, but I'm in the way when she has a visitor. Today it's an important one and maybe she'll get a good job if she's nice to him. If I stay quiet, she'll let me back in when he's gone."

"She does love you, of course she does, but this can't go on. One day you'll really get hurt." *Poor little waif. Hard to believe he's eleven. So thin. So unhappy. He deserves a bit of love, but he's not going to get it from her.*

"It doesn't matter. It's my own fault. I was making too much noise."

"Ach, my poor boy." Frau Gruber put her ample arms around Karl and drew him into the warmth of her matronly body, muffling his sobs.

Karl's mother, Alana, had told Frau Gruber months ago that she expected a promotion at work. Nothing had changed, however, in her part-time position at the government office where she did occasional translation work from Russian or Polish to German. One official after another, and many of their friends, had trailed through Alana Werner's revolving door. She bragged of their promises, but Frau Gruber saw the derisive smirks on the men's faces as they left the building.

"Come, Karl, let's go over here to the sofa and have some bread with jam. Maybe a little tea? You sit and I'll get a cloth to tidy up your face."

22.

October 1923

Alana applied another layer of powder and rouge to disguise the haggard, pinched face that looked back at her from the mirror. She pulled on her woollen jacket and left the apartment.

Her boot heels clicked along the broken sidewalks. The war had made Berlin look as shabby as she felt. But she did what she had to do and took pride in doing it well; her customers were always satisfied. And maybe, just maybe, she wouldn't have to work so hard at supplementing the pay from her government job if she could hang onto her most recent catch.

Brisk autumn gusts swirled the linden leaves around her feet and pelted the brown leather boots with fine pebbles. She pulled her scarf up to cover the front of her throat. The solid walls of tenement buildings along each side of the street loomed above her, their greyness adding to the chill of the air. It felt almost cold enough to snow, but most likely it would be icy rain again.

At last she stepped up onto the tram. Oh, it was good to be out of the wind. Alana unbuttoned her jacket and let it hang loosely. She sat and, with practiced detachment, ran her hand down the length of her leg, enjoying the feel of her chic, new silk stockings. The appreciative gazes of the male passengers pleased her. She smiled smugly at the women, inviting their disparaging glares.

Hermann Wasser was on her mind a lot these days. She would have to try to hang onto this one. He could be her ticket. He had money and influence. Who cared if he was a bit overweight and balding? He still had a healthy sexual appetite and that was what she would use to snare him.

"Darling, let me help you with the rent," Hermann had said. "And I don't want to see you working in that beer hall in the evenings either. I want you home waiting for me." She would miss opportunities with men who paid, but most of those were one-time encounters. With Hermann, she hoped to make the relationship last longer. Besides, his gifts—hard-to-get, luxury items that most people had all but forgotten—were a welcome fringe benefit.

As she stepped off the tram, the icy wind sharpened her senses. Damn, it was cold. She grabbed the lapels of her jacket and pulled them together for warmth. Across the street she entered the stone building that housed the Internal Security Office. She and Hermann both worked there, although his work often took him out of the office.

"Just in time, Alana." The clerk gestured with his head towards a desk at the back of the room. "Herr Essler has some important papers he needs translated right away."

"Thank you, Rudi." Alana swished past him with a smile. She hoped he noticed her new stockings.

Herr Essler smirked as Alana approached. He admired her figure. She had a tight ass for a woman who kept it so busy, but what did he care? Once was enough. He didn't need all her baggage.

He had passed her on to his friend, Wasser, who had just transferred in from Stettin. He owed Hermann a favour and this one cost him nothing.

Straight to the meeting, Herr Wasser?" his driver asked.

"Of course." Hermann settled back in his seat, folding his hands on his ample belly. Things were going well. He had it all sorted out—almost.

He smiled to himself and wondered what Alana would say when he brought her his next gift. He had stopped a well-to-do French couple at an impromptu checkpoint that morning and confiscated their belongings. The red velvet dress would be stunning on her. He could hear her now.

"Hermann, darling," she would croon, "where do you find such treasures?" Her frown wrinkles would disappear and her weary eyes would sparkle. "How did you know that red is my colour? It is perfect with my blond hair." Yes, she would love the dress, but more than that, he was counting on the obligation she would feel towards him. She would do anything for him when she saw this dress.

It was a convenient arrangement he had with her, for now. Housing was scarce in post-war Berlin and although his friend, Essler, had found him an apartment, it was shabby. It served as a refuge when he wanted a peaceful evening alone, or privacy for a night with some stray kitty, but at Alana's, a warm bed was guaranteed and he could satisfy his urges any time. She wasn't a bad cook either; best homemade pasta he'd ever tasted. But most importantly, she knew better than to make demands on him. A bit of perfume here, some stockings there, a piece of chocolate or a sip of brandy; a small price to pay for the comforts of an uncomplicated bed.

There was only the one snag—that snot-nosed boy of hers.

After receiving the dress and giving Hermann what was probably the wildest ride of his sexual life, Alana was surprised to see him arrive early one afternoon while Karl was playing outside in the street. With an inviting smile, Alana unbuttoned and dropped her skirt. She loosened Hermann's tie and pulled it off while he unbuttoned her blouse as he kicked off his shoes. Their clothing littered a trail from the apartment door to the small bedroom. She thought afterwards that Karl should have known she was busy—he must have seen their clothes on the floor.

"Alana, you sure know how to please a man," Hermann said, between kisses. He pulled her down onto the bed, cupping her breasts as she leaned towards him. His erection told her he was ready for her but she would make him work for his pleasure today. She straddled him, keeping her bottom high in the air, and nibbled on his earlobe. Her tongue ran around the curled edge of his ear and lightly probed the passage into his ear.

"Oh-h-h, Alana," he moaned, arching his back in an effort to reach her. He unbuttoned his pants and her hands were instantly inside, teasing, tracing, circling.

He kicked at the entangling pants, finally flinging them onto the floor. Hermann put both hands on Alana's firm cheeks. He had just begun to pull her down onto him when they heard the apartment door open. Karl called out, "Mutti! Mutti! Where are you? Can I have something to eat?"

"Shit!" Alana and Hermann said together. Hermann almost threw her against the wall in his haste to get up.

"For Christ's sake, Alana! I told you I'm not putting up with this crap."

Alana scrambled to regain her balance and grabbed a sheet to cover herself. "It's all right, Hermann. Please don't go. Please! Wait! I'll fix it." He snatched his clothes viciously off the floor and stuffed his pale, hairless legs into his pants. Hermann looked up. Karl stood in the doorway wide-eyed, mouth agape. Alana's panic rose. Would he hurt the boy? Instead he took out his rage on the bedroom door as he kicked it shut. He whirled around to face her, his face distorted in anger.

"Just get rid of him or I'll only be back once more and that will be to pack my things," Hermann hissed. He tucked in his shirt under his pot belly and crammed his tie into his pants pocket. In the living room he grabbed his suit jacket and stormed out.

The slam of the apartment door reverberated in Alana's head as she collapsed on the shabby living room couch, stunned by the turn of events.

Karl was not a bad child, but she couldn't look at him without thinking of the man who had deserted her when he found out she was pregnant. Every year Karl resembled his long-gone father more. At times his face had an expression that took her back twelve years and she felt her bile rising all over again.

She had thought that with Hermann she had one more chance to catch a man who would stay and take care of her. Now it could be ruined. The insane rage building inside propelled her off the couch. "Karl! Come here!"

"I'm sorry Mu—" Karl started to say, as the first open-handed smack spun him around.

"How dare you barge in like that?" she screamed. "What did you think you were doing? You're supposed to stay outside until I call you." She seized the poker from beside the coal bin and whacked at his bony legs as he ran for the door.

On the landing, tousled and only half-dressed, Alana raised the poker over her head and flung it over the railing. Frau Gruber slammed her door shut just in time to avoid being hit with the iron missile. Her sturdy wooden door repelled the flying poker and sent it skittering across the hallway floor with a clatter that echoed up the stairwell.

Immediately Frau Gruber re-opened her door a crack and shouted to Alana, "This time you've gone too far. I'm contacting Youth Services and you should be thankful I'm not going to the police."

"Go ahead then. See if I care. Nosy bitch!"

Alana shrank back into her apartment and leaned her back on the door. She brought her palms up to her cheeks and stared straight ahead. *Oh, my God, what have I done?*

November 1923

At the sound of knocking, Alana ran on tiptoes to the door. She paused, ran her hands over the red velvet dress, and fluffed her hair. She felt like a princess. She was sure Hermann would fall in love with her now. But her face dropped when, instead of Hermann, an unsmiling woman in a long grey coat stood in front of her, a "Youth Services" tag prominently displayed on her lapel.

"Frau Werner?"

Alana nodded.

"I'm from Youth Services."

"I can read."

"There has been a complaint and I have been sent to collect your son. He will be taken to a good home." The stern-faced woman raised her chin and looked down her nose at Alana.

For several days Alana had watched the boy limping around, an ugly reminder of her quick, cruel temper. When guilt crept through her mind, she told herself to think of Hermann and choked back her growing trepidation.

"Please don't make this difficult, Frau Werner." The woman forced the words out through compressed lips. "It's best for the boy."

Alana stepped back from the door, let the woman in, and pointed to the alcove off the kitchen. Karl sat cross-legged on a cot, playing solitaire.

"This lady wants you to go with her."

"What? Why?"

"Never mind, Karl. Just get your sack and put in your clothes. You have to go with her. They have found a good family for you." Tears welled up in her eyes, surprising her. "Hurry up now. Throw those clothes into that sack. Here's your jacket, boots, playing cards...."

"Mutti!" Karl screamed, and tugged at her arm. "Don't let her take me. Mutti, don't! No, Mutti, ple-e-ase!" His eyes were wild and his thin arms so strong. Alana and the Youth Services worker dragged the struggling child down the stairs. Frau Gruber's door snapped shut as they passed. The driver of the waiting wagon jumped down to help.

"Up we go. There's a good boy," he said. Pinned between the driver and the woman, Karl turned his head to look behind the woman's shoulder at his mother.

"Mutti-i-i-i...." Great sobs tore out of his throat. Alana only glanced back once and saw Karl slump over in resignation, but the sound of his crying pursued her until she shut the outer building door.

Alana hurried upstairs to her apartment. She stared unseeingly at the place where the wagon had been and caressed the red velvet dress. "It was the right thing to do," she told herself. "The right thing to do." Tears stained the expensive dress.

23.

Karl stared through his tears at the horse's massive rear end and wondered how much longer till they got to...? He had no idea where they were going.

The rutted road was frozen hard and the wagon lurched along jostling the passengers. The woman from Youth Services winced with every bump. She was dressed all in grey. Even her face looked grey. Wedged between her and the driver, Karl was glad for the bit of warmth their bodies provided, but still he squirmed. In every breath he tasted the driver's stale tobacco mingled with the woman's rank body smell. He felt his throat tighten up as he tried not to gag. How he wished he was sitting close to his mother instead, with her sweet smell of delicate perfume. The thought of his mother brought forth another bout of sniffling. Karl tucked his nose into the front of his jacket and scrunched his eyes shut. He clenched his fists.

They turned down a narrow lane that led to a farmhouse. "Don't worry, Karl. The Bauermans are very kind people." The grey woman was trying to be friendly, but Karl didn't believe anything she said. It was her fault he was being taken away. "You will live with them and they'll take care of you," she continued. "Just behave yourself, try to be helpful, and everything will be all right."

As if to contradict her, a snarling German shepherd ran out and savaged the wagon wheels. Karl cringed and pulled back. The driver spoke to him for the first time. "He's all bark. When you get to know him he'll be friendly." Karl shrank down and pulled his jacket tighter around himself.

The dog barked and lunged at the wagon as the driver pulled to a stop in front of the tall white-washed building. A stout man with tousled blond hair stepped out of a brightly lit doorway and raised a hand in greeting. "Duchsie! That's enough!" he snapped. Duchsie's tail drooped and he slunk into his doghouse beside the porch.

"So this is the young fellow, is it? Come right in. What's your name, son?"

"Karl," he whispered. He hoped Duchsie would stay in his doghouse.

"Karl it is then." He put his hand out for Karl to shake. "You can call me Herr Bauerman. Ah, here comes Frau Bauerman. Liesl, will you take young Karl inside with you. He's just in time to join us for supper."

Karl kept Frau Bauerman between himself and the doghouse. In the warmth of the porch, his mouth watered at the smell of roast pork that wafted his way. He hadn't realized how hungry he was.

Herr Bauerman took the boy's sack down from the wagon.

"This one's a sad case," the driver said between puffs on his pipe.

"Aren't they all?" Bauerman said.

"We'll fill you in on the details when we get our report written up."

"Fine. No hurry. They all need the same thing—food, shelter, a bit of love, and a purpose. Have a good trip back to town." Bauerman stepped back from the wagon and sighed as he noted the small size of the bundle. He tossed it over his shoulder and returned to the house. Another little waif needed a decent home. He was more than willing to provide for their needs, but he did expect something back from these children. The government cheque helped cover some of their expenses but there was plenty of work to be done—in the farmyard for the boys and in the house for the girls. But this one was so thin. And that limp.... Bauerman was not at all sure he would be much help in dunging out the cattle stalls and slopping the pigs.

Karl sat at the long wooden table with the other foster children. There were six of them—seven counting Karl—mostly around his own age of eleven.

"Children," Frau Bauerman announced, "this is Karl and he is going to stay with us as your brother now. He—"

"No, I'm not," Karl blurted out. "I'm not your brother. I'm not going to stay here. They made me come here."

"Karl, please." Frau Bauerman's eyes narrowed under her wrinkled brow and she glared at him. "We are all polite here and it would be a shame if you had to go to bed without supper on your first night with us."

"I don't care!" Karl pushed away from the table, squirmed out of his space on the bench and stood, casting about for an escape.

Frau Bauerman was quick to grab his arm. She was as sturdy as a tank and there was no resisting her as she pulled him up the stairs to the bedroom. "I know it's all new to you and you feel you don't belong, but you are here with us now and this is where you must stay. You have a choice; you can say you're sorry and eat supper with us, or you can go to bed without supper."

"I'm not sorry," he shouted. "Everyone is mean to me."

"Fine. This is your bed. Go to sleep and we'll talk in the morning. Good night."

Karl tossed and fidgeted on the straw-stuffed mattress, muttering to himself, "I wish I never had to come here. She made it sound like I'm here to stay. No way! I'm going back to Mutti in the morning."

His throat ached from crying. When he heard the children coming upstairs to their beds, he pulled the pillow over his head to muffle his sobs. The last thing he needed was for them to hear him crying.

In the morning he was too tired and too cried out to make much fuss. Frau Bauerman had laid out clothes for him. "We'll have to wash the clothes you brought with you so you can wear these until then," she told him. Obediently he stepped into the knee socks and knickerbocker pants. He was thankful for the warmer shirt but was careful not to let Frau Bauerman know that. He was still angry with her for telling the other children that he was their brother and would be staying there. First chance he got, he was going home.

Moments later he heard Frau Bauerman call, "Karl, come and have your breakfast." He hated the idea of going downstairs to face everyone, but he did not intend to miss another meal.

"Good morning, Karl." A chorus of voices greeted him.

He mumbled a "morning," determined not to be their friend, much less their brother. But the children of the Bauerman household seemed eager to make Karl feel better after his bad start the night before. Each tried in his own way to be helpful.

"Our school is not so bad," Fritz said. "You can walk with me if you want. I can show you the way."

"All right." Karl shrugged. "Thanks."

"We'll have to get going right after breakfast," Peter said. "It's a long walk."

"You're going too then?" Karl asked.

"Oh, yes! So are Winfred and Albert. We all go to the same school. Trudy and Gerlinde go to the school for girls."

Although Karl hated porridge, he hurried to eat his fill of it for breakfast. He wasn't crazy about milk either, but he drank it thirstily. Moments later the boys flung their leather schoolbags onto their backs and left the house together, leaving the girls to clear the table.

"Do you feel better today?" Fritz asked Karl.

"I don't know. A little bit, I guess." Karl kicked at rocks on the road.

"We felt like that when we first came to the Bauermans," Peter said. "But they're pretty good to us."

"We have to work after school to help out on the farm," Fritz said, "but after all, they do feed us."

"I won't be staying long enough to do farm work. I'm going back to my mother."

"How?" the boys said together.

"I'll walk."

"Do you know where to go?" Fritz asked.

"I know it's in the city and I know my street and number."

"The city is too far away for walking. You'd better forget about that idea and do what we do." This was not what Karl wanted to hear, but these boys knew where they were, so he had to admit that Fritz was probably right.

"Yeah," Peter added. "It's not hard work and you get good food."

"What kind of work would I have to do?"

"You'll start out like I did, dunging out the stalls."

"You mean shovel ... you know ... animal shit?" He couldn't imagine being hungry enough to heave dung. A black cloud moved into his mind as he brooded over the thought of cleaning stalls.

"At first, yes. I've been here the longest," Peter continued, "so I do other jobs now like helping Herr Bauerman curry the horses. And I get to clean the reins and bridles."

They walked along the country lane briskly to keep warm. In the distance Karl could see buildings closer together like the beginning of a little town.

"One thing you need to be careful of though," Fritz said. "Stay clear of the bull. He can only go as far as his chain reaches from the post in the middle of the field, but don't get too close."

"Don't worry. I don't like animals so I won't go near any of them if I don't have to. That dog looks mean too."

"Duchsie?" Peter asked. "He's harmless."

"It's our job to give him food and water." Winfred pointed at Albert and himself. "He's really a nice dog."

"He didn't seem very nice last night. I'm going to keep out of his way."

Near the edge of the township, Peter pointed at a huge building. "There's the school." The cold, imposing two-storey brick building towered over Karl, who suddenly had to pee. He was afraid to ask where the bathroom was, but he need not have worried. All four boys headed straight for it as they entered the school.

At the office, Karl handed in a paper from the Bauermans and he was taken to his classroom. Forty heads turned to stare at him. Karl felt his face heating up. He looked at his feet and plunked himself down in the empty desk he was shown.

The teacher, tall, bald, and wearing spectacles, sighed and turned to the class. He straightened his wrinkled brown suit jacket and silenced the boys with a slam of the cane on his desk. "Now, let's begin. Take out your reading book—and Werner, you follow along in Schmidt's book beside you. I'll see if I can find you a book during the break."

As the lesson went on, Karl found it hard to focus on the reading and even harder to listen to the teacher's droning voice. He lost his place in the book and let his thoughts wander. Images whirled through his mind— Hermann scrambling for his clothes, his mother half-dressed, Duchsie snarling at him— "Werner ... Werner!" His head snapped up.

"I asked you what the dog's name is."

"Duchsie," Karl said, wondering how the teacher could know about the dog.

"Duchsie! Duchsie? How in the world did you come up with that answer? Page 23, at the top. Read, please!"

"Max barked at the horses," Karl read.

"Fine. Now what was the dog's name?"

"You mean the dog on the farm?" Karl asked. Snickers surrounded him and Karl felt his face getting hot again.

"Werner! This is not a good start. Since it's your first day, we'll *all* overlook it and carry on, but see that you pay more attention from now on." Karl hung his head.

"You will say 'Yes, Herr Solberg' when I speak to you."

Silence.

"I'm waiting."

"Yes, Herr Solberg," Karl whispered.

"Such a little mouse," Herr Solberg said, under his breath, but loud enough for everyone to hear.

All he thought about was going home. The previous November, he had traveled for a long time in the wagon to get to the farm. The city was left far behind. Could he walk that far? And what if he headed in the wrong direction? At the Bauermans he had food and a bed and, well … friends. Each day he said to himself he would find a way tomorrow. And so the weeks and months passed.

"I'll get out of here someday," he told Peter. "I'm only here for a short while."

Peter shook his head sadly. "Yes, you keep saying that, Karl, but it's not so easy to go home."

"And Herr Solberg makes me want to leave even sooner. He doesn't like me—picks on me all the time."

Peter shrugged. "He likes boys who behave."

"I'll get even with him one day."

Herr Solberg nagged him. "Karl! What's this? Did one of those farm hens run across your page? Who is supposed to be able to read this? You'll copy this work again after class." Karl smirked and lapped up the attention he received.

The next day at recess, the boys, as always, paraded two abreast around the inner court of the schoolyard. Karl had what he needed—an elastic band and one of Frau Bauerman's hairpins. In the middle of the yard, Herr Solberg stood, hands behind his back, ever watchful, his gleaming pate bobbing back and forth as he teetered back and forth from toe to heel. Karl kept his hands down and to one side as he loaded the hairpin and drew back on the elastic band between his thumb and pointer finger. He released the stretched elastic and immediately dropped it on the ground. Karl used Peter's body as a screen to hide the laughter he couldn't keep inside.

Herr Solberg's hand flew to his temple, slapping himself. His bald head swivelled. Eagle eyes searched the line of boys. In seconds he had traced the path of the flying object and pointed to several of the boys around Karl.

"You four. Step out." Karl, Peter, and two other boys stepped out of line. "Empty your pockets." The boys all had various small items in their pockets, but Karl had nothing. "One of you did this." Herr Solberg pointed at the red welt on his temple. "You will tell me who did it right now, or you will all be punished."

Peter had a pained grimace on his face. Karl could see him struggling with his conscience. Although Peter mostly looked at the ground, his eyes constantly flicked over to look at Karl as if he was waiting for him to confess. Moments later Peter broke down and pointed at Karl.

Herr Solberg took Karl by the scruff of the neck and hauled him into the school, lifting him so that the tips of his toes were all that touched the ground as he walked. Karl tingled with excitement. At the end of the break, the class had to witness his punishment. Karl stood at the front of the classroom looking at the faces of his classmates. Some covered their mouths to hide their expressions of horror at the pain they knew was coming, while others beamed openly in gleeful anticipation.

Herr Solberg pointed. "Bend over the table." He took his cane and smacked the table beside Karl. The knocking of knees on desks appeared to give Herr Solberg pleasure. His lips stretched back into a sadistic grin. He wiped a bit of drool from his mouth and proceeded to give Karl's backside three hard whacks.

Karl winced but didn't cry. When it was over, he sauntered back to his desk with a smirk.

"I'm really sorry, Karl," Peter said on the way home, "but he was going to cane us all if someone didn't speak up and I was the only one who knew you did it."

"Don't worry about it." Karl threw back his shoulders and pulled himself up as tall as possible. He walked with a swagger.

"But it must have hurt like hell, getting your bottom hit like that."

"It wasn't too bad." Karl stopped abruptly and reached down inside the back of his knickerbockers. He pulled out a huge handful of straw. "I expected to get caught." The boys shrieked with laughter as they ran home.

Karl hated the stink of the stalls. It made his eyes water and his nose run. He pitched out the soiled straw as fast as he could. The smell of manure followed him everywhere. He caught whiffs of it on his clothes, especially in the warmth of the classroom. He scrubbed himself often and it became his habit to add a drop of Herr Bauerman's aftershave to the water.

One thing he knew for sure. He never wanted to be a farmer. He hated animals and he hated having to care for them. Why should he care about them? Nobody cared about him.

He was afraid of them. The bull, the cows, the dog. Duchsie especially terrified him. When he looked at the dog, he saw teeth—huge teeth, like those of the wolf in the fairy tales. At first he always made sure that he was with another boy when it was time to go clean the barn, in case Duchsie was nearby. On the way back to the house, he picked up several rocks to have in his pockets, in case he met Duchsie alone. Sometimes Duchsie was tied to the doghouse and Karl threw rocks at him anyway, to show him who was boss. It gave him satisfaction to hear the dog yelp when his rocks found their mark. Herr Bauerman once remarked to Karl, "How strange that Duchsie always runs from you." Karl shrugged.

One day Karl threw a rock that clipped Duchsie behind the ear. The dog's yelp alerted Frau Bauerman. She flung open the kitchen window and stuck out her plump face. "Karl!" she shrieked. "You get in here right now." He was only half sorry he'd been caught. It was almost worth it to see Frau Bauerman's red face get redder in anger.

Karl spent the rest of the week doing roadwork as punishment. He still had to dung out the stalls and then, instead of playtime, he had to level the ruts in the road with a pick and shovel. He grumbled to himself as he drove the pick into the stubborn ground and plotted his revenge. She was always going on about this little plant or that one in her garden. He would show her.

Frau Bauerman called him to wash up for supper at the outside wash basin. Around the back of the house, he was out of sight of both the kitchen window and the barn door. He dashed over to the edge of the bull's field.

Chained to a heavy stake, the bull stood motionless, staring straight ahead, dripping threads of mucous from his thick lips. With one last glance over his shoulder, Karl summoned up his courage and ran in a half-crouched position, as fast as his limp allowed, to the bull's post. He grabbed the heavy stake and was disappointed to feel that it was firmly anchored in the ground. He threw his weight into his work and rocked the stake back and forth, back and forth, until he felt it loosen. The massive bull turned his head in slow motion and blew steam through his wet nostrils. He began to shift his heavy body. Karl gave two more quick heaves back and forth on the stake. *There!* he thought. *That should do it.*

He raced to the side of the house and dipped his hands into the wash basin just as Frau Bauerman stuck her head around the corner. "What's keeping you, Karl? Supper is almost on the table."

"Be right there."

Karl enjoyed his meal that evening. He went upstairs afterwards to do his homework without argument. He was eager to go to bed on time that night. He couldn't wait until morning.

Gustav!" Liesl shouted. "Gustav! The bull!"

"What on earth? What's wrong with the bull?" Gustav puffed and wheezed as his heels pounded down the stairs.

Liesl pointed out the open kitchen door. "He's right here. Just outside the door."

"Holy shit! How did that goddamned bull get loose?" Gustav looked out the front door and surveyed the yard. "Damn! He's torn down the fence."

"Not my *garden* fence?" Her voice went up an octave. "My vegetable garden?" She pushed past her husband and looked towards her newly sprouted garden. "Oh NO-O-O!" Liesl grabbed Gustav's arm for support. "All that work! Our food!" Tears welled up. She wanted to run out to look for survivors among her plants, but the bull had not moved from the door. "Gustav, get that bloody bull out of here."

Gustav pulled on his boots and hurried out the door. He took hold of the chain and led the bull away. Liesl followed at a safe distance. In the backyard she couldn't believe what she saw. The wooden fence, meant to keep the dog and chickens out, was piled in a broken heap. Long gouges in the soil told of the dragged stake, chain, and pieces of wooden fence. The tidy geometric garden of young shoots was no more. A square of razed ground remained, dotted with potholes the size of the bull's feet. Liesl's garden was in ruins.

She came back into the house to the stares of six children standing open-mouthed in the kitchen. The seventh had an undeniable brightness in his eyes and a poorly hidden smirk.

Liesl's hands trembled and her eyes stung, but it was breakfast time and she still had to see that the children got to school. She took several deep breaths to try to regain her composure, and busied herself with serving the porridge.

"We can help you fix the garden, Frau Bauerman," Gerlinde said.

"We'll all help," Trudy added.

The boys nodded, all except Karl. Liesl watched him now when she thought he wasn't looking.

"And the boys too?" Liesl asked.

Four boys were quick to say yes, they would help, but Karl was slower to offer. When he did say he would help, Liesl was sure she saw that self-satisfied smile again.

After the children had left for school, Liesl called her husband to the kitchen. "Sit down, Gustav. I need to talk to you."

"You look so serious. Is something else wrong?"

"When did you last see the bull at his stake?"

Gustav thought for a moment. "Late yesterday afternoon."

"And this morning the damage was done. Late yesterday afternoon all the children were in the house. Trudy and Gerlinde were helping with supper. The boys were doing their homework upstairs, except for Karl."

"I thought you told him to work on the road."

"For throwing rocks at Duchsie, yes, but then I told him to go around back to get washed."

"You don't think he pulled the stake out? He's too thin."

"All it needed was a bit of rocking back and forth to loosen it. The bull could do the rest. And Karl has enough anger in him to do such a thing. Maybe to get back at me for punishing him."

"What do you think we should do?"

"It's time for him to leave. Fritz has been asked to deliver notes to me at least three times about Karl's unruly behaviour at school. He has been cruel to the dog, and now this. I've had enough. I want him gone."

Gustav looked at the floor and hesitated. "I suppose you're right. I hate to lose a helper in the barn, even one who doesn't do a very good job, but I can see that you have your hands full with him. I'll take the buggy into town today and go to Youth Services. They'll have to find another placement for him. If they can."

"If they can't, I don't care. He can go back to his witch of a mother."

"Now, Liesl, you know you don't wish that. I'll see what can be done for him. But who will tell the boy?"

"If I take another look at my ruined garden, I will be able to tell him the bad news without losing a wink of sleep tonight."

24.

Berlin 1933

Karl put his shoulder to the side door of the small repair shop and shoved to open it. No wonder it hadn't wanted to budge. Several boxes blocked access. "What the hell?"

"Morning, Karl." Herr Lehman's perpetually friendly mood matched his looks. He was a man with gently rounded features, a pot belly, and a pudgy face. Dark hair had said goodbye to the top of his head years ago, preferring to live on the fringe of his cranium. A mighty moustache, like a brush, helped to sweep away thoughts of baldness when one first looked at him. "Lots of jobs today. Two of them in those boxes by the door."

"Were you afraid I wouldn't notice them?"

"I knew you would grumble about them if I put them in your way, and then I wouldn't forget to tell you about them. The two little hand-operated sewing machines need fixing right away."

"No problem, Herr Lehman. That's the kind of machine my Aunt Paula had when I lived with her. I kept it running for her."

"I remember that." Herr Lehman nodded and smiled. "I remember the day she asked me to take you on as an apprentice. 'He's a magician when it comes to fixing things,' she said."

"I was pretty nervous that first day."

"You sure were. But no wonder. You were just a skinny fourteen-year-old. No experience. Little more than a street urchin. But you've done fine these past seven years."

"You must have known my aunt for a long time."

"Many years. I met her when I was doing machine repairs like you're doing now. She invited me to have a cup of tea with her and it turned into a friendship. Just friends. Nothing more." Herr Lehman stood lost in thought for a moment. "Where did the time go? Seems like yesterday when I was sitting in her living room. She always had a little piece of cake and interesting conversation to offer. Very nice lady."

"Aunt Paula's a good person. She took me in when I really needed a place. I've tried not to let her down. Or you."

"And you haven't." Herr Lehman gave his head a shake as if to bring himself back to the present. "Now let's get busy here. The owners of these machines will be coming by this afternoon and I want them to go home satisfied."

"Any house calls to do today?"

"Three. You should be able to take care of at least one of them today."

"Right. Any young ones?"

"Too old for you." Herr Lehman's fat belly shook as he laughed.

Karl had the machines fixed in half an hour. He grabbed his jacket and his worn tool satchel and headed out the door to make his first house call.

A well-maintained building near a park matched the address he was looking for. It was not in a rich part of the city, but the building looked much more respectable than his own apartment block. Someday he hoped to be able to afford something like this.

A chubby woman of about forty answered the door. Rolled down stockings cut into the ankles of her stovepipe legs. Her light brown hair, streaked with grey, fell to her shoulders. Karl thought a good haircut would better suit her jolly face and friendly manner. "Come in, come in," she said. "It's my daughter's machine. She stepped out to pick up her assignments for today. She does alterations for a dress shop and needs the machine fixed right away."

"Let's have a look. If nothing is broken, we can probably have the machine running very soon."

"She would like that. Oh, here she is now." A slender, red-haired woman with moss green eyes came into the room carrying a huge bundle of clothes. Karl suddenly became aware of the shabbiness of his only jacket. He stood up as tall as he could and congratulated himself on having had the forethought to run a comb through his blond hair before making this house call.

"Erika, this is the man from Singer. He's here to fix your sewing machine. Young man, you didn't give your name."

"It's Karl Werner. Pleased to meet you, Erika."

Karl tipped the body of the machine back to look inside and underneath. He groped in his tool bag, did some adjustments to the sewing machine, and a few moments later had it stitching smoothly.

"That is amazing, Herr Werner," Erika said. "Is it fixed then?"

"All fixed."

"What was the problem?"

"Lint, mostly. But this is what stopped it from working completely." He held up the pincette. His favourite tool held a black button between its fine prongs.

"A button! Imagine that. Thank you so much, Herr—"

"Please call me Karl." He hoped that he had interpreted her appraising glances correctly. He knew he was a bit on the thin side, but handsome enough. Well, why not take a chance? He wouldn't know if he didn't ask. "Say, Erika...."

"Yes?"

"I was wondering...." Karl lowered his voice. "Would you like to go out with me? I'd be honoured if you'd let me call on you tonight." He hoped she didn't think he was too fast and pushy.

Erika glanced around and, not seeing her mother, leaned towards him and said, "What did you have in mind?"

"A stroll in the park, maybe a beer or a coffee. 7:00?"

"I'll be ready."

He had dated a string of girls after Erika. And then he found Thea. She was an alluring woman. Her petite shape gave her a girlish look, but at twenty-one, she could trade quips back and forth with the patrons of Anton's Bar like a regular. She struck a seductive pose with her dark, short-bobbed hair and her cigarette holder. Thea appeared to be striving for that Piaf look that was all the rage, and in Berlin's nightclub life, image was everything. She sat cross-legged on a barstool bobbing her shapely leg up and down like a lure. It snared Karl's attention.

"Come on home with Daddy," he had told her. "I'll keep you comfortable. All you need to do is be there when I come home from work." To his surprise, she did.

Lying back on Karl's threadbare sofa, Thea stretched her arms out in front of her, spreading her fingers tautly to inspect her nails. "I painted my nails a different colour. Do you like it?" Karl nodded. "And I did my hair. You didn't even notice." She pouted and blew smoke rings in his face.

As he repaired machines during the day, Karl thought about Thea waiting for him, warm and sexy. Sex in the evening before a night out in the bars and more sex in the early morning when they came home—it was a never-ending adrenaline high. But after a couple of months, Karl was finding the pace hard to maintain.

He had thought this was what he wanted, but when Herr Lehman confronted him, he began to have doubts. "What's going on with you, Karl? You're dragging around here not getting much done. I need you to be sharp, not falling asleep on some woman's sewing machine."

"Did that old biddy complain?" Karl snorted and waved off the accusation. "She's an old half-blind bat. Maybe I yawned once or twice. Won't happen again."

"Well, I'm warning you. If you start losing customers, I'll have to look for someone else. Someone who isn't burnt out before the day begins."

"Yes, all right. Don't worry. I can manage. I just haven't been getting enough sleep for a few nights. I'll fix it." *Jeezus! I'd better get a grip! I need this job to keep that little minx happy.*

Arriving home that evening, Karl walked into a fog of cigarette smoke. A whine emanated from deep inside the smoky cloud. "Ka-a-rl! What took you so long? I've been ready to go out for hours."

"Aw, Thea." Karl dropped his jacket on the unmade bed. "I'm too tired. Why don't you fix us some supper while I have a nap?"

"What!? Me? Cook?"

"What's the matter with that?"

"Are you crazy? Course, if you can't afford to keep me and take me out...."

"No, that's not a problem. Just let me get my jacket back on."

"That's my boy," she crooned.

With a sigh Karl looked longingly at his bed and closed the apartment door behind them.

The friendly familiar faces of other regulars welcomed Thea and Karl in the small bars of Berlin. With shouts, nods, and waves, they exchanged greetings. Karl joined a noisy group at a table, seated Thea and called for beer. A three-piece band played and several couples danced. By eleven that night, Karl was ready to go home, but judging by her enthusiasm, Thea was just getting warmed up.

"C'mon, Karl, let's dance another one." She jumped up and pulled on his arm.

"Thea, I'm so tired."

"I'm not."

"You probably slept half the day."

"I had a little nap. Oh, come on. Let's dance." She waited. "All right then." She flopped down on the chair and folded her arms across her chest. "Buy me another drink and we'll sit this one out." As an afterthought she added, "And get me another pack of cigarettes too, will you darling?"

Karl had used up almost all his savings, every extra mark being spent on Thea's cigarettes. "I need to smoke as much as possible," she had told him. "I'm saving the coupons that come with the cigarettes to trade for collectors' cards. I really like Birds of Germany. They're my favourite this year."

Three months later Herr Lehman took him aside. "Karl, I don't know what's going on with you, but if things don't improve immediately, I'm afraid I'll have to let you go.

Karl listened in stunned silence. "What do I need to do?"

"Get some sleep. Put in a good day's work each day like you used to and try to win back some of the disgruntled customers you've lost."

Karl nodded. He had been warned months ago, but he had been weak and let Thea control him. Now he would pay, unless he took back his life.

Sit down, Thea. We have to talk."

"Don't look like that, Karl. You're scaring me."

"Things have to change. I need sleep. I need food. I need clean clothes and clean air. I need to have someone who is interested in looking after my needs. Dammit, I need more than a party girl!" He wished he could control his rising voice, but it frustrated and angered him that he was so weak where Thea was concerned and that Herr Lehman was right.

"But honey, I do look after your needs." Thea stroked his cheek, batted her blackened eyelashes, and then took time out to blow a smoke ring before continuing. "Don't I take care of your needs every night ... if you haven't already fallen asleep, that is."

"Stop it, Thea! You haven't heard a word I said."

"Of course I heard what you said." She snapped at him, in a temper now. "The whole apartment block heard what you said. But if you think I'm going to stay here just to cook and clean and do your washing, well, you know I can't cook and I don't clean and the thought of doing your washing ... Ugh!"

"Then we're finished. Pack your cosmetics and get out." There. He'd done it.

"What? You can't just throw me out."

"Can't I? Just watch me."

"But Karl, I ... I'm ... pregnant."

"What!?" His stomach turned over and his lungs forgot to breathe.

"You heard me. I'm not happy about it, but we need to get married."

"Married? What are you thinking? Men don't marry women like you!"

The few dishes that Karl had in his kitchen cupboard were soon in pieces on the floor. As he ducked one last time, Karl wondered whether, with the ashtray now broken as well, Thea would see that she really couldn't stay. Almost as if reading his thoughts, Thea swept her makeup into her cosmetics bag. She tore her nightclub dresses off the hangers and gathered up the bits of clothing and underwear that littered the bed. She rammed everything into a cloth satchel and stormed out the door. Its slam set the dangling light bulb swaying.

Karl opened the window. The fresh air felt good. It seemed as if a huge weight had been lifted from his shoulders. With a sigh of relief, he turned the lock on the door and fell into bed looking forward to his first good sleep in weeks.

Months later Karl began to wonder about his child. Guilt weighed on his conscience as the time for Thea's delivery drew near. She had gone home to live with her mother, that much he knew, but since he had stopped frequenting the bars, he had not seen or heard anything of her. The more he thought about it, the more he was convinced that maybe marriage with Thea wouldn't be so bad. He'd have a real family. But what was he thinking? He would be the one having to change the diapers, or worse yet, wash them. There'd be nothing to eat unless he cooked it himself. Still, he berated himself for being a rat, abandoning a girl in a difficult situation that he felt partly responsible for. And then there was macho pride at having fathered a child. That counted for something, didn't it?

The smells of old, damp wood mixed with sauerkraut and musty carpet runners filled the apartment hallway. Karl stopped on the fourth-floor landing to catch his breath before knocking. He had dressed in his only suit to make a good impression. He rapped on the battle-scarred door. It opened a crack.

"Good afternoon. Are you Thea's mother?"

"What of it?" The door opened wider.

"My name is Karl," he began. "I came to see Thea." The woman's eyes narrowed into slits, her lips puckered as she pressed them together, and she inhaled through her nose. Her face reddened. Karl took a step backwards. "I wondered if she had the baby."

"Yes, she's had the baby and she never wants to see you again, you lousy shit!"

25.

February 1936

Berlin Singer Repairs at your service," Karl announced to the pleasant-looking young woman who opened the apartment door.

"Am I glad to see you! You can't imagine how frustrated this machine has made me."

Hmm. Frustrated woman. Glad to see me. This sounds promising. "We'll have it fixed up in no time. Don't you worry your pretty little head, Frau ... er...."

"Fraeulein, actually. Just call me Evelyn."

"A pleasure, Evelyn." He took her delicate hand in his own rather large one. "Karl Werner." He raised her hand and studied it briefly. As she pulled her hand away, he quickly added. "You have very fine fingers. Do you sew much?"

"It's my living. I take in sewing repairs and I do alterations. I *need* this machine to be working. It's what feeds me and pays my share of the rent."

"Let's have a look here." Karl set his leather tool bag on the sewing table next to the machine. He worked the treadle several times, watching the action of the needle. In seconds the needle bent and broke. "I see." He flipped the machine backwards on its hinges, exposing its underbelly. With his magnifying glass, he focused on the bobbin case. He took out his pincette and reached into the inner workings of the bobbin case. Like a pair of forceps the pincette could reach into tiny spaces, places where his large hands could not go, to poke, prod, pick up, or retrieve all manner of materials from the intricate assemblies of small machines. Retracting the tool slowly, Karl straightened up. "And here we have the little devil that has been causing you so much grief." It was one of his favourite lines with the young ladies whose machines he repaired. It never failed to get their attention.

"A straight pin?"

"It must have become caught in the feeder teeth and got dragged down into the workings of the machine. That's what has been breaking your sewing needles."

She had a look of surprise and admiration on her face. "That's it then? It's fixed?"

"It should be, but let me try it out to be sure." Karl replaced the bobbin case, threaded a new needle, and worked the treadle of the machine. It ticked and sang as stitches of perfect size and tension appeared on his scrap of cloth.

"That's wonderful! And it didn't take you any time at all. You really are a genius."

"Thank you, my dear." He loved the way she acknowledged his skills. "And since it was so quickly repaired, I'll just give it a quick cleaning and oiling so you shouldn't have any trouble for a long time. Provided you keep the pins out of the way of the moving parts." He grinned, hugely pleased with himself.

"I'm so happy to have it working again. I've been struggling with it for two days and the work is piling up. I'll have to get busy and catch up now before my brother comes home from work. He expects me to cook and clean for him and that cuts into the time I have for sewing, which I need to do if I'm to pay my share of the rent. Oh!—" She stopped and clamped a hand over her mouth. "I'm sorry. I don't know why I'm telling you all this."

"That's no problem. Listen, you don't need the burden of another expense. What do you say to going out for a cup of cocoa and I'll take care of the bill?"

"Now?"

"Why not? Think of it as time you don't have to spend sewing to pay the repair bill."

She covered her mouth gently with the tips of her fingers as she considered. "Well, if you put it that way. All right. You have been kind. Just let me get my coat."

"Yes, it's chilly but the cocoa will warm us up." He thought he felt things heating up already as they left the apartment together.

"Here we are." Evelyn stopped in front of the door of a tiny bakery and coffee shop. "It's a small place, but it's very good."

"You come here often?"

"Once in a while—the prices are very reasonable."

"I suppose that's a consideration."

She gave him a questioning look.

"I mean times are tough for many people." He hurried to explain his blunder. "I visit a lot of homes to do repairs, and the way people suffer just trying to survive these days.... Well, I know it's hard."

She folded her arms holding onto her elbows. "Of course. I'm working hard to pay expenses, and you've seen my apartment. But, I get by." She shook her head. "Let's not think about that. It's nice to enjoy a little escape."

They sat at a small table and chatted. Karl studied her while trying not to be obvious. She was pretty in a plain sort of way but she didn't seem to be concerned about how she looked. Not at all like Thea.

Their cocoas were soon gone and as Karl stood up, he reached over to Evelyn. She pulled back slightly. "If you'll excuse me," he put one hand under her chin, smiled and ran a finger of his other hand over her upper lip, "you had a cocoa moustache." Evelyn looked down as if embarrassed, but then Karl saw that she was looking for something on her lap.

Napkin in hand she stood and said, "So do you." She wiped Karl's upper lip and they both laughed.

Karl cut slices of rye bread for his supper. He had picked up some salami at a meat shop on his way home. As he prepared his open-face sandwiches, his thoughts returned again and again to Evelyn. She was so different from Thea.

"I *need* this machine to be working," Evelyn had said. "It's what feeds me and pays my share of the rent." It was refreshing to meet a woman who concerned herself with coping with real life—rent payments, deadlines, and responsibilities.

She was a plain girl with her mouse-coloured hair and washed-out blue eyes, but her nose was fine and she had a warm smile that made her look prettier than she really was. He had a feeling that Evelyn would be sympathetic toward his own imperfections and the slight limp he had learned to live with.

Karl had no illusions about his shortcomings. He was only of average height and less than average weight.

He was not a physical person; no Johnny Weissmueller, that was for sure. If he could capture the interest of someone like Evelyn, mousey or not, he thought he would be doing all right.

Evelyn couldn't compare to Thea in looks, but her pleasant, easy manner more than made up for that. He realized, after meeting Evelyn, that Thea, in spite of her good looks, had in fact been self-centered and shallow, a star in her own fantasy.

Karl bit into his salami on rye and decided to try to see Evelyn again. It had been over two years since his involvement with Thea and he had taken out only a few girls since then. The sordidness of one-night stands was unsatisfying. He wondered what Evelyn's delicate hands were doing now? Sewing, most likely. Sewing! That was it! That was what he needed to have her do. He rummaged around in his sparsely outfitted wardrobe and easily found a shirt needing repair. Maybe there was something she could do about that frayed collar.

The next day he appeared at Evelyn's apartment. A thin, pale man with sandy hair opened the door. He looked Karl over, his red-rimmed eyes locking on the shirt bundled up in Karl's hands. "Sewing?" he asked.

"Excuse me?"

"Sewing. You have sewing for my sister?"

"Oh, yes. Is she here?"

"Evelyn!" he called over his shoulder.

Karl twisted the shirt in his hands while he waited for Evelyn to appear. As she came into the small vestibule, her hands fluttered shakily up to her hair, patting it into place.

"Karl! How are you? What brings you here?"

"My feet." He smiled at his own joke, but instantly looked at the floor. *Oh, God. How stupid! What's the matter with me? Pull yourself together, Karl.*

Evelyn giggled. "Well, I'm glad they did. Come in, please."

"Actually it was my shirt that brought me. I wondered if you would do this little sewing job for me." He held out the shirt to show her the frayed collar.

"I see this kind of thing a lot."

"Can it be repaired?"

"Not really, but I can turn the collar so the worn part can't be seen, and it will look like a new shirt. I hope you're not in a hurry for it." She pointed to the stack of clothing on her sewing table.

"Take all the time you need. Is it all right if I come and check the progress once in a while? Say, tomorrow? About this time? Another cup of cocoa?"

Evelyn smiled and Karl felt emboldened. "Or perhaps you'd like to see a film with me?"

Evelyn's head tilted to the side and her shoulders came up ever so slightly in a shrug that suggested she might be open to the invitation. "Saturday then?" he asked.

"All right."

"I'll pick you up at 6:30."

They shook hands warmly and Karl almost walked into the doorframe as he left.

Karl licked his ice cream and glanced down at the slim figure beside him. "You know, Evelyn, I feel comfortable with you."

"Me too. I mean with *you*." Evelyn's shoulders rose to meet her ears as she buried a little giggle.

"I was thinking, we've been to films, the zoo, the park, and your apartment." Karl hesitated. "Do you want to come see my apartment? I've only lived in this new place for a couple of months."

"I guess?" She sounded unsure, as if she wondered what his real intentions were.

"Don't worry. I don't mean anything else by that. I thought you might like to see where I live. It's not fancy, but on rainy days, we could have a cup of tea there and not disturb your brother."

"That would be nice. To have a private place to go. Besides, Wilhelm likes his time alone. I don't think he's well."

"I'm sorry. I hope he feels better soon. Now what about having a look at the apartment?"

Oh, Karl! This is nice." Evelyn turned around and around in the small apartment. "It needs a woman's touch, but you have plenty of room here and I can see the possibilities."

"What do you think about this as a little sewing corner?"

Evelyn swung around to stare at Karl. "What are you saying?"

"Why not move in and do your sewing here? At least you could be sure your sewing machine would be kept in perfect running order."

"What about my brother?"

"I don't think I can manage to keep him in running order, but he can probably look after himself."

"Karl!" Evelyn gave him a dig in the ribs. "You know what I mean."

"Wilhelm can find someone to move in with him. There are always people looking to share an apartment."

"But what if it doesn't work out with us? My sewing machine and I would be out on the street. No, Karl, much as I like the idea, I'm afraid I couldn't risk it."

"Well, what if we got married?" *Where in the world did that come from?*

"What!? Are you serious?"

"Why not? It would be a good arrangement for us both. We get along well and we'd be good for each other, don't you think?"

"I guess so. It's just that it's rather sudden. I'd have to talk to my brother."

"But do you like the idea? I mean if your brother is okay with it?"

"Yes, I think so. I like you a lot, Karl. I think we'd get along well."

He was encouraged by her shy smile. "All right. Think about it until next weekend. You can tell your brother that you'll give him a month to find someone else to share his apartment. Then at the end of that month, we can get married." Was he pushing too hard? He watched her face closely. She stood still, gazing at the floor and chewing on her lip, as if she were working things out in her mind. "Evelyn?"

"I'll let you know next weekend, but I hope my brother doesn't get all in a dither. He has coughing fits if he gets excited." Her face, happy at first, had clouded over again.

"He'll get used to the idea." Karl pulled Evelyn closer and landed a kiss on her forehead. "It will be all right. You'll see." He smiled and tried to look confident.

"Yes, I suppose.... I hope so," she said. He took her hands in his. They felt thin and cool.

"You have big hands, Karl. And warm." She looked up at him and smiled. "I feel like I'll be safe with you."

Karl glowed inside. "I'll do my best to take care of you. I promise."

She nodded. "We'll take care of each other." She turned her face up to meet his lips. Karl was surprised at the heat those thin lips of hers generated in him. He pressed closer, enjoying contact with her body.

She pushed him away and gasped. Her face was flushed, but she was smiling. "I'd best be getting back now." She laughed nervously.

"I'll see you home. We can continue this another time if you like."

"Yes, I think I like. Another time, yes."

As he walked home from Evelyn's apartment half an hour later, Karl's nerves trembled with emotion. His life was about to change. He liked Evelyn a lot. In fact, he liked her more than he had liked Thea. It was a good feeling to be with someone who didn't contradict him all the time. He could relax and be himself. Best of all he liked that she accepted the way he took charge. He gave his head a shake. He still couldn't believe he had offered to marry her, but he wanted to end the loneliness of his empty life. She would turn his bare apartment into a home, and that was what had always been missing in his life, what he had always craved—a home.

Karl slapped down the jack of clubs.

"Damn you, Karl! How do you do it?" Otto ran his fingers through his curly brown hair. He readjusted his metal-framed glasses. "One of these days, I'm going to beat you at this game."

"One day, maybe, but looks like today's not your day." Karl winked at Franz who tossed his cards down and reached for his schnapps glass. The three friends finished the last round of cards and Karl leaned back in his chair smiling. He was good and usually won the small pot of change they threw in for bets. "You need to brush up on your math if you want to win at skat. You need to think and plan. But that's never been your strong suit, has it Otto?"

"What hasn't?"

"Thinking."

"You're an ass, Karl," Otto said. "Why don't you just take your winnings and go home?"

Karl stubbed out his cigarette and scooped up the money. "Your place next week, Franz?"

"Sure." Franz shrugged his shoulders and let out a sigh.

Otto didn't bother to get up to see them out. Franz and Karl walked down the block together in the warm night air. "This is my street. I'll see you next Wednesday. And, Karl?" Franz put his hand on his friend's shoulder. "Try to take it easy on Otto, will you? He's not as smart as you, but he's a good guy."

"He needs someone to wake him up. He can be so stupid. Maybe I was a bit hard on him, but he's so transparent in his bids. Can't he see that he has to be more devious in his strategy?"

"I guess he can't and it hurts him when you point it out so ruthlessly."

"Bah! He can take it. If not, he will have to learn to be tougher." *Nobody babied me.*

Franz looked at the ground and shook his head. "Well, see you next week. My place, don't forget."

Kristina made some poppy seed cake. I told her it doesn't go with beer, but she insisted we have some." Franz glowed with pride as the men took their places around his table. He winked at Kristina.

"Looks tasty." Otto reached for a piece.

"Who could say no to cake?" Karl took a large bite of cake and wiped the crumbs off his mouth with the back of his hand. "This is one of the advantages of having a woman around."

"One of them." Franz grinned. "And when are you going to get yourself a little woman for the house, Karl?"

"As a matter of fact, I've asked Evelyn to move in with me, but she didn't want to risk it—"

"Can't say I blame her," Otto said.

"So I asked her to marry me."

"Oh-ho! So that's why we haven't seen you on the weekends anymore. It's getting serious, is it?" Franz leaned across the table and looked up into Karl's face. "So tell! What else have you been keeping from us?" His deep blue eyes twinkled as he waited for Karl to speak.

"Oh, not much. But if she says yes, I'll need you fellows to stand up for me."

"Of course!"

"I'm not sure I can." Otto shifted his heavy body in the chair, stuck out his lower lip, and studied the contents of his beer glass.

"Why not?"

"Well, what if I have to do any thinking? It's not my strong suit." He looked up directly into Karl's eyes.

"Okay, Otto. Point taken. I apologize. Friends?" Karl reached out his hand. Otto shook it energetically.

"You're smart, Karl, but you would be smarter if you kept it to yourself."

"The wedding?"

"No, being smart."

"I see. I'll take it under advisement." Karl smiled to hide his discomfort. "Now, did you bring plenty of money to lose? Let's play."

September 1936

The fresh stains on the white tablecloth at "The Golden Lion" told of an excellent wedding supper—pork roast with homemade pasta and red cabbage. Soufflé and coffee for dessert. Karl sat back beaming at the group of friends around him. Franz and Otto had witnessed the civil ceremony. Evelyn's brother, Wilhelm, and her friend Gisela had stood as witnesses for her. Now the four guests raised brandy glasses to the bride and groom.

"To a long and healthy life," said Wilhelm. A cough suddenly escaped him. A fine spray of blood coated his glass.

Shocked silence settled on the group. "Excuse me, please." Wilhelm pulled the glass close to his chest and tried to cover the blood with his hands. His hasty effort only made things worse, as the bloody sputum dappled the front of his white shirt.

I know he's sick, but he's not your responsibility. You should be looking after me, not him." Karl wished she would get over this obsession with her brother, always looking after him like a mother hen.

"I can't simply forget about him. The doctor said they would take him to a sanatorium as soon as they had a bed for him, but until then, I have to look after him. It's bad enough he has to spend nights alone with no one to call if he needs something."

Karl took her by the shoulders. "Look, Evelyn. I know you feel you should help him but there's nothing to be done. There's no cure for tuberculosis. The doctor said he needs to rest and you're not to get too close or you could get it too. I don't want you to get sick."

"I'll be careful."

"And try to get something done today. You haven't done a thing for days."

"That's not fair!"

"I meant with the sewing."

Evelyn spun away from him and grabbed at the shirt that lay on top of a huge stack of folded clothes. She dropped heavily into the chair in front of the sewing machine, shook out the shirt, and shoved a torn seam under the needle. She threw her hands up in exasperation. The small drawers at the side of the sewing cabinet were almost torn off their tracks as she yanked them out and rummaged for thread.

Karl stood rooted to the floor. *What is going on with her? Did I say something?* He took a tentative step towards her. "Evelyn? I...."

Evelyn put her face into her hands. Her shoulders jerked up and down. Karl gently stroked her back. "Evelyn, dear. I didn't know how much this has been affecting you. Forgive me for being an insensitive fool. Come here." He pulled her up and embraced her. The sobbing increased and Karl wondered if he was doing the right thing, but as he rubbed her back and whispered, "Shhh-shhh-shhh...," he could feel her calming down. "Let's not fight over this."

"But you said—" She turned away and coughed, unable to continue.

"I know, I know. Never mind what I said. Let's try to get this sorted out. How about if you go over there for a quick visit in the morning to make sure Wilhelm is okay? Make him a cup of tea or whatever he wants, and then you come home and you can catch up on your sewing. After supper you and I will take a quick walk over and check on him again. Maybe we can get a friend to go look in on him in the afternoon."

"All right." Evelyn sniffed and wiped her nose. "We can try that. I hope it will be enough."

April 1937

Franz and Otto arrived together for the Wednesday night card game. "Hey, Karl! How's married life?" Franz asked.

"Good, good. Come in. Sit down. Beer or schnapps?"

"How about beer today?" Otto said. "I had a bit of a hangover from the schnapps at Franz's last week."

"Same for me," Franz added.

"Fine. Beer it is."

In the kitchen Evelyn cut up an apple cake and put it on a platter. "Karl, I'll leave the serving to you. I'm going to carry on with my sewing."

Men's voices talking and laughing, the slapping of cards and sudden outcries of surprise filled the rooms of the apartment. The rocking sound of the treadle stopped now and then, replaced by the sound of coughing. Evelyn hurried past the card players on her way from the bathroom. "Evelyn, are you feeling all right?" Karl asked.

"Oh, I'm fine. Just a bit of an upset stomach."

"How long has this been going on?"

"Couple of weeks."

"Why don't you leave the sewing and go on to bed?"

"Yes, all right. I'll just finish up this blouse repair. Good night, Franz, Otto. 'Night, Karl."

She hurried out of the room, coughing again.

"She looks pale," Otto said. "Are you sure she's all right."

"Throwing up for two weeks? Sounds like she's pregnant."

Karl sat up and looked straight at Franz. "What did you say?"

"She's pregnant. She's got that pale greenish tinge to her face. She's been throwing up a lot. She's pregnant. That's how it was with Kristina."

Karl lost at skat that evening.

In November of 1937, Evelyn's baby boy was stillborn. The doctor took Karl aside. "I'm very sorry, Herr Werner, but there was not much hope that the boy would live, under the circumstances."

"What do you mean?"

"She is barely able to provide for her own body, let alone a baby. She's very weak and the birth took too long. I assume you're aware that she has tuberculosis."

"Tuberculosis? No! That bastard!"

"Herr Werner, please. What are you talking about?"

"Her brother died of tuberculosis last winter. I told her she shouldn't spend so much time with him. Now she's got it too."

"I'm very sorry. I'm afraid it's not easy to find a place in a sanatorium. They're all full, but I'll see what I can do. Please sit down, Herr Werner. You're looking pale yourself."

Karl couldn't believe his bad luck. He had grown fond of Evelyn. Maybe it wasn't real love like in the films, but he did care for her. "What do I have to do to take care of her at home?" he asked the doctor.

"I'm afraid there's not a lot you can do except see that she rests as much as possible."

"I'll do what I can. Meanwhile you'll put her on the waiting list for the sanatorium?"

"I will, but don't get your hopes up."

"It's all I have." Karl turned away whispering to himself. "It's all I've ever had."

Karl, what's wrong?" Evelyn asked.

"Josef isn't well and business has been slow. He told me today he has to close the shop."

"I still have my sewing," Evelyn said. Karl rolled his eyes. She really had no idea what it took to get by these days. The rent alone was going to be difficult to manage, never mind finding enough to eat.

"I know it's not much, but it's something."

"I'll have to see what I can hustle up. If I have to go door to door asking about sewing machines, so be it."

"Why not ask about other small appliances? You know you can fix anything." Evelyn had one thing going for her, he had to admit, she was an optimist. She didn't seem to realize how hard it was to get people to part with their money these days. It wasn't just themselves who were hurting. Everyone was struggling to survive.

"I'll start tomorrow." He gave her a quick hug. "Try not to worry. We'll manage."

Karl felt confident about his ability to talk people into anything, and he knew his way around the streets of Berlin. He hustled odd jobs to pay the rent. Backstreet trading was his forte. He'd buy a pound of butter, make a few swaps around the corner, and come home with enough food for several meals for himself and Evelyn. They got by.

September 1939

War. The limp he'd had since childhood was reason enough for the army to reject him. For the first time in his life, Karl considered the limp a blessing. He needed to be home to look after Evelyn. Her tuberculosis was getting worse. She still took in sewing but she tired easily and the pay was meagre.

"Karl, you need to take those ration cards and get in line before they run out of food." Evelyn was always a step behind Karl in her thought processes.

"Don't worry. I have Otto standing in line for me."

"Why would he do that?"

"I always make sure I give him a little something from my black market deals. While he's standing in line for me, I can go to the meat shop. I have a good arrangement with the butcher's son. He gives me some trimmings through the back door of the shop and he knows I'll get him what he needs too when I can.

"That's something I've always admired about you. You find all sorts of ways to get a deal."

"With enough swapping I can find us the best deals and the most variety. There are even people who are happy to give me an extra ration card in exchange for something I offer just so they don't have to stand in line."

"That's great, Karl." She rubbed his shoulder and looked at him adoringly. "I'm so proud of the way you take care of us." She did know how to make him feel good.

"I know these streets and I know how to get what I want."

"Lucky for me," Evelyn said, and kissed him on the cheek. "You're a real survivor."

November 1943

The air raid sirens wailed. Karl and Evelyn sat bolt upright in bed. They fumbled for the nearest clothes and stuffed their feet into shoes, not bothering with laces. "Grab a jacket," Karl said, "and a blanket. I'll get a bottle of water." Seconds later he grabbed Evelyn's hand, turned off the lights, and rushed out the door with her. Karl could already hear the woofing booms of faraway explosions.

Around them people as hastily dressed as themselves stumbled and jostled down the stairs. Karl tightened his grip on Evelyn's hand and cleared a path for them. "Come, come, come," he urged. "We're almost there." In the dank cellar, they found a spot on a bench and huddled together.

He put his arm around Evelyn and pulled her closer to make room for the others now crowding through the small cellar door. Above the crying of young children and old women, Karl heard the explosions—more frequent now and louder.

"Do you hear that dull roar?" he said quietly to Evelyn. "Feel the vibration? Hear the bombs? Way more than last time. This could be a bad one." He pulled her closer.

Evelyn's shriek was one of a chorus of shouts and cries when the bomb hit. Karl felt the air sucked from his lungs. A searing heat replaced it in the next second. His skin prickled hot and dry. He threw his arms over his head and covered Evelyn with his own body as much as he could. Rubble dropped from the cellar roof in chunks. Karl coughed and gasped for air in the thick cloud of brick and mortar dust. Evelyn's coughing continued long after he had regained control of his own breathing. "Here, breathe through the blanket." His voice sounded strange to him, almost as if he were talking under water. Evelyn's lips moved soundlessly. Gradually the ringing in his ears subsided and he became aware of the warmth of the cellar. As long as it didn't get any warmer it would be all right to stay. He would rather run out through fire than be roasted alive in a dungeon oven. After half an hour, he judged the cellar to be slightly cooler. They had escaped this time.

The sound of explosions and anti-aircraft fire faded at last. The first feeble rays of the cold November sun greeted them as they crept out of the cellar. People gasped in relief that their building was still standing. But daylight in the foyer? "Look, Mutti," one little boy cried. "The big door is gone."

Karl and Evelyn stepped outside and stumbled. Debris and rubble littered the street and sidewalk. "Karl! Oh my God! The building next door. It's gone! It's completely gone."

"That could have been ours," he said numbly. His relief at finding their building still standing was short-lived. In their apartment their feet squished across the soggy old carpet. The water pipes had burst. All windows were blown out. Their few pictures had been blown off the walls. Scorched wallpaper hung in shreds over the windows while at the bottom it had lifted, waterlogged. The bookcase and china cabinet lay face down on the floor, soggy books and broken dishes everywhere. The whole place had the smell of a recently snuffed out giant match. Only the sewing machine looked unharmed.

Evelyn sank down to sit on the bed. She stared at the floor and cried. Karl sat beside her, stunned. "We have to leave here," he said.

Karl and Evelyn joined hundreds of homeless and injured survivors who picked their way through the rubble of the previous night's bombing. Masses of distraught Berliners milled about at the main railway station. Lists of names and messages overflowed bulletin boards. Shouts and cries of exasperation and despair filled the air. Some wondered why they couldn't get on the train. They had the money. Others had none and pleaded desperately for transportation out of the bombed city. The maimed and wounded cried for special consideration. Some children wailed for their mothers who had gone to look for train tickets. Others wailed for mothers who were simply gone. Chaos ruled.

"We'll never get a train out of here," Evelyn said. She looked so spent that Karl took yet another bag from her to add to his load. Her condition hampered him now, and although he resented that, he was overwhelmed with pity.

Officials with megaphones directed the crowd according to needs. The injured were sent to a medical tent set up by the Red Cross. Temporary shelter for those with children was available at several nearby sites, transportation provided. Still, a large group remained.

Karl left Evelyn to guard their belongings. He came back with a spring in his step. "Don't worry," he said. "I've just talked to a fellow who told me extra trains have been rerouted to deal with the huge numbers heading south." Before the day was over, they managed to squeeze onto a railway car. Karl had used Evelyn's illness as a reason for needing priority consideration.

They dozed minutes at a time, waking at every stop. The official who helped Karl get his wife onto the train had told him, "Don't get off until you get to Goerkau. They have a sanatorium. Better chance of getting your wife a bed there. Good luck."

February 1944

Karl stepped out through the big double doors of the sanatorium. It was good to be outside again and even better, he thought with twinges of guilt, to be free of his burden. They had found a room with a kind family in the little town of Goerkau. Two months had passed since he had put Evelyn's name on the sanatorium's waiting list. Since then her tuberculosis symptoms had become difficult to ignore. She tired more easily and coughed more frequently. He hated looking at her pale face and feverish glassy eyes. It frustrated him to hear her cough. He didn't like not being in control and, in this case, he had no control whatsoever.

He leaned on the railing and gulped fresh air thirstily. For months he had been afraid to breathe for fear of inhaling the dreaded tuberculosis bacteria. Now that Evelyn had been accepted in the sanatorium, he slipped free of that encumbrance like a snake shedding its skin—free of fear, free of his responsibilities, free of his ailing wife.

He felt sorry for her, deeply sorry, but he didn't love her. Not enough. Not the way his conscience told him he should.

26.

June 1944

He hadn't planned to come to Goerkau. Never would he have chosen such a small town. Its backwater pace was too slow for him at first. He had grown up in the city and nothing compared to city life. But the air raids, Evelyn's illness, his unemployment, and hunger—they had all taken their toll. The bustle of city nights had been exciting at one time. Now they belonged to another life. He had little energy to spare these days. In body and soul he felt as battered as his beloved city of Berlin. But in time the quiet routine of village life began to calm his raw nerves.

Since Evelyn's hospitalization, his days, for the most part, were spent alone. His visits at the sanatorium were always short. She tired easily, he rationalized, but if he was honest with himself, he had to admit that he was selfish. Being around sick people made him feel helpless. Sickness took away his control.

He had no work and no connections, but he was resourceful. He went house to house looking for jobs. At every home and business, he left his contact information: Karl Werner, Small Appliance Repair. Each day he chose a new section of town for his door-to-door canvass.

"Yes, I have plenty of odd jobs that need to be done," a war widow told him, "but I have no money to pay you."

"That's not a problem," Karl said. "I'll take whatever you can spare in trade. I see you have a few chickens. Perhaps you would like to pay me with eggs?"

At the end of the day he often brought a variety of things home to his lonely rented room; bunches of green onions, a piece of sausage, half a pound of butter, a fallen soldier's shirt, home-knitted socks—whatever the woman of the house had to spare and thought to offer in payment. His landlady too was happy to take payment in goods rather than money. He hustled to pay his way.

Unlike the Berlin neighbourhoods he was used to, these small town homes often had rabbits, ducks, and chickens in their backyards. *Pfui! How can they live with the smell of the barnyard right under their noses? Reminds me of the Bauermans' place.* He shuddered involuntarily remembering the unhappy days of foster care on the farm. He yearned for the city life, but as he reminisced, he realized that many of his years there had also been filled with ugliness. The difficult years after the stock market crash, followed by the ongoing war and destruction.... No, there was nothing to go back to.

"Giddup, Trude!" Karl snapped out of his reverie. A ruddy-faced farmer slapped the reins on the horse's behind again and again until the farm wagon lurched forward over the cobbled street. The rattle of the heavy farm wagon must have masked the honking of the goose as it was caught beneath one of the wagon wheels. The farmer didn't so much as turn his head and the wagon trundled on down the street. The goose flapped a wing one last time and lay still.

Karl scanned the street and the houses. Seeing no one, he grabbed the goose by the neck and hurried to the end of the block. He knocked on the door of the last house. It was as good as any. A sturdy young woman opened it and looked out at him.

He held up the goose and gave the woman what he hoped was his most charming smile. "It's yours if you invite me to dinner."

The following day, Brigitte and her two young children sat at the table, eyes wide as Karl told wildly embellished stories of his life in the big city. The goose was delicious and all declared what a treat it had been.

Brigitte brought out the after-dinner entertainment, a zither in a black wooden carrying case. Karl pushed back his chair and jumped up to inspect the instrument. "I remember my Aunt Paula's zither. It looked very much like this one—even had the same design of gold angels under the strings."

"Do you play?" Brigitte asked.

"A bit. Do you?"

"No. It was my husband's. He's off fighting somewhere, so no one plays it much now. But we can sing."

"I can try to force a melody out of it, but you must be sure to drown out my playing with your singing. Let's see. Do you know this one?" Karl played a popular folk song and soon all four of them were singing. They smiled at the end of the song, glowing in the nostalgia of better times. Karl used the big winged key to tighten some of the strings. "It hasn't been tuned for a while."

"That's true. But how wonderful to hear it played again." Brigitte sniffed and turned away. She patted her pockets. Karl offered her his handkerchief. "I'm sorry. My husband always played it." She sniffed again and dabbed at her eyes. Karl felt a bit awkward, but he remembered that Evelyn liked to have her shoulders rubbed when she was upset. He let his hand hover over

Brigitte's back while he waffled over etiquette. To be on the safe side, he gave Brigitte a polite little pat on the back.

"That's all right. The war is hard on everyone." He struggled to bring her back to the present. "You have a good voice, Brigitte. And you too, children."

"Thank you, but if you want to hear a really good voice, you should hear my sister sing. She's the talented one."

"Oh? Does she live in town here?" She had his full attention.

"No, but she visits sometimes. Why don't I invite her to come over next Sunday? Come for supper and play for us."

Julia rummaged through her closet. Several pretty dresses beckoned to her, but it was not appropriate to wear anything other than black. She would wear black for at least a year. It bothered her sometimes that she couldn't remember Lukas's face. Five months had passed since he died. It felt more like five years. She had only seen him for a few days each year during the war. At least she had that one precious picture of him to remind her. She dug it out of its secret hiding place in the linen closet and touched his face yet again. The photo paper was getting limp from handling. His letters too were precious. His last words to her. How often had she read them and cried? She knew them by heart now. And always she came to the same realization—he would never come back. Never. Never. Never. The finality of death. It was like trying to understand what was beyond the stars. Impossible to comprehend. All she knew was that she had been too lonely, too long.

Brigitte's letter sparked Julia's imagination. "I'm inviting a special guest for dinner," she had written, "someone I think you might enjoy meeting. Stay a few days. The change will do you good. Ask Ingrid to feed the rabbits and chickens for you."

Sofie came into her mother's bedroom and watched her pondering the clothes in her closet. "Who is the special guest, Mutti?"

"I have no idea, but I hope you'll remember to mind your manners tomorrow and be on your best behaviour."

"I will, but I don't know about Steffie. She still acts silly sometimes. You should remind her to act more grown up. Are you going to wear a pretty dress?"

"I'm going to wear the same dress I always wear, Sofie. It's what I wear because I'm a widow. I explained what that means, didn't I?"

"Yes, it's because Daddy died." There was a long pause. "Will you be sad forever because Daddy died?"

"I don't know. Right now I feel like I'll always be sad, but forever is a long time and we have to keep living. This weekend let's try to think about happier things and enjoy a visit with Auntie Brigitte. You and Steffie can play with Kurt and Frieda."

"I like Frieda but Kurt always wrecks our games when we play."

"He's still quite little, but maybe if you play something that he can do too, it will be more fun. Now, we have to get things ready for tomorrow's trip."

Julia and the girls got off the train at Komotau and set out on foot the rest of the way to Goerkau. An hour later they arrived at Brigitte's house, tired but happy.

While Sofie and Steffie played outside with Kurt and Frieda, Julia and Brigitte had a cup of tea and brought each other up to date.

"And who is this special guest you are inviting tomorrow?" She tried not to sound too interested. After all she was a widow, and she did love Lukas, even though he was gone. She felt a pang of guilt for even asking about the guest.

"It's going to be a surprise. Don't try to make me tell. But I think you'll be pleased."

"Do I know him?"

"Not yet. He's from Berlin."

"Well then, he'll be too high and mighty for the likes of us."

He stood in the doorway holding a bouquet of flowers in each hand. "For the lady of the house," he said. A wave of his blondish hair fell forward as he inclined his head in a quick bow to Brigitte. Julia took a deep breath as Brigitte motioned for her to come closer.

"This is my sister, Julia Feldmann. Our new friend, Karl Werner." Karl gave the second bouquet to Julia and shook her hand.

"So happy to meet you, Julia. I hope you like flowers too."

"I love flowers. Very nice to meet you, Karl." He was charming. No doubt about that.

"Mutti, Mutti!" Steffie ran into the house, gasping for breath. "I saw a man picking the neighbours' flowers."

"Psh-sh-t! Steffie!" Julia said.

"That's him!" She pointed, mouth agape, and hid behind her mother.

"They were being wasted over there and I knew there were two lovely ladies in this house who needed them. Now, Steffie—is that your name? What a pretty name. You won't tell on me, will you?"

"No." Steffie peeked at Karl from behind Julia's dress.

Julia watched the smile playing around Karl's lips as he wooed Steffie into becoming an accomplice in his crime.

"Let's get these lovely flowers into water so they haven't been picked in vain," Brigitte said. "Why don't we sit in the living room? Steffie you can go on back out and play."

"Don't forget to keep our secret," Karl called after her.

"I won't," she said, skipping out the door. "Sofie! Guess what!" they heard her call.

Julia shook her head and smiled to herself. Karl smiled back at her and chuckled over Steffie's impending betrayal. In the living room, Julia let Brigitte lead the conversation, only interrupting occasionally to ask a question. She studied Karl intently between bits of conversation. Sky blue eyes. Small straight teeth. Thin lips, but a big smile.

"I'm going to get a few things ready for supper," Brigitte said.

Julia tore her eyes away from her assessment of Karl. "I'll help you."

"No need, Julia. I have most things already prepared. You stay and talk to Karl."

Julia found it hard to know where to begin. This was exactly the kind of thing she hated. She was no good at making meaningless small talk. Oh, she wished she had stayed home. Here she sat in this drab black dress with a complete stranger. She couldn't be bothered to go through the "getting-to-know-you" motions. What was that he said to her?

"Have you been widowed long?"

"Since this past March. No, to be honest, it feels like since September 1939."

"I know what you mean. The war has disrupted all our lives."

"What about you, Karl? What are you doing here?"

"I'm meeting a lovely lady for supper tonight. And what a breath of fresh air after the ordeal my wife and I have come through."

"Your *wife*?" The sky blue eyes, the small teeth, the big smile evaporated. "Wh-where is she tonight then?"

"Ah, Brigitte didn't tell you? She's in the sanatorium. Tuberculosis. She hasn't got much longer."

"Oh, I'm so sorry."

"Yes, she's had a hard time but at least now she's looked after in the sanatorium. There's nothing anyone can do for her except keep her as comfortable as possible." He sighed. "Ach. The whole world is turned upside down and no end in sight. Not much hope for a bright future, but we have to try to make the best of every day." He dipped his head and smiled as if to hide his embarrassment. "I'm sorry. It's all so sad ... but I'm very happy to have met you today."

"Thank you. Me too. I often feel like there is no point in going on, but I have the two girls—you'll meet Sofie shortly—and they depend on me."

"I'm renting a room not far from here, and perhaps next time you come to visit your sister, I'll see you again. Just friends. Mutual moral support."

She gave him a tentative smile. "Yes, that might be very nice. Something to look forward to. Now I should help Brigitte get supper ready. Why don't you come into the kitchen and talk to us there?"

Karl and the two families enjoyed a dinner of potato dumplings and gravy with a thin cutlet of pork for each of the adults and just a taste of pork for the children. Pickled cucumber slices served as a vegetable.

"A fine meal, considering the hard times our country is going through," Karl said. "My compliments to the cook."

"Thank you," Brigitte said. "Now why don't we get that zither out and see what tunes we can revive on it?"

Karl's playing was adequate. He smiled broadly when Julia sang. She was surprised at the sound of her own voice. There had been no music for such a long time. While she sang, her mind was transported to the old times before the war, before despair. She heard the sweet notes of Michael's violin. He had stolen her heart with his music in those wonderful summer days at choir practices. Michael. Dear, dear Michael. Where was he now? What if she had married him? Would they both be dead? Or maybe living and loving somewhere else? Somewhere safe? They were singing one of Michael's favourites, the song about the workday coming to a close, when her throat closed. She swallowed and blinked to keep the emotion from escaping her.

"Mutti? Are you all right?" Sofie sounded scared.

"What? Oh. Yes. My goodness. I ... I was just lost in thought. The music took me back so many years." She looked at her two sweet daughters and felt her face get hot. Oh my God. To be thinking of Michael like that, when it was Lukas she had married. Lukas she had loved. Lukas. And now he was gone. She had to get used to that idea. *He is gone*, she told herself. She shook her head to clear her thoughts and return to the present.

"Let's sing another one." She hoped the singing of other songs would mask the distress the memories awoke in her.

One song led to another. The children added their voices until one by one they nodded off to sleep on the sofa and the big chair. Brigitte put them to bed while Karl continued to play for Julia.

"Julia, your voice is wonderfully mellow."

"Aren't you the smooth talker." Julia looked down at her hands but then turned to look at him, wondering how sincere he was. "But go ahead. Tell me more. I'll sort out what's flattery and what's honesty later."

"I must definitely see you again," he said. "I've never seen anyone look so radiant in a black dress."

March 1945

Brigitte, would you mind giving Julia this letter for me next time you see her?"

"Karl, come in. You don't need to stand in the doorway. Come in." Karl sat down at the kitchen table. "What's happened? You look upset."

"I've been drafted."

"Oh, no. When do you have to leave?"

"Tomorrow. Not even time for tying up loose ends. Hah! What's left to tie? Evelyn died months ago. I have no family left that I know of. In a way, that makes things easier. But I've come to like Julia very much and I thought maybe you'd be kind enough to give her this letter for me."

"Of course I will. But she'll be so upset."

"Will she, do you think? Does she care about me?"

"I know she does. Even Sofie has said to me how nice it is to see her mother smile again."

In spite of the conscription looming over him, his spirits lifted when he heard Brigitte's response.

"I'm going to miss all of you very much. You've been very good to me."

"Can I make you a cup of tea?" Brigitte asked.

"I would love that, but I'll have to say no. I still have to settle up with my landlady and get my things together for an early start tomorrow. Thank you for everything." Karl put his hand out for Brigitte, who ignored it and gave him a warm embrace. Karl swallowed hard and blinked back tears.

"Take good care of yourself and come back safely," she said. "I'll be sure to give your letter to Julia."

"Ask her to write to me, please."

27.

The war was lost. Couldn't they see that? Why should he be target practice for the Russians? Karl spat out a mouthful of dirt. He crawled on his belly, following another soldier's boots snaking across the field. They were to protect the crossing of the river Neisse, but Karl had no interest in military strategy. Pinned down under Russian rifle and mortar fire, survival was uppermost in his mind. He didn't believe in Hitler's policies and had no illusions about the man himself. Certainly he wasn't prepared to die for him. That was for fools and heroes and he was neither. If he could just make it across that field, he would have the protection of the trench.

If his commander hadn't had a reputation for shooting deserters, Karl would gladly have kept right on crawling all the way back to Goerkau and Julia. Anger raged through him. How had he ended up here crawling in the dirt? For what? All he wanted was to live an ordinary life. He had escaped the draft for a time because of his leg. They must have been desperate to enlist him, with his disability. He hoped that meant the war would soon be over. And in the next moment, it was—at least for him.

He felt the explosion, much closer than previous ones. His ears rang, the field blurred. As his vision cleared, he could see the boot soles of the man in front of him, but by their awkward twist he knew they wouldn't be snaking across the field anymore. The man's bloodied head was half gone.

Karl scratched at the irritation in his ribs. Seconds later, it turned into a sharp burning pain. He lay still trying to assess the damage without making himself more of a target. Blood seeped down the right side of his shirt. It was only a trickle. For several minutes he didn't move, trying to decide what to do. The gunfire stopped. What did the silence mean? Ahead of him he saw movement—men scurrying for the safety of the trench. He decided to make a break for it. As he raised himself to a sitting position, the world spun and he fell sideways. His ribcage throbbed, his head pounded, and his vision swam again. He wanted to lie down and sleep, but he knew if he stayed there, he would die. He took a deep breath and immediately regretted it. *Ow! Son of a bitch! All right, Karl. Get up. Not too high. Keep low. You can do this. Small breaths, small steps. Just another hundred metres to the trench. One foot in front of the other. Again. Again. For Julia.*

He found the trench occupied by Russian soldiers, the surviving Germans, now prisoners, lined up ready to march. Their weapons had been confiscated. Karl gave his up, glad to be rid of its weight. He was exhausted and barely able to stay conscious. He arrived at the Russian POW camp on a stretcher carried by fellow soldiers, Fredi and Heinz.

"You're damned lucky to be here," Heinz told him. "Those sons of bitches wanted us to leave you behind when you passed out. Fredi was quick with the stretcher and they let us put you on it."

"Lucky?" Karl said. "Look around you. It's not exactly home."

"They've been shooting anyone who couldn't keep up," Heinz said.

"Oh, Jeezus! Bloody bastards." This was serious. "Well, in that case, my thanks to you and Fredi."

At the Stalag they learned to scrounge for every scrap of anything edible. Nourishment was negligible. Flour soup one day; thin potato peel soup the next. They hoarded crusts of stale bread and broke them into the watery soup. They scooped up used coffee grounds discarded by the Russian guards. Even though the grounds might consist only of roasted barley or chicory, they were boiled over and over to make a watery drink.

Work parties were sent out, some to the fields, others to the open pit coal mines. After a day in the fields, Heinz said under his breath, "This should improve our potato peel soup today." He unbuttoned his shirt and pulled out three small potatoes.

"Well done, Heinz. I have a contribution too." Fredi pulled a turnip out from under his jacket.

Karl escaped the fieldwork for the first week until his rib wound began to heal. Heinz and Fredi gladly shared their fortified soup with him.

"I really appreciate this, fellas," Karl said. "I'll make it up to you when I get back on my feet." He wanted to show his comrades that he was somebody to be reckoned with. After a few days, he joined the work party, and the number of turnips and potatoes in the soup increased dramatically. He was brazen and daring when it came to foraging for food under the noses of the Russian guards.

Evenings were long and although they were tired, none of the soldiers wanted to spend more time than necessary on the hard plank beds. "Come on, Karl," Fredi said. "Let's have a game." He brought out a roughly made checkerboard and lumps of wooden figurines barely recognizable as chess pieces.

"What'll you give me if I win?" Karl asked. "Do you have anything left?"

"Cigarettes," Fredi offered.

"I have plenty."

"Right. You don't smoke them."

"I gave it up, but I can use them to trade for something else. All right. Set them up."

Karl won game after game, taking on many of his fellow prisoners. He swapped the cigarettes he won for small items—a piece of soap, a spoon, whatever was available. At times he was able to use these winnings to make a trade for a bit of the most precious commodity of all—food.

Each night after the games, Karl suffered pounding headaches from the strain of concentrating. His need to win overpowered the voice in his head that told him to stop inflicting pain on himself. His injured rib, the head trauma caused by the grenade, and the starvation diet had turned him into a mere shadow of his former self in both body and mind. By the end of three months, he tired easily and his shirtsleeves and pant legs flapped in the breeze. An uncertain winter still lay ahead. He wondered if he would soon join the corpses that were removed from the Stalag each day. Dysentery spread through the camp. So far he had avoided it by boiling everything he put in his mouth. But gnawing hunger evoked the greatest desperation. When he looked into the small shard of mirror he bought with his latest cigarette winnings, he was shocked to see his sunken face. What would Julia think if she saw him looking like this? Ha! What did it matter? She hadn't written a word to him the whole time he had been away. Maybe the attraction was all one-sided and he had only imagined that she cared for him.

August 1946

Karl! Heinz! Have you heard the news?" Fredi hurried over to them. "We're to be released soon."

"Is it possible?" Karl felt his heart trying to jump out of his ribcage. "When? I've almost stopped hoping."

"Next week. Monday."

"Next week. I can hardly believe it," Karl said. "The war has been over for more than a year. I was starting to think they would keep us imprisoned forever."

"God be praised." Heinz's chin compressed into dimples and tears filled his eyes. "I never thought I'd see the day. I wonder if my family is still alive."

"Family," Karl mumbled to himself. "Family. Humph! Lucky bastard."

Three days later the POWs gathered their few possessions and lined up at the Stalag gates to have their passbooks stamped on their way to freedom. The last distribution of mail was done as the soldiers passed through the gates. Only a handful of POWs had mail. Karl thought he must have heard wrong when his name was called. The Russian guard tossed a tatty bundle of letters to him and read the next name. Karl was stunned. Not a single letter for over a year and now, on the last day, a bundle of ... thirty-one, he counted. All from Julia.

He was frantic with wanting to open them, but nothing, not even these special letters, could make him lag behind in the POW camp. *Out! Out! Just get out first, and then I can look at them.*

As soon as he was out of sight of the prison camp, he sank down on the ground beside the road. His hands trembled as he opened the first letter. Through tears he saw her lovely handwriting, so perfect and neat; words that spoke of loneliness and longing. Each letter contained a small anecdote of Julia's home life and ended with the hope that they would see each other again. Around the edges of the pages his name was written over and over in a border design, "KarlKarlKarlKarl. I miss you, Karl."

He wasn't sure how long he sat there. Other recently released POWs walked by. No one stopped. They had seen it all and there was nothing unusual about a man sitting in the dirt crying his eyes out as he read his mail.

28.

The early autumn sun continued to warm the land during the daytime, but nights grew colder. In spite of Red Cross donations of warmer clothing and household goods, life in the dank old castle of Sternberg was dreary and uncomfortable.

"Frau Hahn and her two young boys left today. They've been given accommodation in Koenigshofen," Katerina said when Julia came back from working in the fields.

"Oh, that's good. Another family saved from this misery."

Katerina had little patience left these days. "Our turn can't come soon enough."

Julia's shoulders slumped. "I know, Mother. I wish they could find a place for us, but I've heard the women talk in the fields. They say Bavaria is overwhelmed with refugees like us and they don't know where to put us all."

"Almost any place is better than this," her mother grumbled.

One family after another received accommodation in nearby townships. Single people were placed more quickly than families. But the end of September was near, and the Sommer family was among many who were still waiting. Although the war had been over for a year and a half, Julia, always so positive, was losing hope for an end to their ordeal.

In the castle, hunger, cold, and bleakness prevailed. The children had no schoolwork or books or radio to entertain them. Julia was tired of being the one who kept everyone's spirits up, but what choice did she have? Run away? Leave her girls? Never.

"I'm so sick of being cold and hungry all the time," she said to her mother. "There won't be much more work in the fields once the potato harvest is in. A bit of cleanup around the sugar beets maybe, but once it freezes, that will be it for work."

Katrina put her arms around Julia's shoulders. "We all have to work harder at being patient. We'll take it one day at a time—and look at how lucky we are. We're alive and together. So many didn't make it."

"I know. I know." Julia sighed. "I should be thankful. I am. But I wish Lukas was here to take some of the responsibility."

"Don't worry, girl. Our turn will come and we'll all have a home again. It can't be too much longer now."

Julia couldn't expect her parents to do more. They were already looking after the girls while she worked. And there was no one else. Lukas was gone. Sole responsibility for her family's welfare lay on her shoulders. She desperately wished for a husband to help share her burden.

Each day she put on a brave face. She had to look happy for her girls. Story time helped to cheer her daughters during the long boring evenings.

"Mutti, tell us about the time Steffie fell down the stairs," Sofie said.

"No! Don't! Sofie, that wasn't funny." Steffie pouted, but a smirk played around her lips and both girls began to giggle.

"I wanted to bake a sand cake," Sofie said. "Mutti always made them and they were good."

"A week's worth of ration cards used up."

Steffie giggled. "But then you put sand in the cake."

"It's called a sand cake." Sofie shrugged and her face turned red. "But that's only because of the colour, I guess."

"What a disaster," Julia went on. "Eggs, margarine, and sugar spilled. And do I need to say where the sand was?"

"Everywhere!" the girls said together.

"Do we have to have the next part of the story?" Steffie whined.

"Of course! It's the best part," Julia said, "and you are the star of the show. After I recovered from the shock, I sent you girls to your room. I filled a bucket with warm soapy water and mopped up the mess on the floor. Just then you, Steffie, came down the stairs ... too fast. When your feet hit the wet floor at the bottom, they went out from under you and you landed—"

"Right in the bucket," the girls finished for her.

"Bum first!" Sofie giggled. Steffie's face glowed red again.

"And there you were with your legs and arms sticking straight up. You were stuck!" Both girls laughed at the memory of the scene. "Sofie held the bucket and I picked you up by the legs and arms. But the bucket didn't want to let you go.

"Finally you came out with a whoosh and a pop." Julia smiled at the memory and hugged Steffie. Then she put her arm around Sofie too. "Our house may be gone, and all our nice things gone, but we still have each other. And what would I do without my girls?"

With a hoe Julia chopped at the roots of stubborn weeds that popped up between the rows of sugar beets. As she raked the wilted weeds into small piles and smoothed the paths, the sun warmed her back. It seemed as if the sun was trying to help her body heal from the hardships she had endured. If only the sun could heal her soul.

Julia wondered if Karl had received her letters; wondered if he ever thought of her. He might be dead for all she knew. Probably he was. She had never received an answer. It was hopeless. Even if he was alive and even if he thought of her, he had no idea where she was. She resigned herself to never seeing him again.

Later in the day, Julia moved on to another field to help with the potato harvest. Once in a while she took a moment to stand up and straighten her aching back. The field was dotted with workers. Frau Schiller, digging in the next row, laughed. "Julia, you should see yourself. You've powdered your face, I see. With dirt."

Julia smiled. "I think I have a pretty good idea what my face looks like, judging by yours."

"You have a big smear of dirt across your cheek too."

"Well, it doesn't matter much out here." She pulled out the wilted yellow potato stalks, threw them onto a pile to be burned later, and dug around in the dirt for every precious potato she could find to put in the burlap sack that sat between the rows.

On the long cart track beside the potato field, a thin man walked towards them, shading his eyes with his hand to scan the fields. For a second she thought she recognized the slight limp, the swaggering gait. Her heart pounded against her ribs. But no. It couldn't be. She must have been out in the sun too long. She squinted to see better, and as he came closer, she knew his beaming smile. Julia felt as if all her blood rushed to her head and then instantly drained to her feet. Karl threw his arms around her and planted kisses all over her dusty face. She clung to him. Words didn't come, but laughter and tears mingled—all the communication they needed.

29.

In the half-light of morning, Karl watched Julia put on her thin cotton dress with the green and blue paisley pattern. The dark brown apron disguised her youthful figure. She glanced over at Karl on the bed, put on her only sweater for warmth, apparently oblivious to its baggy elbows and shabby appearance. Days were chilly and fashion was not an issue for refugees in the old fortress of Sternberg. Finding enough warm clothing took precedence. More than once Karl had heard Julia say jokingly, "I may not be pretty, but I'm warm."

If you only knew. "No, you're not pretty," he would say. "You're beautiful through and through."

"What are you going to do today?" she asked.

Karl propped himself up on one elbow. "I'm going to Koenigshofen to remind them that we are still here waiting for housing. I'll check the businesses again for work. Sooner or later there has to be something." He had to find work. What if Julia lost faith in his promise to provide for her? Unthinkable to lose her now.

"Good luck. I'll see you this evening then. We're harvesting the last of the potatoes. I hope the farmer will feed us something decent for lunch so I can bring us back some food."

"I'll see what I can come up with in town too. Sometimes I get lucky."

"Every bit helps."

He reached for Julia's wrist and pulled her back down to the bed.

"Karl," she whispered. "Not here. The girls are just on the other side of the curtain."

"They're sound asleep. Come give me a hug before you go." He pulled her close and mumbled into her hair, "Julia, without you I'd have given up long ago."

"Same for me, Karl. You make everything easier to bear."

"We'll make it, sweetie. Things will get better in time." He stroked her hair gently. "You can count on me. I'm here for you now and I always will be." He silently prayed that her trust in him wouldn't be misplaced. He needed her to believe that he could take care of her.

Julia stood up, took Karl's face in her hands, and kissed his forehead. "Love you," she said quietly, then slipped out the door.

"And I adore you," he whispered after she had gone. Karl put on his suit. The seat of the pants was shiny with wear, the jacket elbows threadbare. It annoyed him that the image he presented these days was a far cry from the distinguished look he would have preferred. Today he would see what could be done about clothes for them all.

And food, always food. Somewhere along the way to town there must be a vegetable patch that wasn't being watched too closely. He was tired of living on next to nothing. Tired of goddammed potatoes.

Katerina had heated up the last bit of thin potato soup from the night before. She tried to convince Sofie and Steffie that with a bit of imagination, the soup would be thicker and the added bits of stale hard bread would make it tastier. *Good luck with that*, he thought.

"I'm off to Koenigshofen," Karl told Katerina and Thomas at the breakfast table.

Thomas set down his cup of weak tea, raised his arm, and started to get up. "I'll come with you."

Karl shrugged. "Sure. Fine. I have a number of stops to make."

"Fine, fine. All right then, let's go." Thomas picked up his cane. He was almost as thin as the walking stick he had whittled for himself. Having lost his normal muscle tone, Thomas was a bit unsure of his footing. A year and a half of starvation diet could do that to an old man.

The walk from Sternberg to Koenigshofen was long, but the air was fresh and clean. Karl was not a person who loved nature, but after being stuck in the gloomy castle, it felt good to get out. He savoured the earthy smell of the steam coming off the land as the sun warmed it. On either side of the road the fields stretched out like a checkerboard of yellow and green, lovely colours after the dark browns and greys of the castle rooms. Even the birds showed their appreciation for another beautiful day as they hopped from shrub to shrub along the ditch, singing and scolding.

"I'm going to stop at the Red Cross office first," Karl said when they reached the outskirts of Koenigshofen. "I need to make them see that we have to get out of that ice castle. Either that or they can damn well give us warmer clothes."

"Yes, and I need to ask again if there is any word of Elisabeth and Ingrid," said Thomas.

"It's good we came early. I see a small lineup already. Let's split up so we can get twice the value for our efforts."

Half an hour later, Karl pushed open the heavy doors of the building. Thomas got up from the bench and approached Karl. "So? How did you do? It looks like you made some progress this time, judging by the smirk on your face."

"I got some clothes for each of us. We can pick them up in an hour."

"That's fantastic, Karl. Julia will be happy about that."

"And ... we have housing!"

"NO!"

"Yes. It's only one little attic room above a leather shop, but they will take you and Katerina, Julia and me and the children."

"But how did you convince them, after all the times you've been here to ask?"

"Well, it just happens that the Red Cross man I spoke to has a damaged sewing machine. I think he got it from some bombed out place. I promised to fix his problem for him if he would fix mine for me."

"Trust you, Karl. You have a nose for these things."

"Yes. Yes, I do. Now how about you, Thomas? Any news about Elisabeth and Ingrid?"

"As a matter of fact, it's our lucky day. Elisabeth and Andreas are in Coburg and will be contacted in the next days. They will join us here, but they will need accommodation right away. Perhaps your Red Cross man has a friend with another sewing machine that needs fixing." Thomas picked up his cane. He was beaming with happiness. "Oh, and Ingrid has gone to Mainburg to be with a distant cousin of hers."

"So, a good start to the day. Now wasn't it a good idea I had about splitting up? Just leave these things to me. I know my way around these ignorant bureaucrats. You farm people just don't have the street skills you need for these situations."

Thomas stood rooted to the spot. He pressed his lips together as if to bite back a response.

"You know I'm right, Thomas. Just leave these things to me. And now I have some other business to attend to, so you run along home without me. I'll see you later." Karl spun on his heel and marched away. "Oh, and the clothes," he called over his shoulder, "you can pick up yours and Katerina's. I'll pick up those for me and my family." A few steps along the way, Karl glanced over his shoulder and noted with satisfaction that Thomas still had a shocked look on his face.

At the corner store, Karl pushed his way in through the spring-loaded door. He said good day to the few patrons and headed for a table near the back where three men were playing cards and drinking what he assumed to be ersatz coffee, the substitute coffee that was all most people could afford.

"Good morning, gentlemen." He nodded cheerfully. "Who's winning?"

"Oh, it's you again," said the one with the bulbous nose. He pushed a greasy shock of hair out of his face. "Are you going to let us win our goods back? Sit down. You won't be so lucky this time."

"That's right," said the bald man to his right. "We've been practicing and this time we're going to win."

A red-headed man sat farther away from the table to allow room for his belly. He motioned for Karl to sit in the empty fourth chair. "What have you got to wager?"

"I'll wager a man's suit of clothes. And what do the rest of you have to offer?"

"Four kilos of cabbage," said bulbous nose.

"Some electrical cords and switches."

"A kilo of bacon from my pig, but I think I'll be going home with my bacon and a new suit too. I hope that suit is size large. It practically has my name on it."

Thomas dropped a bundle of clothes on the chair and poured himself a glass of water. He pressed his lips together and shook his head. "Katya, I tell you, I have a bad feeling about this Karl."

"What do you mean?"

"Haven't you noticed how cutting he can be with his comments? One moment you think you're having a friendly conversation and the next, you feel like you've been punched in the guts." And he wasn't even telling her the whole scene, how Karl had belittled his right to be the head of the family. Hadn't he provided for his family all his life? Hadn't he raised them to be good people? Protected them? How dare that young dandy talk down to him like that. Shocking how little respect Karl had for his elders. He unclenched his fists and shook them out.

"Did you have an argument in town?" Katerina put down the shirt she was mending and gave Thomas her full attention.

Thomas shrugged. "I thought everything was going well, and all of a sudden, he was saying he knew best because he's from the city and I'm a stupid farmer."

"How rude!" Katerina rubbed Thomas' back. Suddenly her hand flew to her mouth. "Oh, my God. Julia. She adores him."

"You should have a talk with her. I don't think it's good for her to be so involved with Karl. I just don't understand what she sees in him."

"I'll talk to her today when she gets home," Katerina agreed, "if I can find a chance to have some privacy."

"Take her to visit Frau Messmer. I'll keep Karl and the girls busy while you're gone."

Karl shuffled along the last hundred metres to Sternberg castle. The ten-kilometre walk always took its toll on him; the stitch in his ribs from his shrapnel wound nagged at him. He was gaunt and without stamina. The Russian POW camp had not been kind to him.

Even with the loan of a small wagon, the load was almost too much for him. He was exhausted from the effort of pulling it from Koenigshofen to Sternberg. He plunked two huge cabbages and a hefty chunk of bacon on the table. He dumped the clothes from the Red Cross on the bed and put the box of electrical cords and switches under it. While Katerina exclaimed about the cabbage and bacon, he grabbed a quick drink of water and with a wave to her, hurried out the door again.

The sun was dipping low in the sky and Karl walked as briskly as he could towards the potato fields. He strained his eyes for the first glimpse of Julia returning from the farm. He ran the last few metres waving a paper in his hand. "We've got it!" he called. The short run sapped the last of his strength. "We've got a roof over our heads. One big room upstairs in the back of a leather shop. We're moving tomorrow." He gasped for air, giddy with joy.

Julia set down the heavy pot of soup she was carrying. "Oh, thank God! Karl, you're wonderful!" She flung her arms around his neck. "But will we all fit into this room? My parents, us, the girls?" She kissed him with complete abandon. He loved the way she made him feel so good.

"It won't matter if we're crowded for a while. They've promised to look for a place for your parents right away. Elisabeth and Andreas will be in town soon and I think your parents will want to be with them." He didn't tell Julia he'd been doing his best to make sure Thomas would prefer that arrangement.

"I can hardly believe that my life might be normal again one day." Tears gathered in the corners of Julia's eyes. Karl gave her another quick squeeze and picked up the small pot of pea soup. In spite of his fatigue, he felt a lightness in his step as they walked back to their lodging.

"You're amazing, Julia. You've managed to survive and provide for your family all this time. You could have eaten this yourself after a hard day's work, but here you are bringing leftover food back to your children and your parents."

"The farmer tries to give us enough so we can bring some home. These Bavarians are not all as unwelcoming as some have been."

"I managed to bring home a bit today too. Still, I admire the way you provide and how you never gave up. But now you will always have me and we can make it together."

"Always?"

Karl stopped and put down the pot of soup again. He took Julia in his arms. "I want you to marry me, if you will."

"I will, Karl. Yes, I will." After a moment Julia squirmed away from him and said, "Now let's get this soup home before it gets cold."

"Always the practical one, aren't you?" He smiled at her and shook his head, but his heart was bursting with joy.

Julia and her mother strolled across the courtyard towards Frau Messmer's room. On the far side of the yard, Katerina took Julia's arm and pulled her around the corner where they sat on a bench.

"Mother? What's going on?" Her mother had been behaving strangely ever since Julia had come home from the fields.

"I have to talk to you, Julia, in private."

"Is something wrong?" Her mother seemed nervous and the serious tone of her voice alarmed Julia. "Did the girls misbehave today?"

"No, no. The girls are wonderful, as always. It's about Karl...." Katerina hesitated.

"Has he done something? What is it?"

"I'm concerned you and Karl are ... your father says ... well, we're not sure he's right for you."

Julia stared at her mother. What in the world had brought this on? "What makes you say a thing like that?"

"I don't like the way he treats you. He can be very hurtful with his comments and ... and ... well, he's just so different from Lukas. Even your baker friend would be a better choice."

"As it happens, neither of them is available to me," Julia said bitterly.

"Oh, Julia, dear. I'm sorry. You know I'm not trying to hurt you. I'm only worried that you'll make a mistake you'll regret. Haven't you seen how he snaps at the children? Don't you notice how short-tempered he is with your father? He acts as if he owns you and you aren't even married."

"Well, I'm sorry Mother. I know he's not perfect, but Lukas and Michael are gone and I need a man who will help look after us. Karl loves me and he can be very charming."

"But—"

"And I've already said I would marry him."

"Oh! Oh, Julia. I'm sorry."

"I thought you'd be happy for me."

"Of course, I'll be happy for you if you're happy. I—" Katerina sighed and dropped her arms slackly at her sides. "I suppose time will tell."

"I'm tired of carrying the whole load myself. I need him." Julia shrugged. "It's as simple as that."

Katerina pulled Julia into an embrace. "Just remember to stay true to yourself. And never let any man abuse you."

"I won't, Mother. No one is going to hurt me."

PART FIVE

Canada

1947-1973

30.

Julia marvelled at the beauty of springtime—the first spring of her new life with Karl. Snowdrops and crocuses seemed to say, "Look how pretty we are. We're frail, but we've survived." *Just like I did.* The last years had dragged on interminably. Julia thought of how she had lost Lukas, her home, and all her belongings, how she had fought to survive each day never being able to count on seeing the next one. The days in the barracks, the forced labour at the brewery, the terrible train ride, and the winter spent starving in the cold rooms of Sternberg castle—those days had threatened to last forever. Spring in Koenigshofen was a miracle, a new chance at life, a soothing balm on her battered soul.

Their room was tiny, but it had what they needed: table and chairs in the center, a small counter with a hot plate, and a cabinet for dishes, pots, and pans. The bathroom facilities were down the stairs at the back of the house, but Julia kept a big jug of good water in the kitchen area for drinking and for washing up and a slop pail for the dirty water. She put a curtain in front of her parents' bed as well as one in front of hers for privacy. The girls shared a bed and slept one at each end, their legs side by side in the middle. It was a temporary arrangement they tolerated cheerfully.

The clean sharp smell of leather seeped up through the floorboards from the tack shop below. She heard the shop owner tapping at his leatherwork, cutting, pounding, shaping, and polishing. He kept late hours, but the awareness of his presence lent a certain security to their lives.

Karl found odd repair jobs around town and Sofie and Steffie were happy to be in school again. Within weeks, Elisabeth and Andreas arrived from Coburg and her parents moved in with them into their larger living quarters. Life was returning to something closer to normal.

Julia often spent the days with her parents in their allotted communal garden plot outside of town. She loved to feel the texture of the earth in her hands. *How ironic that soil could smell so clean.* The first radishes were up and onion shoots had sprouted. The twittering of birds and the peace of the garden soothed her. She was lost in thought as she prepared the ground for what she hoped would be a good crop of potatoes.

"Don't you overdo it now, Julia," Thomas said.

Katerina looked up from her hoeing. "Are you sure you should be doing this in your condition, dear?"

"I'm fine, Mother. It's not like I haven't been pregnant before."

"Yes, I know, but you weren't so thin when you had the other babies."

"I'll be fine. The only thing that may not be fine is that Karl and I won't be able to get married if those papers don't arrive in time. I can't believe it took six months to verify Lukas's death certificate. And now we have to go through the same endless waiting for the marriage licence."

"Don't you worry about it." Thomas put his hand on his daughter's shoulder. "There's no shame in it. If the baby comes before the wedding, it can proudly carry the Sommer name."

"I'm sure I'll survive, but you know how some people are, especially these religious ones. They're the first to point fingers at an unmarried woman having a child. But they will have to call me Frau anyway, not Fraeulein. After all, I am married, even if I am a widow."

"They already gossip about you living with Karl," Katerina said. "It won't matter that much more when you have his child."

She detected a hint of disapproval in her mother's tone, even though her words seemed to be supportive. "He really wants to marry me. You must know that."

"Yes, of course. Don't you worry. It will be fine. Now come sit down and rest for a bit." Thomas led her to the garden bench. "And remember that any time you need us, you come over to Elisabeth's place and visit us there." Her father understood. She felt lucky to have him.

"Sometimes a woman needs to get away from her man for a little while." Katerina ignored Thomas' raised eyebrows. "We've seen how Karl can be."

At Katerina's words, Julia looked at her sharply. *Oh God. Here it comes.*

She was about to object but her mother held up a hand. "Shhh-sh-sh-shhhh. You don't have to say a word."

Julia swallowed the lump in her throat. Of course they had heard his cutting comments. Of course they had seen Sofie and Steffie cringe when he snapped at them. *I cringe myself. But he can be sweet too. He loves* me. *Really loves me. And I need him. Lord knows, I need him. I'm worn out doing everything myself.*

"Yes, I'll come over," Julia said. *Best not to get into this conversation.* "It's nice to have a place to visit. I'm happy that it's working out well, you living with Elisabeth and Andreas, and it gives us much-needed room." What she didn't say was that life with Karl was easier now. Without someone to compete with or prove himself to, he was less often the strutting peacock demanding acknowledgment, and their relationship had calmed considerably.

February 1949

Lena Sommer-Werner came into the world in the summer of 1947. Karl was ecstatic. At last he had the family he had craved since the days of his youth. As the child grew, Karl lavished attention on her. Nothing was too good for Lena. She was the cement that bound Julia to him.

"Karl, you do have other children," Julia said.

"Not really. Those two girls are yours. I'll support them but they're not mine. Lena is mine—"

"Ours."

"Yes, all right, ours. And I like Sofie and Steffie too, of course, but Lena is my own blood." Why was she always going on about him treating her girls the same as he treated Lena? Didn't she know it would never happen? He could tolerate the other man's children, even like them, but he loved his own. What could be more normal?

"I don't want Sofie and Steffie feeling left out. I think you should make an effort to include them in your admiration."

"Fine, fine." He waved the air in front of him as if to swish away a pesky fly. Julia closed her eyes. Her shoulders sagged.

"What?" Karl asked impatiently.

"You might as well get used to sharing your affections. We are going to have another baby." She sighed and chewed her lip, watching his face as she told him the news.

"No! Really?" Karl pulled Julia close and hugged her. He could feel Julia pulling away. "What?" He thought she would be as happy as he was.

"I know you love Lena and there is no doubt you will love little Juergen when he is born, but I want you to promise me you'll be good to *all my* children. Promise me."

Oh, that again. Not a big deal. He would tell her what she wanted to hear. "I promise. So is it really for sure? We are having another baby? You think it might be a boy this time?" Although, he loved little girls, a boy would make him proud.

"A baby, yes. A boy, maybe. It's not what we need— another mouth to feed, but babies don't ask. They just come."

Karl hugged Julia again. *Oh, but it is what we need. It's what I need.*

Julia knew that Karl had tools in his briefcase for his town business, not papers as he liked to pretend, but she didn't comment on it. She knew his big talk was a cover for his insecurity, and although it embarrassed her to listen to him bragging, she overlooked it and forgave him. He still had not landed a steady job, but thousands were unemployed in this postwar time. What she admired about Karl was his resourcefulness; he was always thinking and planning.

"Julia," he said one day, "where did you put that wiring I brought home when we were still in Sternberg? You didn't throw it out, did you?"

"Of course not. It's in that box under the bed." Karl pulled out the box and brought it over to the table.

"What do you say to this idea? I make up the wiring, and you sew cloth covers. We'll put together little heating pads that I can trade for other things we need."

"I can cut up old clothes that are worn out and use the scraps to make the covers. I'll have to do them by hand, but that's no problem. Do you really think it will work?"

"Why not? You and I can do anything we put our minds to."

Karl dressed meticulously before going out on his job searches and business dealings. He firmly believed that if you wanted to make an impression, you had to dress and act the part.

"Where are you off to?" Julia asked.

"Where else? Town. Job hunting."

"You smell like you're going to the opera."

"Good, huh? Give me a kiss." He put his arms around Julia, kissed her head, her ear, her cheek.

"My God, you smell like a perfume factory." She pushed him away gently.

"It's the city boy in me. People I do business with respect a person who has city experience. It wouldn't do to smell like an old turnip like some of the farmers around here."

"There's nothing wrong with being a farmer."

"Sure, sure, but I'd rather not smell like one."

Karl liked to dab on aftershave lotion before going to the weekly card games. His hard facial stubble was the antithesis of the fine silky blond hair on his head. He felt tough and refined at the same time.

He cultivated his residual Berlin accent, determined to make an impression among the lowly farmers of the small Bavarian town. He was convinced that his city image helped him win at card games. The trio of Robert, Rufus, and Harold still played cards with him in the corner store as they had back in the days of the Sternberg refugee camp. Once a week they wagered and lost to Karl.

Between heating pad sales, small appliance repairs, and winnings from the evening card games, Karl brought home enough food, clothing, and supplies to keep his growing family fed.

One day, Karl came home and placed a box wrapped in newspaper on the table.

"What's in the package?" Steffie asked.

"I bet it's a bunch of wires for heating pads," Sofie said. Fifteen now, Sofie was a serious girl with an abundance of self-control.

"Too small," Steffie said.

"This package," Karl said, "is for two girls who have been a big help to their mother."

"For us?" The girls pressed closer to the table. Karl loved the way he had their attention. They were darling girls and he felt bad about the times he had snapped at them lately when he was feeling frustrated about other things—things that were not their fault. Also he had sensed Julia pulling away from him afterwards. He needed to get back into her good graces.

"I'll give you each three guesses."

"Me first," said Steffie. "Is it candy? Or clothes? Is it a puzzle?"

"No."

"Is it books?" Sofie asked. Karl shook his head. "Shoes? School bag?"

"No. It's something that you can play with and share. Something that two girls can play with at the same time. Go ahead. Open it."

They tore off the newspaper and looked at a wooden box, eyebrows wrinkled in puzzlement. "It's a little wooden suitcase." Sofie picked it up and looked at it from all angles.

"Open the suitcase," Steffie said.

"Wow! A chess set. Look at the chess pieces, Steffie. And see how the suitcase turns into a chessboard?"

Karl beamed when he saw their faces light up.

"What do you say, girls?" Julia had been watching as she sat in a chair in the far corner of the room, sewing a heating pad cover.

"Thank you," they both said, and smothered him with hugs.

Karl smiled over their heads at Julia, happy to see her smile back. "Now," he said, "how would you like to have a game and I'll help you out if you get stuck?"

"All right!"

May 1952

Tall alders lined the sides of the country road that led from Koenigshofen to the communal garden outside of town. Julia pushed the stroller while Lena chattered along beside her.

"Mutti, can I push Juergen for a while?"

"All right, but not too fast. I know you like to run, but with a baby you have to be careful."

"He's not really a baby anymore."

"Do you remember how old he is?"

"Of course. He's two." Lena held up two fingers and the stroller began to veer to the left. Julia smiled and corrected the stroller's path.

"That's right. And how old are you?"

"I'm four." She held up four fingers and the stroller again veered to the left. Again Julia corrected for her and this time kept one hand on the stroller. "But soon I'll be five." Lena held up five fingers.

"That's right." Julia smiled at her daughter. "Hear the birds, Lena?"

Juergen turned his head to his mother and pointed a finger to the trees. "Brs."

"They're talking to you."

"Birds can't talk," Lena said.

"Of course they can. How do you think they tell each other what they want and when it's supper time?"

"But they can't talk like we do."

"No, but if you listen you can hear them trying to talk to us. Listen! That one just said, "Oh, Juergen. Oh, Lena." Julia put just enough singsong lilt into her voice that it was a good imitation of birds singing.

The children turned their heads to the side and listened intently. "I can hear it!" Lena stopped walking to listen. "He said it again. Did you hear it, Juergen?"

"And hear that little one? He's calling to his mother, 'Feed me! Feed me!'"

Lena clapped her hands in delight.

"Oh, there's another one. Do you hear that one that starts to sing and his voice goes higher and higher. There! That one! He's saying, 'You're pretty. You're pretty. Oh, really!'"

Lena's eyes were wide as she pressed her hands over her open mouth. "I can hear it."

At their garden plot, Julia put Juergen on a grassy area and asked Lena to keep an eye on him. The morning sun warmed Julia's back as she sat on the garden bench. Before starting the hoeing, she surveyed her work of earlier that spring. Radishes were ripe. The kohlrabies had sturdy leaves, each plant with a tiny lump beginning to form. Strawberries had finished blooming and now bore tiny greenish-yellow fruit. Best of all, the many potatoes she had put into the ground and hilled up were now leafing out into healthy plants. *Life is good.* As Julia had that thought, she realized how little it took to make her happy. A bit of sun, a garden, her children.

But what of her children? It would take more than a bit of sun and a garden to fulfill their lives, their future. It was a question that had begun to nag her. Sofie and Steffie were eighteen and sixteen. Both of them were growing into lovely young women, each in their own way. What would they do as adults?

Sofie was turning into quite the academic; constantly reading a book or writing in her journal. She had talked about how she wished she could go on to university. In another lifetime when their lives were not so uprooted, this might have been an option, but now...?

Steffie would be happy enough to work as a clerk in a store or even some kind of garden work. She enjoyed talking to people and plants alike. Her prospects were slim. Even in these jobs that required little training, there wasn't much hope of finding employment. People were still starving everywhere. Jobs were scarce. Was there any future worth looking forward to—for any of her children? She mulled over these thoughts as she cultivated the soil.

After clearing the paths between the vegetable rows, Julia left the hoeing. She placed Juergen back in the stroller and wheeled it to the shade of a lilac bush at the edge of the garden. He was asleep in minutes. Then she showed Lena which plants were radishes and gave her the job of pulling out anything in that row that was not a radish.

"Is this a radish, Mutti?"

"No, you can pull that one."

Seconds later Lena called, "Mutti, can you come here? Is this one a weed? It looks different, but it has a thing that looks like a radish on it and a flower on top."

"What a smart girl you are, Lena. Yes, that is a radish, but see how the leaves have changed? This is a radish that got too old and the fruit is too hard and woody now. We can pull this one out, but if you find any more like this, just leave them for now."

They worked for a while longer and as the sun began to beat down on them, Julia said, "I think that's enough for one day. Time to go home." She looked over at Lena. "Were they good?"

"What?"

"The radishes. Were they good?"

Lena's face went as red as the radishes she had eaten.

"I only ate a couple."

"That's all right. Come here. Let's clean up your face." Julia took the corner of her apron and spat on it. With it she wiped the dirt from around Lena's mouth. "There we go. Now you are presentable again."

Vati!" Lena called as she ran into the house.

"Hello, sweetheart. What have you been up to?" Karl asked.

"Vati! The birds can talk to us."

"Really? What did they say?"

"They called to us and they knew our names. And they said 'You're pretty. You're pretty. Oh, really!'"

"Well, if they said that, then it must be true." Karl picked her up in his arms. He gave her a kiss, put her down, and told her to go wash her hands. He patted Juergen on the head. "How's my little man?"

"Brs," he said.

"Julia. I think that bird was talking about you."

She smiled. "Oh really?"

"And by the way. There's a letter for you. From Canada. Who is M. Hiebert?"

31.

Julia stared at the name on the back of the envelope. The script was not familiar to her, but why would it be? She couldn't recall ever having seen Michael's handwriting. Who else could M. Hiebert be though? What must Karl be thinking? She glanced up to see him staring at her intently. A flush of heat spread over her face.

"Who is M. Hiebert?" Karl's left eye twitched ever so slightly, a sure signal to Julia that he was angry.

"I-I'm not sure, but it could be a Michael Hiebert I knew a long time ago."

"Well, what are you waiting for? Open it and find out." He made no move to give her privacy.

"I think I'll just wait." Julia tucked the letter into her pocket.

Karl's eyebrows rose. He stood absolutely still for a few seconds. "Do as you like." He spun around, picked up his briefcase and left.

Julia pulled back the curtain ever so slightly and peeked out at Karl. He had one hand gripped tightly around the briefcase handle, the other jammed into his suit-jacket pocket. His stride was purposeful and he looked at the ground. It was already late afternoon and Julia guessed that Karl was heading for the corner store for a game of cards if he could round up the players.

She let the curtain drop and reached into her pocket. The letter burned in her hand. What on earth was Michael doing in Canada of all places? He might as well be on the moon, it was so far away. She was surprised to see that her hands were trembling. *Thank God I didn't open it in front of Karl.* She slipped her fingernail under the envelope's glued flap. It was a firm seal and the blue airmail paper was thin, but she managed not to tear it much. She sank down into the armchair and began to read.

April 30, 1952

Dear Julia,

I hope that I've found you at last and that you are well. I've been writing letters and looking for you since the war ended. I didn't know if you were dead or alive. I was so happy when the Red Cross sent me this address for you. They told me you are listed as a widow, so I presume that Lukas did not survive the war. I'm sorry for your loss. He was a good man.

I've been in Canada since 1938 when Hitler's enforcers came looking for anyone who had opposed him politically. I was lucky to escape. I couldn't even say goodbye to Marlies. I heard later that she died in the Dresden bombing. She had relatives there and was visiting at that terrible time. Sadly, they all perished.

A group of us, who feared for our lives, went into hiding. We managed to slip out of the country and come to Canada via Britain. There are a lot of German people in the Dawson Creek area.

Would you and your daughters consider coming to Canada? It is a land of hope and opportunity, they say. I believe it. It has been good to me. I have a bakery here in Dawson Creek and it is doing well. Why don't you come? There are hard times ahead for you in Germany. Life is better here. Say you'll come.

Michael

Julia's hands dropped limply to her lap. She sat, dazed, for several minutes. In her mind she was nineteen again, skipping along the path, giving Michael a playful nudge that had him tripping into the potato patch. She felt his lips explore her face, his hands in her hair, pulling her closer, pressing himself into her. Juergen's cries brought her back. *Oh my God! What is wrong with me?*

"Juergen, sweetie, are you all right? Show Mutti where it hurts." He pointed to his knee and sniffled. Julia kissed her finger and pressed it to his knee. She picked him up and hugged him tightly. "There, there. Mutti's here, sweetie."

"Mutti, you dropped a paper," Lena said. "Is it a letter?"

"Yes, give it here. I'll put it away."

"Who is it from?"

"No one important. Now let's see what we can make for supper. You can be my helper, all right?"

"All right. Where's Vati?"

"He'll be back soon." *I think....*

32.

Late in the evening, Julia heard Karl's footsteps—she would recognize that uneven gait anywhere. She was prepared to face Karl with all sorts of arguments: *I had a life before I met you. So did you. What did you expect? That no one had been interested in me before you came along?*

She got up from the sofa where she had been trying to read. Karl looked tired and pale. He dropped his briefcase by the door and took off his jacket.

Julia took a step towards him. "Karl, I—" She couldn't finish her sentence. Karl had covered her mouth with his.

"Never mind," he said. He pulled her close and leaned his head on the side of hers. His hand caressed her hair. "I'm a jealous fool."

"Karl, there's no problem. I'll just tell him I'm married now and I can't come to Canada."

"What? He wants you to come to Canada?" Karl stood, incredulous. "Let me see the letter."

"Of course you can see it. It's just that earlier, I wanted a little privacy. It was a shock to hear from him—from Michael—after so many years. Here. Read it for yourself."

Karl sat at the kitchen table and read Michael's letter. "So this was the first boyfriend?"

"Yes, but nothing came of it. We were more like good friends."

"Obviously he has been thinking about you." Karl frowned. "So what do you think about his offer?"

"It's flattering to be invited to Canada, but he doesn't know that I'm married again. It goes without saying that I'm not going to take him up on the offer. I don't know why you even have to ask me that."

Karl said nothing, so Julia went on, "I'll write tomorrow to thank him and tell him that I'm married and can't come."

"Fine. That's good." Karl gave a curt nod. "Now let's go to bed. I'm tired. I hope that will be the last we hear of him."

Julia put on her nightgown and washed her face and hands. She hesitated, then locked the bathroom door and took out the letter one more time, reading the lines over and over, tracing the words with her finger.

The next day she waited until Karl went out and then, as promised, she sat down to write.

May 18, 1952

Dear Michael,

What a surprise to hear from you after all these years. We thought you were dead when you disappeared so suddenly that night. I have no idea where this Dawson Creek place is, where you ended up, but I'm happy to hear that you are alive, that you have a bakery again, and that you are successful.

You're right about Lukas. He never made it home from the war. Times were hard for us

after that—when the Czechs drove us out—too
terrible to write about.

I appreciate your kind invitation to come
to Canada, but I have married again and have
two more children. Your letter came addressed
to Julia Feldmann, but I am now Julia Werner.
Karl and I were married four years ago.

Thank you for thinking of me. I wish you all
the best.

Fondly,

Julia

33.

Michael tossed the bundle of mail onto the table. The airmail envelope with a German stamp caught his eye. Julia! It had to be from Julia. *Please God, let her say yes.* He swished the other envelopes aside and tore the letter open. His eyes scanned quickly to the end of the letter.

"Thank you for thinking of me. I wish you all the best," did not sound like a yes. Crestfallen he sank onto a kitchen chair to read from the beginning. In spite of the rejection he now knew was coming, he needed to savour Julia's every word.

"Times were hard ... Czechs drove us out...," he read. No wonder he had so much trouble finding her. "Married. Two more children." Damn! Why? Why did she have to go and get married again? Why did it take the Red Cross so long to find her? Now it was too late. Married again. And two more children. Shit!

"Oh, Julia," he mumbled. "Seems I'm always too late." Elbows on the table, he pressed the heels of his hands into his eyes, dropped his head and let his fingers slide through his thinning hair. A tear dripped onto the arborite tabletop. And another. Suddenly he pulled his head up with a jerk. "No. I may be late, but I'm not finished yet. If I can just have her near me, maybe something will happen. Maybe her husband will.... No,

I can't wish that on her. But if I can just have her near. Yes, I must get her over here any way I can. Another letter. One more try."

June 13, 1952

Dear Julia,

It doesn't matter that you are married again. I want you to have a chance for a better life. I've heard how hard it is to find food, jobs, and housing in Germany, even now that the war is over.

I have a place for your family to live, an apartment behind the bakery, and there is a very good chance of finding work for anyone who wants it. What does Karl do? I can find out what jobs there are for him and let you know. I will sponsor you and pay for your passage to Canada. I will pay for you all—you, your husband, and all your children.

Please reconsider.

Michael

34.

August, 1952

"What do you think, Karl?" Julia asked.

"About what?"

"About the letter. About Canada. Would you consider going?"

"I guess you would like to see this old boyfriend, hmm?" He raised his chin ever so slightly in challenge.

"Karl! We're married. I haven't seen Michael since 1938, when he disappeared. We went out a few times twenty years ago." *And I really cared for him then.*

"It looks like he still thinks of you."

"The point is that we would have a chance at a fresh start. What do we have here? We're existing, that's all. Sofie and Steffie are getting to the age where they will need to choose a career or get married. There's nothing for them here. Lena and Juergen will go through school and then what? There's only a life of poverty waiting for them."

Karl sighed. "I know. You're right. We'll never have our own place or much of a future here."

"What would we be leaving behind? Neither of us are from here. These Bavarians are not our people. Of course I would miss my parents, but they have Elisabeth. And we never see the rest of my family. They live so far away."

"Are you saying you want to go?" Karl asked.

"I'm saying we have nothing to lose and everything to gain." Julia couldn't believe her own argument. She was terrified at the thought of leaving home. She was starting to wish she had never tried to convince Karl. She hadn't really thought he would consider it.

"For sure there is no employment here and I'm not getting younger. All right. I'm willing to try it. What have we got to lose?"

September, 1953

Karl! A letter from Michael."

"Open it. What are you waiting for? What does he say?"

Julia couldn't conceal the excitement in her voice as she shared the contents of Michael's letter with Karl.

August 25, 1953

Dear Julia,

I have found a job for Karl if he wants it, with the local appliance repair shop. All is set. Your tickets are enclosed for passage on the Canberra. You leave from Bremerhaven on October 20. Bring the basic necessities and sell the rest. You can buy what you need when you get here. When you get to Quebec City, take the train to Edmonton and then to Dawson Creek.

I'm so glad you have decided to come to Canada—you won't regret it, I promise.

Michael

"That sounds good about the job," Karl said. "It looks like it's really going to happen. We were smart to get our vaccinations and medical exams and to have the emigration papers approved. The only thing left is to pack and sell what we're not taking."

"I'm afraid I won't be much help to you in packing except to say what goes where. This baby wants to have its own ticket to Canada." Julia clutched her huge belly as if to hold up the baby inside.

"You just do what you can and when you need to rest, you rest. I'm going to see where I can scrounge some trunks to pack our things. You could start making a list of what you think we should take. Now that Sofie is back from Munich, she can help you."

"I hope there is a place where she can continue college in Dawson Creek."

"Don't hold your breath waiting for that to happen. It sounds like Dawson Creek is just a little backwater. It's so far from everywhere. I looked on the map and even the distance from there to Edmonton where we change trains is farther than our trip across all of Germany to Bremerhaven."

Julia stared at him incredulously. "Oh my God. That far? What have we done? I know Canada is a big country, but that is unimaginable."

Karl opened his palms and shrugged. "Well, it's too late now," he snapped. "We've made our decision and we're stuck with it."

Oh my God, she thought again, after Karl left. *Oh my God. I had no idea! And Michael said it gets cold in the winter. I can't imagine what minus 40 degrees feels like. Oh dear God. I think we made a big mistake.*

Julia didn't sleep well that night. She couldn't push away the fear and doubts. If it didn't work out, there was no coming back. They had no money for a change of heart once they stepped onto that ship. It would be unthinkable to waste the money Michael had spent for their passage. She resolved to try to go to sleep. Although her mind settled down at last, the baby inside her did not.

Finally she decided to get up and make herself a cup of tea. Before the kettle had boiled she knew she had to wake Karl. "Go for the doctor, Karl. It's time."

35.

October 1953

Reinhard Werner was four weeks old when Julia held him in her arms and waved goodbye to the friends and relatives who had gathered at the bus station in Koenigshofen.

"Julia, you look so pale and tired," Katrina said.

Tired? If her mother only knew. She was so tired she wanted to lie down right there on the cobblestones and go to sleep. She knew she was close to an emotional breakdown, but she also knew that her family depended on her, so the option of giving up was out of the question. "It was a long day yesterday, not only getting everything ready, but dealing with Steffie's fall on the steps. We were lucky to get her arm put in a cast late last night. I hope the bus ride won't be too painful for her."

"I'm worried about *you.*"

"I'll be fine, Mother. I'll be able to sleep a bit when we get to the train. Please don't worry, or I'll have to worry about you. You just take care of yourself."

"Maybe it's best that your father is no longer with us. He hated the idea of you emigrating, but if he had lived to see you actually leave, he would have been heartbroken." Katerina's eyes brimmed with tears. "It's hard enough for me ... but women are stronger than men."

Julia put her hand on her mother's shoulder and let it slide gently down her arm. "Yes. He was always there for me. Lena will miss him too. She sat on his knee on our garden bench so many times." Julia dabbed at her eyes with her handkerchief. "I'm glad you have Elisabeth to take care of you, Mother. I'll miss you so much. I'll write often, I promise."

"Me too. You can't imagine how much I'll miss you." Julia heard the catch in her mother's throat.

"I'd better go. Here, give your grandson one more kiss." The two women hugged one last time, sobbing. "Goodbye, Mother. I love you so much."

Julia dabbed at her eyes again and took a deep breath, determined to put on a brave face as she stepped onto the bus. Karl helped her up. They turned to wave one last time to their family and the crowd of friends and curious onlookers. Julia was touched by the turnout of so many townspeople who came to wish them well on their voyage.

Julia stifled a sob as the bus doors closed, ending a chapter of her life. Karl took a deep breath and smiled at her. She returned his smile, tears threatening to spill. Karl's chin dimpled as he pressed his lips together tightly. *So he's feeling it too, even though he has no family of his own to leave behind.*

Such a mix of emotions—misery at leaving her mother and sister, an empty ache of sorrow for her recently buried father, exhaustion after giving birth to her fifth child, anticipation of a new world, hope for a new beginning, fear of the unknown, and worry for her marriage when Karl and Michael would meet. She spent most of the bus ride blowing her nose and dabbing at her eyes. It was Karl who brought her out of her tailspin.

"Julia, dear, try to think of all the good reasons we're doing this. We have the children. We have each other. The rest will work itself out." He put his arm around her shoulders and pulled her closer on the bus seat.

"You're right, Karl. I'll be fine. We'll all be fine." She blew her nose one more time. "I just had a moment there where all I could think of was everything that could possibly go wrong. I'm so glad I have you."

At Bremerhaven, port for the city of Bremen, they jostled through the crush of the crowd to present passports and emigration documents at the Customs checkpoints. In the waiting room beyond, postcards of the ships were for sale. Julia bought one of their ship, the Canberra.

"It looks very nice, don't you think." She held the card up for Karl to see.

"Clean and white." Karl pointed to a poster displayed on the wall. "Look. Here it is too. It says the ship is about 138 metres long and 17 metres wide. That's not very big compared to some of those fancy ships crossing the Atlantic these days. But good Lord, look at this. It says the ship was built in 1913. It's almost as old as we are."

"We're not really old."

"Forty is not old for a person, but for a ship, it's ancient."

"It looks like new on the postcard. I suppose we'll find out soon enough." *Oh, God. I hope the old tub doesn't fall apart halfway across the Atlantic.*

Julia sat on a bench in the waiting room. "When are we getting on the ship, Mutti?" Lena asked her.

"At two o'clock. Another hour," Julia said. "Steffie, why don't you take Lena and Juergen for a walk, all right? I'm so tired. I could use a little break."

"Let me take Reinhard for a while," Sofie offered.

"Thanks, Sofie. I feel like I haven't slept in a week."

"You probably haven't. All that packing and worrying, not to mention having a baby and selling everything to go to a strange land. But still, we're lucky to be going on this adventure." Julia could hear the excitement in her voice. It seemed so long ago since she had felt such optimism about her own future. Sofie had gone through hard times too since the war was over, more than any child should have to deal with. Julia marvelled at the strength and resilience of youth, still able to rebound from life's setbacks. She wondered when she had lost her own will to take challenges head on. She hoped she would feel rejuvenated in the new country and find herself again, but for the moment it seemed all she could do was worry.

"I hope I didn't make the wrong decision. It's so far and we can't afford to come back." *As it is, we'll be lucky if the money lasts till we get there.*

"But Mutti, it can't be worse than staying in Germany. It's getting harder and harder to feed us all. Won't it be nice to have good food in Canada?"

Julia sighed. "I'd be happy if we had *enough* food. Good food would be a bonus.

"Do you see Karl yet, Sofie? He went to find some water for me. I hope he didn't get lost. It's such a huge building and so many people milling around." She wondered if all her worrying was upsetting Sofie. She hadn't intended to sound so apprehensive. But when she glanced over at Sofie, she saw only a young fresh face, full of happy anticipation.

Karl came out of the crowd, one arm in front of him to prevent a spill. "Here you are, Julia." He handed her a cup of water. "Where are the children?"

Julia pointed as she sipped her water. "Steffie took them for a walk. They were getting bored waiting."

"We'd better find them. I heard someone say they were going to start loading passengers soon."

"I'll go look for them," Sofie said. She handed Reinhard over to Karl. Within minutes she was back, Steffie, Lena, and Juergen trailing behind her.

"Attention, all passengers bound for Quebec City," a voice crackled over the loudspeaker. "The vessel Canberra will begin loading in fifteen minutes. Please have your boarding passes ready."

Julia got up slowly and reached for her suitcase, but Karl touched her arm. "Here, you take the baby and we'll get the suitcases."

Moving forward amidst the crush of other passengers, Julia felt a thousand butterflies in her stomach. They were going so far from home—to a place where she couldn't even speak the language. Sofie and Steffie knew a bit of English from school. That should help. But oh, what if this move was all a big mistake? Misgivings whirled around in her head.

As she stepped out of the waiting room onto the loading platform, the brisk sea air teased a few tendrils of her hair out of the kerchief tied under her chin. The salty iodine smell of the seashore came to her on a cold breeze. She unfastened the top two buttons of her coat and put Reinhard inside, next to her body. Julia shook off a shudder that sent goosebumps over her skin; a shiver that had nothing to do with the chilly wind.

Last chance, her inner voice cried in desperation. Her legs were carrying her forward but her mind was pulling her back. Once she stepped onto that ship, there was no going back. The ocean would separate her from her family roots, her culture, her friends, her life as she had known it, probably forever. On the gangplank Julia took a deep breath and said a quiet goodbye to her past. Ahead of her lay all things unknown. Except for Michael.

No more than a few hours from land, the Canberra began to roll and pitch in the grey North Sea. Karl noticed a sallow greenish tinge creep into Julia's pale face. He settled her on a deck chair in a sheltered corner of the promenade deck, covered her and the baby with an extra blanket and hurried to find a crewmember. Moments later he returned with a uniformed man who led them to a large room in the lower deck of the ship.

"They put the ship's hospital in the best place," Karl said to Julia, once she was put to bed. "It's in the center and at the very bottom of the ship, so the motion is less noticeable and it's not as bad if you think you might get seasick."

"The way I feel, I'm already seasick. I'm sorry to let you down, Karl. And what will Lena and Juergen think when I'm not there for them? And how will I look after the baby?" Julia began to cry softly.

"There, there, Julia. Everything will be all right. The nurse will help you with Reinhard. I'll come see you every day. Don't worry about us. Sofie and Steffie will sleep in a cabin with Lena and Juergen, and I'll be there to help give them a hand during the day."

"Yes, of course. I keep forgetting they aren't little girls anymore. Seventeen and nineteen—they're almost adults. We must be getting old."

"Nonsense, Julia. We're only as old as we feel."

"In that case I'm about a hundred. I'm so tired and the trip is only beginning. Oh, Karl, are we doing the right thing?"

It worried him to see her like this. She had always been so strong in adversity. Was she just worn down from the stress of the move and having the baby, or was she really sick? Like Evelyn? *No, that can't be. She just needs me to get us through this move.*

"It will be fine. We have each other. That's all that matters—you, me, Lena, Juergen, and Reinhard—our children."

"*All* our children. You will be good to Sofie and Steffie? It's all new to them too, this trip."

"Yes, yes, Sofie and Steffie too. I'll keep an eye on all of them."

Karl kissed Julia's cheek. She looked so frail and tired. Her eyes were closed already. Poor thing. She looked exhausted. At least she could get some rest here. He would just have to do what he did best—take charge of the situation and see them through. He took a step away from Julia's bed and looked at her sleeping form. There was something so fragile about her now. A wave of love washed over him. *You're mine. Mine!* "Do you know how much I love you?" he whispered. "Do you know I'll do anything to keep you?"

36.

The Canberra bucked through the rough North Sea
chop for three days before reaching Southampton.
While the ship stood in the harbour, passengers crowded
the rails to admire a colossal passenger liner docked at
the wharf. Karl had brought Julia upstairs for a walk
on the deck. "The fresh air will be good for you and the
baby," he said. "You'll be stuck in that room downstairs
long enough once we start across the Atlantic."

Sofie and Steffie smiled and chatted happily with
their mother. Julia felt Lena tap her hand for attention
as Juergen pulled on her coat. *They missed me like I
missed them.*

"Look at that." Julia pointed at the black-hulled ship
with its white upper deck. "Isn't that a beautiful ship?"

"It's named after the Queen," Sofie said. "See, it says
the name on the front, Queen Elizabeth II."

"So clean and so big." Julia smiled admiringly. "That
must be only for the rich."

"Not us, that's for sure," Karl agreed. "But in a few
days we'll be in Canada and it won't matter how we got
there."

"Oh! Feels like we're moving. I'd better go back
downstairs before I turn green again. Sofie and Steffie,
thank you for taking care of Lena and Juergen. You're
my angels." Julia sensed Karl watching as she hugged

them. It unsettled her to think he was jealous of any affection she gave the girls.

The two younger children clung to Julia's coat. She gave them each a hug. Karl gave Julia a hug and kissed baby Reinhard on the head. He asked the older girls to walk their mother downstairs and meet him in the restaurant afterwards.

"I'll come see you later, Julia," he told her. Turning to Lena and Juergen, he said, "And now my darlings, let's go to the restaurant and see what the cook is doing. Maybe he will have something for us to eat. Who likes pancakes?"

In the mid-North Atlantic the wind picked up. Karl planned to take Lena and Juergen for their usual walk around the ship. He stepped onto the promenade deck and immediately tightened his grip on the children's hands. He noticed that the bow of the ship was cordoned off by a thick rope.

"Whoa!" Juergen yelled. "Vati! Look at the big wave."

"It's coming right over the ship," Lena shouted into the wind. Her hair whipped her face.

The waves washed over the bow and ran across the foredeck to rejoin the ocean through the scuppers at the side. *Holy shit!* "Let's go back inside," Karl said. "Yes, we'd better go in."

"Where is everybody?" Lena looked around in the restaurant.

"Seasick in their cabins. We can sit wherever we want." Karl held his children's hands firmly as the ship pitched and shuddered in the breaking waves of the late October storm.

"I'll sit by the window," Juergen said.

"Watch out, Juergen." Lena put her arm around his shoulders and pulled him closer to her. "You'll get wet." Seawater had forced its way in by the porthole seam. The rivulet trickled down the back of the bench seat. Juergen shrugged his shoulders and slid over beside Lena.

The following day, too, the restaurant was nearly empty. Again they sat on the bench seat near the porthole. "Look, Vati!" Lena said, "This is the spot where the water came in. It made a white mark."

"That's from the salt in the seawater."

Lena shook her head and smiled at him. "You're just playing a joke on me. Right, Vati? Water isn't salty."

"Yes, the ocean is salty."

"No, it's not."

"Taste it and see." Karl smiled at her fondly.

Lena licked the tiny white crystals and her eyes grew round. "It's salt!"

Days later the pitching and rolling of the ship subsided. Someone shouted, "Land!" and the railing was once again lined with passengers pointing and talking excitedly, their pale, drawn faces lit up with anticipation.

"That's Newfoundland." Karl pointed out the greenish-grey shoreline to the children. *Thank God. Getting off this tub can't come soon enough for me.*

The excitement wore off as fog settled in. The next day only a thin layer of low cloud remained—no land in sight. For two more days the horizon offered nothing but sea. Standing alone on a sheltered part of the promenade deck, Karl stared out into the mist and felt his mood matching the endless dull mixture of sea and sky.

"Vati!"

Karl turned at the sound. A stewardess had a firm grip on Lena's hand and was towing her towards him.

"Your daughter?" she asked.

"Senk you," he said in an effort to respond in English. She smiled, gave him a nod, and left.

Lena threw her arms around Karl's legs. "Lena, what are you doing here?" Her face was blotchy and tear stained. "I thought Sofie was looking after you? What happened?"

"I got tired of waiting so I went looking for her and then I got lost and there were so many hallways and-and-and I couldn't find her." She sobbed as she recounted her terrifying experience. "That lady with the uniform helped me find you."

"Well, everything's all right now." *God damn that Sofie! When I get my hands on her....*

Seconds later Sofie burst through the door to the promenade deck. "Lena!" she said. "I've been looking all over for you."

Karl felt his bad mood and anger surge. He slapped Sofie's face before he had time to think. "Where the hell were you? You were supposed to look after her. And where's Juergen?"

Sofie raised her hands to her cheeks. She stood with a shocked look on her face.

"Where's Juergen? I said."

"He-he-he's with Steffie because I had to go looking for Lena." Tears ran down her cheeks.

"From now on you make sure you keep a closer watch on the children." Karl stalked away holding Lena by the hand. He sent a quick glare back at Sofie who stood on the deck looking forsaken and miserable. As he calmed down, Karl realized that he had overreacted, but he would do it again, he told himself, if *his* children were threatened.

Later in the day, an island came into view. Then another island, and another, and another. "This must be what those people were talking about in the restaurant this morning," Karl said. "The Thousand Islands. See that, Sofie, Steffie? The Thousand Islands. We'll be in Quebec soon."

The older girls kept their heads lowered, and Sofie grumbled just loud enough for Karl to hear, "Can't be soon enough."

Hundreds of new arrivals shuffled along with their suitcases. All needed to be checked by the Immigration officials at the gate. Julia stood with her legs braced slightly apart for balance. She had been motion sick for eleven days, and even now on solid ground, she was reeling. She didn't realize that her body had adjusted to the motion of the ocean and now she felt nauseated by the reluctance of the land to move with her. She clutched the handrail as they were herded towards the checkpoint. "Sofie, you stay close by. They'll be asking us questions and I won't know what they're saying."

"Don't worry, Mutti. It'll be all right." Sofie patted her mother's hand almost in a reversal of roles.

The official stamped all the papers without much scrutiny, but then he saw the cast on Steffie's arm. "Hold on. What's this?"

"I break arm," Steffie said.

"You'll have to stay here, then, until the cast comes off."

I don't know what jail is like, but I think this is close," Julia said as she noted the barred windows. For a moment her mind went back eight years to their ordeal in Saaz, except that the spartan accommodations of the Immigration House were luxury compared to the barracks.

"At least we can all be together," Sofie said.

Julia had sensed her older daughters' coolness towards Karl. Did Sofie want them to be together for company, or did she need her mother's protection? "Is everything all right, Sofie?" Julia was about to ask more, but Karl spoke just then.

"Well, Steffie, you've really landed us in the soup now!" Julia spun around and gave Karl a sharp look.

"Karl!" She started to say more, but Karl threw down the suitcases and stormed out the door. She knew he wasn't going far; there was nowhere to go but down the hall. Julia put her arms around Steffie who was sniffing quietly. She wiped away her daughter's tears and pulled Steffie's head close to hers in a hug. "Don't you worry. It will all blow over when we get out of here. It's not your fault that we have to wait for your cast to come off. At least we can rest here and we're safe."

Damn him! He had promised to treat Sofie and Steffie with kindness if not love, but time and time again, Julia found herself being the peacemaker between Karl and her two older daughters. It had become her habit to be watchful and protective. Didn't he see that when he hurt her children, he was hurting her too? Did he have no love to spare for them? She wanted to tell him he was cruel and unfeeling to treat her girls this way, but then he could be so loving towards the younger children—his children. She looked down on Steffie's head snuggled into her neck for protection like a frightened animal.

"I hate him, Mutti," she whispered. "Why does he always have to be so mean to us? I hate him." Steffie's chest heaved with spasms of sobs and Julia's heart ached for her daughter.

Steffie's cast was off. Julia was relieved to see the girls sitting together on the train, chatting and laughing. They had been a great help to her, keeping Lena and Juergen occupied and happy. It had been Sofie's idea to buy the big colouring book for the two little ones to share.

The last few days in the Immigration House had been difficult. The air had crackled with tension between Karl and the girls. Julia had been waiting for an opportunity to speak to Karl, but it was impossible to find any privacy. At last they had a few moments to themselves in their train compartment.

"Karl, we haven't had a chance to talk and I really think we need to."

"I knew this was coming." Karl squinted his eyes ever so slightly and his lower lid twitched. It was a facial expression Julia had learned to recognize. She sighed, already expecting Karl's brick wall of defence.

"We have to pull together or this move will be a disaster."

"I'm doing my share. It's your girls who have been sloughing. For years I've been supporting them. The least they could do is help out a bit."

"Karl, come now. It's not about who is paying the bills. And they do help. They always try to do the right thing." She hesitated. "You promised me you'd be good to them." How could she have missed seeing this cruel streak in him? He must have hidden it well when she first met him. She should have listened to her mother's warning.

Karl clamped his lips together, then looked up at the ceiling as if the answer to their problem might be written there.

"They have feelings too," she pressed on. "Can't you just try to be nice to them?"

"I have been nice to them, but you've seen how cool they are."

"Just give them a chance. They're still hurt over the way you've treated them."

"Oh, so now it's my fault."

"Well, maybe it is. Really! You're supposed to be the adult. Surely you can manage to be nice to them even if you can't love them." She looked at Karl for a response, but his lips were pressed shut and his eye twitched.

"Oh, Karl! Please don't be like that. We want things to work out when we make our new start, don't we?"

"The new start, the new start. I'm sick of the new start," he hissed at her.

"I thought you wanted this."

"Sure, I wanted it, but I think we wanted it for different reasons." His eye twitched rapidly.

"How can you say that? I've never given you any reason to think that." *Unless you can read my mind, that is.* Julia often wondered how it would be to see Michael now. They had really liked each other back then....

"I saw your eyes light up when you got those letters from Michael. Why don't they light up for me anymore?"

"Karl, I love you, but you've been so awful lately. You make it hard for any of us to feel close."

"Well, I can't change who I am, so whatever will be, will be." He folded his arms across his chest.

It was hopeless trying to reason with him when he settled into this rigid mood. At times, Julia wondered why she bothered. When he did agree to treat her daughters fairly, it never lasted very long. If she had arranged to come to Canada without him ... Canada and Michael ... waiting for her.... She sighed. As always, reality pushed away her wishful thinking. She had three other children depending on her. Karl would never part with them and she could never leave them behind. Never! They chained her to Karl, but she loved them. She knew that if need be, she would walk through fire for them. *Perhaps that is what I am doing,* she thought, *getting ready to walk through fire.*

37.

Several grain elevators loomed out of the haze of blowing snow as the train slowed to a crawl and came to a stop at the Dawson Creek train station. A small group of people, bundled up against the cold, stamped their freezing feet and beat their hands together as they waited for the arrivals. Julia looked out the window scanning the small crowd for Michael's face. Would she recognize him? Guilt flooded her mind when she remembered that Karl would be watching her reaction. Could he see her heart thumping under her coat? Did he know that her mouth was dry, or that the palms of her hands inside her gloves were damp? She had gone to the small bathroom at the end of the railcar moments earlier and stolen a peek in the mirror. Quickly she had tidied her hair and brushed her teeth. Had Karl noticed her attempts to make herself look pretty? Every time she glanced at him, he had been studying her. She squirmed under his scrutiny. The brakes hissed and Julia's face burned in spite of the cold air that blasted through the railcar as the doors opened.

"This is it. We're here!" Julia kept her head down as she bent to pick up Reinhard and his blankets.

Karl stood to see to the baggage. "Lena and Juergen, hold Sofie's hand." He stepped off the train first with a suitcase in each hand, set them down on the snow, and turned to help Julia and the children.

Julia stood at the top of the train steps, baby in her arms. The wind whipped ice crystals into her face. Even severe winters in Germany were not like this—and it was only November. She gasped at the cold and felt her eyebrows freeze. She turned to the children. "Make sure you have your coats done up. It's bitter cold." Karl reached to help her down the steps.

As soon as her leather-soled shoes hit the ground, Julia's feet slipped out from under her. Karl caught her just in time. She teetered on the hard-packed snow on the station platform, unable to balance herself because of the baby in her arms.

Another hand reached for her elbow to help steady her. "We'll have to find some good winter boots for you, Julia." She could feel the heat of Michael's hand through her coat. Julia looked up at him. His eyes were still deep brown, almost black. She was thankful that the weakness in her knees could be disguised by the fact that the ground was icy. "Come, let's step into the train station until we get ourselves organized."

Once inside Michael introduced himself to Karl, and Julia introduced Michael to her children. "The girls have grown up," he said. "They were only toddlers when I last saw them. I can see Lukas in their faces." He shook his head and murmured, "So long ago." He followed the direction of Julia's arm as she pointed to her youngest children. "And these three little ones are yours and Karl's?"

"That's right." Michael's smile looked pasted on. *Sorrow. That's what's under the smile.* Julia wondered if he wished things had been different "so long ago."

"Thank you for bringing us to Canada," Karl said. "We're in your debt." He sounded like a talking machine—so mechanical—trying very hard to say and do the right thing under strained circumstances. Julia sympathized with Karl and understood his discomfort at that moment.

"You're very welcome," Michael said. "It's good to meet you, Karl, and lovely to see you again, Julia. Just as beautiful as ever." Julia saw Karl's left eye begin to twitch. She took his arm to calm the jealousy she knew smouldered there. "Now, I've brought my station wagon and I'm sure we can all squeeze in. With any luck we'll even have room for the suitcases. Fortunately we don't have far to go."

Karl took charge. "Julia, you sit in the back with Sofie and Steffie and the little ones will sit up front with me by Michael."

Julia did as Karl said and had the guilty pleasure of observing Michael's hungry eyes boring into hers in the rear-view mirror all the way to their apartment.

Julia brushed a fluff of lint from the shoulders of Karl's suit jacket. "You look very fine."

"You look the same as always—gorgeous," he said with a wide smile.

Julia was thrilled, not only to hear the compliment, but to see Karl smiling. He had developed a permanent scowl over the past week while they settled in. *Maybe everything will work out all right after all.* "Let's go meet the neighbours." She grabbed Karl's hand and pulled him out the door. "Oops!" She did an about face. "Coats! We may be going just next door and up the stairs but it's very cold out there."

The gramophone was playing soft music as Karl and Julia entered the warmth of Michael's apartment. The aroma of freshly baked bread from the bakery below filled the room. It was a smell she had always associated with good things. Good food, good friends—Michael in his bakery, Lukas at Dettmeier's—a delicious, comfortable association.

"Would you like a glass of port wine?" Michael asked. They nodded. "Good. It's not overly sweet, but it does pack a bit of a punch. I think you've met Edward and Martha who live next door to you, and Loretta, who lives upstairs here next to my place, just above you. Loretta has a daughter, Linda, who must be about Sofie's age.

Julia and Karl shook hands all around and sat down. The neighbours were all German and they were soon talking of the hard old times and the better new times.

"Have you lived here long?" Julia asked Martha.

"Five years," she said. "We're so lucky we found Michael. He's been very good to us and even helped to find a job for Edward."

"He's always bringing over some kind of baked goods that he says are left over but I know he could easily have sold," said Loretta. "A very kind man."

Julia wondered if Michael and Loretta had more than a casual landlord/tenant kind of friendship, but she had no time to pursue that thought as Loretta ploughed on.

"But Julia, Michael says you have a daughter Linda's age? I'm sure they'll be friends."

"I have three daughters. Lena is only six, but Steffie and Sofie are seventeen and nineteen. It would be nice for them to be friends.

"Oh, I love that song that's playing." Julia turned to Michael. "Isn't that from The Merry Widow? The Vilja song?"

"You still have an ear for music, Julia." Michael handed her a glass of port wine and then turned to give Karl his. "I'm sure you know what a fine voice Julia has, right Karl?"

"Yes, she does. A beautiful voice. But how do you know this, Michael?" Julia quietly sucked in air between her teeth, hoping this conversation wouldn't lead to sharp words. There was something menacing in the way Karl said Michael's name, as if he were daring him to say one thing too personal and give him reason to explode.

"A long time ago in another life, I played my violin for the choir that Julia sang in." If Michael noticed Karl's tenseness he gave no indication of it, as he responded in a casual tone. "It was Julia's honeyed voice that had me looking forward to every practice. But that was a long time ago."

Michael always was the mellow one. Always knew how to defuse tense situations. "Do you still play your violin, Michael?" Julia asked. She tried to redirect the focus of attention from herself. Karl had been so sweet and friendly today, she didn't want to spoil his mood by making him jealous.

"Seldom. I bought one here—well, ordered it from Edmonton, actually—but I don't play it much."

Michael changed the music and Edward and Martha got up to dance. Karl looked at Julia. Michael said, "Please! Go ahead and dance. This is a lovely piece too."

Karl held Julia close and they swayed to the mellow notes of "Vaya Con Dios." Michael danced with Loretta but Julia could feel his eyes on her. She thought about another dance, long ago, when she danced with Lukas. Michael had watched her then too. She wondered if he was remembering it now, as she was, his heart aching as hers ached. She had cared so much for Michael then, but had hurt him badly when she married Lukas. Maybe if she had a chance to dance with him tonight, she could make up for that hurt in some small way. But Karl was being so possessive of her tonight. If she made him jealous he would be in a bad mood for days.

The pastries were delicious and as the port wine flowed, so did the conversation. Julia was feeling relaxed and happy as the evening wore on. Karl started to say something about it being time to go home when Michael put on "Vaya Con Dios" again and said, "I haven't had the pleasure of a dance with your wife. Do you mind, Karl?"

"Not at all, Michael. After all, as you said, the Julia you knew was from another lifetime." The way Karl's eye twitched as he spoke to Michael worried her. He was trying his best to be charming and friendly tonight, but his wild jealousy was only thinly disguised from the guests and not at all from Julia.

Michael kept a respectable distance as they danced. Karl danced with Loretta this time and when his back was turned, Michael leaned close and whispered to Julia, "I'll come see you tomorrow morning." Julia pushed away, but the song was ending anyway. She had wanted so much to pull him closer, but pushing away was safer. She thanked Michael for a lovely evening, said what a pleasure it had been to meet her neighbours. She knew she was babbling to cover her feelings. She was sure everyone could look right into her heart. She took Karl's hand, squeezed it tightly, and asked him to get their coats.

"So nice to see you all." Michael spoke to his guests as they departed but Julia felt his eyes devouring her.

Karl put his arm around Julia as they hurried along the snow-covered walk to their apartment. In front of their doorstep, he stopped and kissed her. "I feel like a young boy out on a date," he said, laughing. "Must be the wine. But you are delicious, Julia."

"Karl! It must be -20 out here. Let's get into the apartment," she scolded, but she knew he could see her smiling. It was only as she took her coat off inside that she let herself think about Michael's words and became afraid. Afraid of her own weakness.

38.

Michael turned huge batches of dough onto the floured worktable. He shaped loaf after loaf, glancing up now and then as he waited for Karl to leave for work. At last he saw his scrawny figure pass by the storefront window, chin tucked into his chest, and shoulders hunched forward against the cold.

Michael placed the last of the loaves in the oven and set the timer. He slapped the flour from his hands and pulled the apron off over his head. With a freshly baked loaf of rye bread from a previous batch under his arm, he hurried out the door.

Behind the bakery he had added on five apartments over the years. Renting out four of them brought in a tidy sum. The fifth one he had set aside for Julia. He had enjoyed choosing furniture for that apartment knowing she would be using it—the yellow arborite kitchen table and matching chairs, the green sofa bed for the living room, and all the other furnishings and appliances he thought she might need.

"You're up early," Julia said as she opened the door to his knock.

"This loaf has a flaw and can't be sold, so I thought you could use it." He handed her the bread. "May I come in?"

"Of course."

"Why don't you make us a cup of tea, Julia? We have some catching up to do." Michael was surprised to realize that he was nervous. He wanted his first private conversation with her to go well, but it had been such a long time since they had known each other. He knew that his nightingale Julia was still there under the surface, but how was he to break through to her? The years were sure to have cooled her feelings for him. She had been widowed and remarried since the days when they were in love. Would he be able to take her back to those days of long ago?

She filled the kettle with water and set it on the stove. A rosy flush was spreading over her face—a good sign— and she smoothed her dress on her hips. Perhaps he had a chance.

"What did you think of your neighbours when you met them last night?"

"They seem very nice. Does Edward work?"

"Yes, he drives a taxi, so he often works at night."

"And Loretta, the single mother, where is her husband?"

"She's a widow like yourself."

"I'm no longer a widow, Michael. I'm married."

This was not the direction he had wanted the conversation to go. "Yes, I know, I know. I know it all too well. I—"

"Michael, we must leave the past in the past. It didn't work out for us then, and it can't work for us now."

She looked as lovely as ever. She still had those gold flecks in her hazel eyes; still had good legs; still that sweet smile. He reached for her arm.

"Michael. Don't!" He heard the fear in her voice, but she leaned slightly toward him, her lips parted, her eyes bright. She must still want him. Her body said so.

"I shouldn't have let Lukas have you all those years ago." He took a step towards her and she was backed up to the wall with nowhere to go. If he were more of a gentleman, he would give her some space, but he remembered that he had backed off too many times in the past and lost her.

"Julia, I love you. All these years I've loved you. You must know that. Why else would I pay for all of your family to come here?" He put his hand on her shoulder.

Juergen came running into the kitchen. "Mutti, do you know where the colouring book is?" He stopped to stare at Michael who pulled his hand away.

"I think it's over here beside the sofa, Juergen. You be a good boy and go colour now."

"Because you have a visitor?"

"Uncle Michael has brought us some bread. He's just going now." Juergen took the colouring book to the table and began flipping pages. Turning to Michael, Julia said quietly, "Let's have that cup of tea some other time, shall we?"

She was right. The admission came with so much reluctance and pain, but could he be anything less than honest with her? Lowering his voice to a whisper he said, "I have no right to ruin your life now that you have a new family. It's just that ... I had hoped.... For such a long time, I thought only of you. You'll always be the only one for me."

Julia started to reach for him, but then let her hand drop. She chewed her lower lip as her eyes welled with tears. She looked down and slowly shook her head.

As he felt his own eyes begin to fill, he turned away quickly. His shoulders sank with hopelessness.

"Michael, don't do this," Julia pleaded. But she was already speaking to his back as he hurried out the door.

Julia was pleased to see that Sofie seemed much happier as the winter went on. She had a job in the bakery on weekends and after school. It provided her with some spending money and the opportunity to improve her English and meet new friends. Loretta's daughter, Linda, knew everyone at school and brought some of her friends around to visit with Sofie at the bakery. Julia had met some of them there.

"Mutti, do you mind if I go out to the Vogue tonight with Linda?" Sofie asked. "She's bringing a couple of friends and we want to go see Beneath the 12 Mile Reef. Robert Wagner is in it."

"As long as you're not late, I don't see why not."

"We're going to the seven o'clock show so we won't be late. Jack is going with Linda and his friend Brent is coming along."

Julia's eyebrows went up. "You behave yourself. You don't know these boys very well." She hoped Sofie didn't fall for all their lines. Young women were so naïve. *And when we're older and should know better, we're still easily flattered. We want to believe we're still wanted. Believe in the dream.* She looked up then and saw that Sofie was standing still, watching her as she was lost in thought. "Well, you're old enough now, Sofie. Just use your common sense." *Did I?* she wondered. *Will I?*

Michael rolled out the pastry and cut it into rounds for butter tarts. As he worked he invented a thousand premises for visiting Julia in her apartment. It was already March and he had yet to get more than a small peck on the cheek from her. A week ago she had hugged him tightly after she and Karl had a painful argument, but she had come to her senses, too quickly for his liking, and pushed him away.

"I'm so sorry, Michael," she had said. "I don't know what came over me. This can't happen again."

With the tarts out of the oven, he made up his mind to go see her even without an excuse. It was Saturday and Sofie was watching the store. He had recently hired Steffie too, to keep her company. He could see Lena and Juergen all bundled up, playing in the yard in front of the apartment. Karl would be working. He had just been home, presumably for lunch, and was gone again.

"Hi, Uncle Michael," the children called as he passed them on his way to the door.

"Hi kids. Is your mother home?"

"Yes, she's doing the dishes," Lena answered. "She said I don't have to do them this time if I look after Juergen instead."

"Good girl, Lena. You do that. Stay out here and watch Juergen play."

When Julia opened the door, he pushed his way in quickly and locked it behind him. Julia stood with the dish towel in her hand, and dropped it when he kissed her long and demandingly. He saw her face flush and pressed his advantage, pulling her into the bedroom. He pushed her down across the bed, gently but firmly, before she had time for second thoughts. "Julia, I love you. I need you so much," he said between kisses to her face, her neck, her breasts. With shaking hands he unbuttoned the blouse of her dress. Julia reached up and put her hands around his neck. She pulled his head down to her.

"I know this is wrong," she said, "but it feels so good and I need you too. You can't imagine how much I need you." He kissed her with a longing that went back to a time before the world turned upside down. He was kissing the girl who sang like a nightingale. He hoped she was kissing the violinist she had loved so long ago. She pulled her feet up onto the bed. Michael reached down to remove her panties. She was already unbuckling his belt. He felt as if he were on fire and only she could soothe the burning. As he entered her, he had to fight to make it last. He wanted her so much right now. Oh damn! He was going to come too quickly, but he couldn't stop now. He had wanted her, waited for her for so long. With a pained groan of pleasure, he sank into her completely one last time. Propping himself up on his elbows, he kissed the place behind her ears and heard her gasping for breath and moaning. "Oh, Michael," she whispered. "Oh, Michael, that felt so good."

"I'm sorry. I wanted to make it last," he said. "But yes, so good, so right." Her body was shaking as she held him tightly around the waist. It took him a moment to realize she was crying.

"Oh my God, what have I done?" She cried pitifully. "Michael, please go. Please. Quickly. Just go."

"But, Julia. It's so right for us. You can leave Karl. You've got me—"

"NO!" she cried out hysterically. "I can't do this. I shouldn't have done this. Oh, God, what have I done?"

She sobbed and sobbed. Michael tried to pull her close but she pushed him away.

"Please, Michael. Just go. What if the children—?" She jumped up, straightened the bedspread, and stood looking at it in horror.

Michael had thought things were going so well. *What just happened?* "Is it because you're worried the children will come in? We can just be having a cup of tea as far as they're concerned."

"No, it's not only that. Oh, Michael, I'm sorry. It's just wrong. I shouldn't have given in to my feelings. Karl—"

"Don't say his name. Please, Julia. Don't spoil it." He reached for her again, but she stepped back quickly.

"No. Don't. Please. Just go." She hung her head and looked so unhappy that he found it hard to turn away. More than ever he wanted to comfort her, but as he stepped towards her, she raised both palms to push him away should he come closer. Her tear-stained face was hard to bear.

"Just go," she whispered. "Please?"

"Julia—"

"Go. Please, go."

He tidied his clothes and slipped out. "I'll be back," he muttered at the closed door.

39.

A little after 6 o'clock, Karl came home from work. He looked pale and tired. "Supper ready? Smells good."

"Five minutes. Just have to thicken the gravy." Julia's heart pounded double time. She kept her head over the stove, certain she had adultery written all over her face.

"Good. I'm tired. I was learning how to fix an electric Sunbeam mixer today."

"Did you figure it out?" She was relieved to talk about Karl's day as a distraction from her own.

"Oh yeah, eventually. It's just that it takes a bit longer to figure out these new appliances. I didn't want to take too long to fix it in case the boss thought I couldn't do it. It was stressful, but I did it." He put away his briefcase, went to wash up, and sat down at the table to wait for his dinner. "What's for supper?"

"The last of the moose that Michael gave us." She almost choked on his name. Julia gave the gravy one more quick stir and shut off the gas burner.

Sofie and Steffie helped dish up the meal and brought it to the table. Everyone had mashed potatoes with gravy. The small piece of moose meat that Julia had browned to make the flavourful sauce was on Karl's plate.

"Julia, this is amazing how you've made a big dinner for six of us from this one piece of meat. The gravy needs some spicing up, and noodles would have been good, but I know you like potatoes. People from the farm always do. In the city they prefer noodles. It's more refined. Not such peasant food."

Juergen said, "I like potatoes."

"Me too," said Lena, "but I like noodles too."

"Well, I've always believed potatoes belong in the cellar." Karl smiled at the younger children. Lena and Juergen laughed, but the two older girls looked down at their plates, tight-lipped.

"What?" Karl looked at the faces around the table in mock innocence. Then he waved his hand dismissively. "Oh, go ahead and enjoy your potatoes. You can't help it if you're peasants."

The rest of the meal passed in silence. Julia's guilt over Michael was quickly replaced with silent anger at Karl. Why did he always have to be so cutting with his remarks? Did he think that by putting them down, he was building himself up? Maybe he was, in his own eyes, but not in anyone else's.

Karl had gone into the living room with Sofie who had reluctantly agreed to play a game of chess. Julia sighed to think she had tied herself to this man who said hurtful things as easily as other people said, "Good morning and how are you today?" He didn't even seem to notice how often and how much he hurt her and her older daughters. But she had three of his children now, and she loved them as fiercely as she loved her first two. She had no wish to deprive them of a father. After all, he was good to the younger children and did his best to provide for them. She would simply have to bear it. *For better or worse. Till death do us part.*

40.

The summer solstice of 1954 came and went. By early evening it was still light enough to read a book outside, but Julia was too restless for any sedentary activity. She put Reinhard into the baby buggy. "I'll be back by 10:00," she told Steffie. "You can put the kids to bed about 9:00, all right?"

"Yes, have a nice walk, Mutti."

A light west wind brought relief from the heat of the day and now the temperature was pleasant for a stroll. Julia craved time alone, away from her constant responsibilities, and had begun to stay out longer and longer in the evenings. She looked forward to these precious fragments of the day when she could indulge in introspection. She argued with herself about her feelings. She owed Michael. He had paid for their trip to Canada; that was a big debt. But she also felt she owed him for what happened twenty-two years ago. She had tossed him aside when Lukas came along. Michael had been busy with the bakery then and it was a long walk to come to visit her. She had been impatient and married Lukas instead. And yes, she loved Lukas. Maybe she was only infatuated with Michael at the time. And yet after all these years, he could still set her heart racing. The evening of the dance, when he officially handed her over to Lukas, she knew he was hurt, but he stepped aside like a gentleman. Did she want someone who would step aside? Maybe she would rather have someone who would fight for her. Like Lukas. Like Karl?

She pushed the buggy past the shops that had closed hours ago; past the post office and the Hudson's Bay store, until she was almost out of the downtown area. The evening stillness of the town calmed her after a busy day of cooking and cleaning. As she left the empty shops behind and followed the wide footpath past the soapbox derby hill, she took deep breaths of the fresh air. A robin sang the last of its evening serenade. In the background she heard the muted sounds of the occasional vehicle. Otherwise all was still. Peace for her mind.

A white Pontiac station wagon pulled up beside her. Julia's stomach fluttered and her face felt hot as she recognized Michael in the driver's seat.

"How do you like my new car?"

"Very fancy. Another station wagon, I see."

"It's handy for delivering the baking to the other stores that sell it. It's also handy for carrying bulky things like baby buggies. Hop in. I'll give you a ride."

Julia looked around. "I don't know. I wouldn't want to be seen in your car. Karl would be furious if he found out."

"I'll make sure no one sees us. We can take a little drive out of town. We're almost out of town already." He opened the back of the station wagon. Julia picked up Reinhard, and Michael loaded the buggy. She sat in the front seat and sank down as low as possible.

Michael drove quickly until they cleared the last of the buildings at the edge of town and then slowed to a leisurely speed. "You can get up now. No one around."

"I don't know what I'm doing here." *I must have been crazy to get into Michael's car. I'm letting my heart do my thinking for me.*

"You're making me happy." He reached over and took her hand.

Michael pulled onto a side road and stopped beside a wheat field. A wooded area on one side of the dirt track hid the car from the main road. "I want to show you how versatile the back of the car is." He grinned. "It has better uses than carrying bread and baby buggies." He got out and removed the buggy. "You see how the back seat folds down. Now there is even more room." Julia had stepped out of the car, leaving Reinhard asleep on the front seat. She watched as Michael arranged the back. "I thought that if I'm ever stranded somewhere I could sleep in it. Would you like to help me try it out?" She was not surprised when he took her in his arms. She tried to tell herself it was not what she wanted, but his embrace was warm and soothing—a touch she craved, a touch that was missing in her life with Karl.

"Michael, I was going to try to avoid meeting you, but—" She felt tears welling and wanted to melt into him.

"Sh-h-h!" He stroked her hair. "Why would you want to do that? I've loved you for so many years, Julia."

"But, Michael." She took hold of the hand that was caressing her. "You've had other women in your life. I mean that's your right, but still, how can you keep saying you've loved me all along?"

"Yes, I have, but when I'm with them, all I think about is you. I missed my chance with you because of Lukas."

"But why did you let me go? When Lukas came along I hardly saw you anymore."

"I-I don't know. Everything seemed impossible at that time. My father died. The bakery was foundering. You lived a good hour's walk away. I should have tried harder to keep you. I'll never forgive myself for that."

"Times were harder then, it's true."

"Then I had to leave or be shot, and before I could find you, you were married again." He caressed her cheek with the back of his fingers and traced the outline of her chin. "But I never stopped thinking about you and, deep in my heart, I never stopped loving you."

Julia glanced at Reinhard sleeping soundly on the front seat. "Still asleep," she whispered as she let herself be persuaded into the makeshift bed.

"Still my lovely nightingale," he said afterwards. "Always my nightingale."

"Michael, we have to stop this. It can never work for us."

Julia started to get up, but Michael put a hand gently across her shoulder. "Why, when we love each other, when it feels so good and so right?"

"I feel guilty. I know this is wrong. Why can't I just say no?"

"It might have something to do with the way Karl treats you. I've heard him put you down, and he never has a good thing to say about your older girls."

"No, he doesn't see how special they are."

"And I know you're not happy."

"Oh, Michael. I have to learn to be happy." Julia sat up and straightened her clothes. "I have three of his children." She slid towards the open back of the station wagon and got out.

"I'll look after them." Michael followed her out and reached for her. "Divorce him and marry me."

"He would never let me have the children and I could never give them up."

"Julia, I can't give you up either."

"It's a bit late for that now. I'm tied to Karl whether I want it or not."

Michael took her in his arms and kissed her. He hugged her tightly until Julia pushed him away.

"It's no use, Michael. I can't lose my children." She picked up Reinhard and held him as they sat in silence for the ride back into town.

"I'll drop you off a block from home behind these buildings. No one would think to be looking for you there. Then you can continue your stroll with the baby buggy and be home on time."

"Yes, thanks." It all felt so sordid, making love in the back of a car, sneaking around in back alleys. "Along here will be fine. But Michael—"

"Don't say it, please." He placed his hand on her thigh.

"We can't do this anymore. And please stop tempting me. You know I want to say yes and you know it's an impossible situation. You're making it harder for me, and there can only be trouble ahead."

41.

In April of 1955 Rosalie Werner was born. Her dark baby hair might become lighter as it grew in thicker, but those eyes…. Julia had been afraid of this. *Oh God! Karl will be furious.* She knew she could remind him that she had dark hair herself and hazel eyes, but Rosalie's eyes were dark as midnight.

Julia held her tiny baby close. The flailing little arms and baby grunts and cries stilled as she nursed her. This baby needed her protection. For a few seconds, Julia was lost in a fantasy of running away to live with Michael, but she discarded that thought almost as quickly as it came. What of her other children? She could never leave them. She dreaded the moment when Karl would see the baby. He would be devastated. If they had any chance of reviving their love, this birth had destroyed it. If they could manage to stay together, there would be turmoil and pain, but no matter how her marriage troubles played out, it didn't change the fact that this baby needed her. Julia loved her children. She would die for any of them, especially this one.

She almost had to laugh when she remembered the doctor telling her that she should not have any more children. Easy to say, but how to prevent them? Her heart was causing him some concern, the doctor had said. He was afraid it would not be able to take the strain. He didn't have to tell her. She knew her heart had broken a long time ago.

Karl appeared in Julia's hospital room smiling. He bent down to kiss Julia in her bed. If he noticed her tears, he didn't say. *Maybe he's assuming they're tears of joy, like his.* She groaned inadvertently, in anticipation of the scene to come.

"Does it hurt?"

"No, I'm fine. Don't worry about me."

"Can I see the baby?"

"The nurse is changing her just now. She'll be right back with her."

"I'm so glad you're okay. I think we should make this our last baby. We have enough now, don't you think?" Karl seemed so concerned for her health. Julia dreaded the moment that would dash everything.

"Here's your little darling." The nurse placed the baby in Julia's arms. "Now, if there's nothing else you need, Mrs. Werner, I'll give you and your husband some privacy."

Karl bent over to touch the baby's cheek. His hand stopped in mid-air. He straightened up again and his eyes flitted from the baby's to Julia's. The twitch in Karl's eye went crazy.

"Why?" he choked out. "Just tell me why?"

Julia turned her head away, her tears soaking the pillow. Her body convulsed with sobs.

"Karl, I'm so sorry." She turned her head to face him again, but he was already gone.

As she expected, their marriage hovered dangerously close to divorce. Julia was mentally exhausted from the strain of worrying for months that this baby might not be Karl's. Now that Rosalie was born, Julia worried that Karl might take his anger out on the baby. Subconsciously she guarded her night and day, ready to protect her at the slightest hint of a threat, not that Karl had ever given her any overt reason to fear for the child's safety.

Karl stayed late at work. He came home to eat and left again to go to his English for New Canadians class. When he came home, he went straight to bed, often on the couch. They lived almost as strangers.

As spring turned into summer, it was Julia who avoided home. She took her children to the school playground to play on the swings and in the sandbox while she pushed the little ones in the buggy.

One day while Lena and Juergen were playing outside, Karl threw his hands in the air and said, "Julia, we can't go on like this. It's not a life."

"Are you saying you want a divorce?" She was annoyed that she couldn't hide the tremor in her voice. The thought of Karl deserting her, in spite of his faults, filled her with terror. Of course, there was Michael. But would life with Michael be all she hoped it would be, if Michael still wanted her, that is. She felt as powerless as a leaf in the wind.

"No, I'm saying we need to talk about our problems. They aren't going away by themselves."

Julia's shoulders relaxed and sagged a bit. The idea of running to Michael had been fleeting and unrealistic. She was relieved that Karl hadn't said he wanted a divorce. She didn't want to lose her children. Karl would never let her take Lena, Juergen, and Reinhard. In spite of her entanglement—entanglement, what a word....

Be honest, Julia, she scolded herself. *You love Michael, always have.* But Karl had been the one who helped her to rebuild her life when she had nothing left. His war wound still caused him a shortness of breath when his lungs had to work hard. Yes, he had a limp, but he was a proud man. He might have a slight streak of cruelty. Still, she admired his strength of character. She knew he must find Rosalie's birth a bitter pill to swallow. And she knew that he needed her to help him mend what she had broken.

"All right," she said slowly. She sank down onto a chair at the arborite table, not trusting her legs to support her.

He took a seat across from her. "I want us to have a fresh start. Move away from this apartment. I've asked about a loan. There's a house being built and the contractor is in a bind. He needs to sell it, so the price is right. We'd have our own place."

"Where?"

"It's on the outskirts of town. There isn't even a road there yet, just a track through a grassy field, but it will have a road by the time the house is finished. What do you think?"

"What about Rosalie?"

"No one needs to know she's not mine. I'll continue to raise her like our own." Julia sensed him swallowing the lump in his throat, struggling for dignity. "You could leave. Take Rosalie and go live with Michael. Sofie and Steffie would like that. But I know you wouldn't leave our children and I'll never let you take them. I think our best chance is to stay together."

Julia got up and went around the table to stand behind Karl. She didn't want him to see the pain or resignation in her face. She put her arms around his neck and put her cheek against his. "I'm so sorry I've hurt you, Karl." She loved Michael, but there was no denying that Karl was being magnanimous and she loved him for that. Her tears dripped down Karl's cheek. "Let's try to make it work."

In October Sofie's husband, Brent, helped the family move into the new house. Julia was pleased to see Sofie so happy. She thought it was very practical of her to marry someone with a skill and a steady job. Brent had his welding ticket, a small apartment, and a new, used truck. They reminded Julia of herself with Lukas more than twenty years earlier. Brent had an easygoing way of indulging Sofie's every wish. They teased each other and laughed and hugged, obviously in love. Sofie had married for the right reasons and Julia hoped it would bring her daughter the happiness that had been so fleeting in her own life.

Karl and Julia's house, though unfinished, was ready enough to live in. The floor was still bare plywood. The walls needed to be paneled. They had concentrated on getting the upstairs completed. The basement with its spare bedrooms could be finished later. They were not needed immediately, since Sofie had married. Steffie too had moved out. She had a job as a clerk in the Hudson's Bay store and had taken a room with a girlfriend.

"This will do for us," Julia said, as she put sheets on their new bed, part of a bedroom suite from Sears. "The children can manage in one bedroom and we have ours. Later, as they get older, they can have their own rooms downstairs."

Karl agreed. "It may be a bit crowded for them right now, but it's just for sleeping. There's plenty of room for them to play in the kitchen and living room."

"It's huge! I've never had such a big kitchen." Julia beamed. Since her home in Saaz had been taken away, she had not owned a house. It had been camps, rooms, or apartments. What a luxury to have so much room, especially in the kitchen. "I'll make you lots of good dinners in it," she promised.

Karl hugged her. "I love you," he whispered.

Julia's eyes filled with tears. It had been so long since Karl had said anything loving. Perhaps he could forgive her in time.

"We'll make it work," she said. As she hugged him, she looked past him through the window and saw a white Pontiac station wagon crawling past on the road.

42.

"Mutti, I saw Uncle Michael at the Five Cents Store," Lena said.

"Oh? Were you talking to him?" Julia stuck her head around the corner of the kitchen into the living room to make sure no one was within hearing distance. Lena often brought home messages from Michael and, although Julia yearned for them, she dreaded them too. What if Lena blurted out something at the wrong time?

"He asked how you were doing and said to say hello to you. That's all."

"Lena, you know that you mustn't say anything in front of your father."

"I know. He doesn't like it that Uncle Michael likes you. I figured that out a long time ago."

"Thanks, Lena." Oh, God what was she doing? Dragging her daughter into the whole mess. Forcing the poor girl to make impossible decisions. Lena loved her father but she liked Michael too. So unfair to put her in that position but ... *I'm that desperate. I need someone on my side.*

"But why does he always drive past our house? I've seen his car go by here lots of times."

"It's hard to explain. Michael and I were friends a long time ago, even before Sofie and Steffie were born."

"Whoa! That's a long time. So was he your boyfriend then?"

"Yes, but as I said, that was a long time ago."

"So why did you marry Sofie and Steffie's dad instead?"

"Well, Michael was sweet. Very sweet. But I was really shy and Michael was much more confident. His voice was strong and clear and when someone said something funny, he laughed loudly. It wasn't really that loud, thinking back on it now, but I was so painfully shy, it seemed loud to me. People would look to see what was so funny and I was embarrassed by all the attention. And Lukas was always there asking me out, while Michael was busy with his father's bakery. When Lukas came along, he was charming and he was much quieter. More like me. So Michael and I broke up. I think he was very sad about it for a long time, especially when Lukas and I got married."

"That would be sad for him," Lena said, "but it's a good thing you finally met Vati, or I wouldn't be here."

"That's for sure." Julia gave her a short fierce hug. She was growing up so fast, almost fourteen now.

They turned at the sound of shouting and looked out the kitchen window. The white car was there again at the side of the road, the driver's door wide open.

Julia watched in horror as Michael and Karl grappled with each other in the middle of the street. It was over before she had time to run to the door. Karl pushed his way into the house, red-faced, and as wild-eyed as an enraged bull. From the window Julia saw Michael jump into his car and take off, tires spitting gravel.

"That son-of-a-bitch!" Karl shouted. "I showed him."

Julia motioned with her head for Lena to leave the room. She got a basin of water and a washcloth and bathed Karl's head and neck. Deep scratches like claw marks ringed his neck and red welts covered his cheeks and forehead. Julia talked to him gently and cleaned his wounds. "It will be all right, Karl," she said softly, over and over. "It will be all right. Why don't you go lie down for a while? Everything will be all right."

Julia! Come in." Michael's eyes were wide with surprise. "What's wrong?"

"What's wrong? Nothing more than the usual. You know the situation is getting ugly and it can't go on like this. Michael, I can't bear to see you and Karl fighting in the street."

"Yes, I know. So have you come to be with me at last?" He reached for her arm and looked so hopeful that Julia hated to tell him the purpose of her visit. She stepped back.

"Karl has allowed me to come here to talk to you one last time." She saw Michael's bruised eye and felt faint. She took a deep breath and tried to relax her tight throat. "It has to stop." Her eyes welled up with tears.

"What has to stop? I can't stop loving you just because Karl says so. Believe me, Julia, if I could have made it stop, I would have done that years ago and saved myself a lot of pain." He had bared his feelings for her and left himself vulnerable to any attack she might launch. But they both knew she would never do that. She fought the urge to hug Michael to take his pain away.

"It has to stop," she repeated. Why couldn't he help her and make this easier? In his eyes she saw a reflection of her own desire to run away together. She had to fight the urge to give herself over to him. "Please, Michael. Stay away." She knew her voice lacked conviction.

"You have our child, Julia. We're tied forever."

"Then what's to become of us? My life with Karl is miserable. Every time he looks at Rosalie he is reminded of my time with you. He can never forgive me." She knew she was being unfair, asking Michael to stay away when deep inside she wanted him. But if *he* would only make the decision to stay away, she could go along with it.

"Then come live with me, Julia. Please! I would take good care of you. You know I would." He reached for her again, but she pulled away.

"I can't, Michael. Please, don't make this harder than it is." Tears streamed down her face. "You know I can't leave my other children. I just can't. And Karl won't give them up. It's an impossible situation."

"But they're getting older. How old is Reinhard now? Eight? And Lena and Juergen must be what? Fourteen and twelve?"

"That's right." She sniffled and stopped her sobbing to stare at Michael in surprise. "But how is it that you remember all that?"

"I think of you all the time. I know that Steffie is married now too, so both Lukas's children are out of your house. You and Rosalie could come live here."

"The children would miss each other. And I know they would be devastated if I left them. Not that I could live without them." She was thinking out loud, probably not making much sense to Michael. "Oh, what's the use of having this conversation? It can't happen. I only need you to stop."

"Julia...."

"Karl doesn't know about Lena passing messages," she pushed on, "but he knows about you driving by. People have been talking and he hears things that make him wild with jealousy. He's always in a temper and it doesn't make him easier to live with."

"What do you mean? Who's talking?"

"Everyone probably. But the other day Karl came home in a rage. He said that when he was delivering a repaired mixer to the Bay, Mr. Pollard, the manager there, took him aside and suggested that he keep a closer eye on his wife. He said he was just trying to offer helpful advice."

"Oh, shit." Michael frowned. "Well, that does it. I'm going to spit on their bread next time Mrs. Pollard comes in for a loaf."

Julia grimaced and wiped her tears. She felt a smile tug at the corners of her mouth. "It's not funny." But she pictured Mrs. Pollard biting into Michael's spit-on bread.

"No, it's not." Michael sighed. "Julia, I've spent my whole life regretting that I let you go. I think if I keep trying, it has to happen for us someday." Julia looked at the floor. He reached for her again and pulled her close. She felt the warmth that was missing in her marriage and it almost broke her resolve. Tears ran down her cheeks and she tried in vain to find something to say. Something to lessen his pain. Something to heal their broken hearts. But it was Michael who spoke first.

"Look. I can see I'm only hurting you more. I'll stop driving past your house hoping to catch a glimpse of you, and I'll stop asking Lena to give you messages, but I will ask her how you are doing. I do promise you one thing, Julia. I will never stop loving you or stop hoping you'll come to me someday, because I simply can't do otherwise."

Julia collapsed in his arms and cried against his shoulder, sobs that came from deep within her. He put his hand on the back of her head and she remembered the first time he had spread his fingers through her hair thirty years ago. He sighed as he reached for his handkerchief and gently dabbed at her tears.

"Someday I'll come for you, my nightingale. Someday the time will be right for us."

May 1963

The children were in school. Julia went down to the basement and filled the tub of the wringer washing machine through a hose connected to the sink. She pushed the lever to start the agitator. When the clothes were thoroughly washed, she fed the laundry, piece by piece, through the wringer into a laundry basket. She drained the washer and refilled it with rinse water, turned on the agitator again, and fed the laundry through the wringer once more to press out as much excess water as possible. She carried the heavy basket of wet laundry up the stairs and outside to hang it on a clothesline strung up between the house and a big conifer on the corner of the property. It was spring and the ground was muddy, but she put on her gumboots and walked along in the muck hanging up the clothes. She hoped the line would take the weight. Just to make sure, she found an eight foot two-by-four in the lumber pile in the backyard and propped up the clothesline with it, planting the two-by-four in the ground while the weight of the clothesline kept it standing fairly straight.

She came in and scraped her gumboots on a boot scraper in the porch. "What a job that was," she grumbled to herself. "Now to see to supper." She brought up a big bowl of potatoes from the cool bin under the basement stairs. In the kitchen she sat on a stool to rest her feet while she peeled potatoes.

"Listen to that wind," she said to herself. "Seems like it's always the same. 'Winds west at twenty' says the weatherman. Oh well, at least the clothes will dry fast." She peeked out the window at the clothes on the line.

"What?" She jumped up. "Oh NO! Oh, no, no, no, no!" Her morning's work lay strewn in the greasy clay gumbo. The ends of the clothesline dangled limply from the tree and the house.

Julia put on her boots and gathered up the muddy laundry, carried it all downstairs again. While the washer refilled, she sat on the edge of the bathtub nearby and cried.

Karl had had a trying day at work. The new boy who had been hired to help him in the repair shop was an idiot and Karl had told him so. He was in a foul mood when he arrived at home.

What the hell? "Julia? No supper? I don't smell anything cooking."

"It's going to be a bit late today."

"The one time I need a good meal to be on time. I had a terrible day. What have you been doing all day? All I ask is that you have a meal ready for me. Is that too much to ask?"

Julia glared at him. "Today, yes. It is too much."

"What's wrong?"

"Oh, never mind." Julia threw her hands into the air. "You don't want to hear all that housewife stuff."

She threw down the wooden spoon and stomped out of the kitchen.

"Have you even been home today?" he said to her back. "Has *he* been here while I was at work? Tell me!" The knuckles of his clenched fists were white and his voice trembled in anger.

"What are you talking about?" She spun around to face him and threw her hands in the air. "And hush, or the children will hear."

"I should have taken them away with me eight years ago." He knew his rising anger was steering them toward another blow-up, but he was too exasperated to care. It had been that kind of day.

"Karl! Damn it! What's wrong with you? I couldn't get supper ready in time because the laundry fell into the muck when the clothesline broke and I had to do it all over again. Now stop all this nonsense talk."

Karl was stunned by Julia's outburst. She rarely talked back to him, let alone used foul language. He slunk into the living room and sat down. The children were in their rooms, he assumed, so he lay back on the couch and closed his eyes. What in the world had come over him? He'd had a bad day and now he would have a bad night too. He had made sure of that with his paranoid accusations. Oh, if only he could turn back the hands of time. Ha! What would he do? How far back would he turn them? No sense staying in Germany. Nothing but starvation awaited them there in those postwar years. What would he do differently? Maybe be nicer to Julia? But he was, wasn't he? Except for just now, but that was her fault. Well, maybe it wasn't this time, but what did she expect him to think if she didn't have his supper ready?

He loved Julia so much but it seemed that all he could do was punish her. She had hurt him terribly. Maybe she hadn't done anything to hurt him today, but she probably thought about *him* all the time. And that child! The sight of her was salt in his wounds. But the affair was years ago. Why couldn't he let it go? He was too tired to think. He closed his eyes and drifted off.

Julia sat slumped at the table in defeat. Supper had been a failure. After her laundry disaster, there hadn't been enough simmering time for the chuck steak and the meat was tough.

She hadn't seen Karl so angry in years. She had thought he was getting over her affair with Michael. He had been tolerable to live with, even pleasant at times, but she supposed that most days, one look at Rosalie was enough to bring it all back. He had tried at first to treat Rosalie kindly, but she had known it couldn't last.

Reinhard and Rosalie were close in age and played together like best friends. Reinhard was a sweet boy and deserved his father's devotion, but it came at Rosalie's expense. Karl made a point of giving Reinhard all his attention. Rosalie got none. In any altercation between the two children, Karl was quick to blame Rosalie and it seemed to Julia that she always had to come to her daughter's defence. Julia tried to make up for the love that was missing in Rosalie's life with extra cuddling and attention. *Sofie and Steffie all over again,* she thought with a heavy sigh.

Vati," Lena said to him one Sunday morning. "How come you're still in bed?" Karl looked at his daughter and felt a surge of love and misery. "And where's Mutti?" He heard the fear in her voice.

"She's gone for a walk with Rosalie." In spite of his effort not to show his emotions, his eyes filled with tears.

"This early?" Lena studied her father more intently. "Is she coming back?" Karl sensed her rising panic.

"I think so." He turned his face away. "Of course she is."

Julia couldn't sleep. She stared at the ceiling in the darkness, mulling things over. She was tired of it all. Tired of trying to make the marriage work. She had seriously considered running to Michael. She and Rosalie had left the house early before anyone woke up. Rosalie asked a lot of questions at first, wondering where they were going.

"Just for a walk. Just you and me," Julia had said. They had a long quiet walk through the fields of prairie grass that started a block from their house and went on forever. Rosalie accompanied her wordlessly. Perhaps she accepted that her mother needed the quiet time. She seemed to enjoy having her mother all to herself, to judge by the loving grip of her little hand. In time the quiet whispering of the long grasses soothed Julia and she was able to go home again.

Except for meeting with Michael after he and Karl had fought in the street, Julia had no real contact with him for eight years. They'd had chance meetings in town when he appeared out of nowhere, but Julia doubted that there was much chance involved on Michael's part.

Those few times they exchanged whispered greetings, usually in the Co-op when she was shopping for groceries.

"How's my little girl?"

"She's fine. Please go away now before someone sees."

"I miss you."

"I have to go now. Take care of yourself." She dared not say more, lest she fan flames that would end up burning them both. That was the extent of their relationship, and after all these years, Karl was still crazy with hurt and jealousy. It was no use. She was too tired to go on.

She got out of bed and went to the medicine cabinet. She took what was left in the bottle of sleeping pills and lay back down in her bed.

Lena! Get up!" Karl shook her shoulders urgently. "Wake up. I need your help."

"What's going on?" She was still half asleep.

"Mutti took the wrong kind of pills last night. We have to keep her walking to make sure she doesn't fall asleep."

Lena bolted out of bed and ran to the kitchen looking to left and right, and then on to the living room. Her mother sat slumped over on the sofa with foam bubbling from her mouth. Karl was right behind Lena. "Let's get her up. You take one arm. I'll take the other." They got Julia walking between them like a drunkard, barely able to put weight on her feet at first. Around the kitchen, out to the living room, back to the kitchen again; anywhere to keep her moving. After half an hour, Julia began to take more of her own weight on her feet and her head stopped lolling around. She still had her eyes closed and bits of foam still bubbled around her lips, but she was more responsive to the questions they kept firing at her to keep her from losing consciousness. As Juergen joined the scene, he was ordered to make coffee quickly. At last Julia revived and the family relaxed.

"What happened to you, Mutti?" Lena asked, once her mother could speak again.

"Got up to take aspirin," Julia said with an effort. "Didn't want to turn on ... light ... wake anyone. Guess I opened ... wrong bottle. Took sleeping pills instead."

But Karl knew. And it shocked him to think that she had tried to kill herself. At the same time he admired her for lying to her children to spare them future worry. He felt profoundly guilty for not letting her forget how she had hurt him. So many years he had tortured her to make sure she shared the pain she had caused him by her betrayal.

Perhaps the time had come to let it go. Perhaps a change of scene? A change of some sort was definitely needed. Why not a move? This town had only brought them unhappiness. Perhaps in a new place without all the old memories he could begin to forgive her.

43.

"Moving?" Julia stopped stirring the stew, put down the wooden spoon, and turned to face Karl. "Moving where? What are you talking about?" Her first thought was that Karl was playing a joke on her, but then she saw the smug look on his face. He was serious.

"I've accepted a job with a repair shop in Nanaimo and we're moving." Karl raised his chin ever so slightly, as if daring her to challenge him.

"Nanaimo? But why haven't we talked about this? What makes you think I want to move?" Julia felt as if the bottom had dropped out of her world. Karl's body language and tone of voice had a belligerent edge that told her she would gain nothing by arguing. It was a *fait accompli*. Helpless frustration was a feeling she thought she had left behind in the war years, but here it was again, her life controlled by others. She wanted to shout at Karl, hit him, fight, but what good would that do? Struggling against the inevitable was futile.

"It really doesn't matter what you want in this case. We have to leave if we want our marriage to work."

Julia stared at the kitchen counter. Her heart pounded and her mouth felt dry. *I'll never see Michael again.*

"You'll never see Michael again." Julia's head jerked up to look at Karl.

"No," she said. "I won't." *I won't ever see him again.*

"You really don't have a choice, Julia. The children are coming to Nanaimo, and if you want to live with them, it will be in Nanaimo."

An invisible weight pressed on her chest. Her heart raced wildly. She cast about for arguments to change his mind, but his jaw was set and she knew it was hopeless.

February 1964

Karl had packed a few clothes, his tools, and his personal toiletry items. He kissed his children goodbye. Julia walked him to the waiting taxi.

"Take care of the children and yourself, Julia. I'll let you know when I find a house for us."

"Phone when you get to Nanaimo."

"Yes, all right. And Julia ... remember that I love you with all my heart." Karl looked near tears. "It's the reason I'm doing this. I feel it's our last chance."

"I love you too, Karl. Now hurry or you'll miss that bus." She gave him a kiss on the cheek and a quick hug. She did love him, she told herself. They had so much history, and not all of it was bad, but this would be the end of any contact with Michael, her one thread of hope when things went wrong. Could she live without ever seeing him again?

Don't worry about everything so much, Mutti." Sofie had come over for a visit when Julia told her about the move. "It will be good for you to have a new start."

"A new start? *Another* new start." Start to what? she wondered. Julia was anguished by the events that Karl had set in motion. Everything was happening too fast for her. Her life was being uprooted again. She didn't know how many times she could keep starting over, leaving parts of herself behind each time. Soon there would be nothing left. She would be lost.

"Won't you consider moving too?" Julia made a frantic effort to hold on to the comfort of having family close by.

"There's no question of me going to Nanaimo. At least not right now. Brent has a good job with the welding company and the children are happy at school with their friends. We're building a good life for them here. If we moved we would have to begin all over looking for a job, a home, friends for the kids."

"Of course, I understand. It's just that I'll miss you all so much. Steffie said she doesn't want to leave either. She's got her friends and her husband." Julia did understand, but it was so hard to leave the girls.

"Sofie, I know Brent is good to you. It reminds me of the life I had for a while with your father when you and Steffie were little. Then the war changed everything." If Sofie had a chance for happiness, Julia wished with all her heart that she could find it and keep it. "I want what's best for you, but I don't know what I'll do without you." She fought back the tears she felt building.

"I know, Mutti. I'm going to miss you too … terribly. But you'll be fine after a while." Sofie hugged her mother.

Julia sighed and resigned herself to losing this battle. "I hope you remember how to write a letter."

"I'll be writing you a lot of letters, Mutti." She gave her mother a kiss on the cheek. "We'll save up our money and come to visit you when you're settled. Steffie said the same thing. Maybe we'll come together."

"I'll look forward to that." Tears prickled again. Would she really see her daughters again? Nanaimo was a long way from Dawson Creek. "I'm happy for you, Sofie. Happy that you have a man you love, who is good to you. I hope you know how precious a treasure that is. Hang onto that and don't let anyone take it away."

The Mayflower moving van was late. Julia, Karl, and the four children had slept on the hardwood floor of the living room for two nights already. Before that, they had slept on the bus for the twenty-three-hour ride. They all wanted their beds.

The house was typical of the style popular in Nanaimo's coal-mining pioneer days. Four square posts supported a huge covered veranda. The massive front door of heavy oak was almost three inches thick. Bookcases with leaded glass doors and brass handles served to partition the living room and dining room. Ten-foot ceilings threatened to trap any heat up high if the hot water radiators ever actually warmed the place. It was an old house, but well built, and Julia could see that it had potential.

For three days Juergen had kept sporadic watch from the front yard. "Here comes the van at last!" he yelled. "Yippee!"

"All our stuff!" Lena bounced up and down on the balls of her feet.

On the veranda Reinhard and Rosalie stared in awe as the huge rig backed up to the walkway and movers unloaded furniture and boxes.

"I hope they're careful with my new violin." Rosalie craned her neck and wrung her hands. "I wanted to bring it with me on the bus, but Mutti said the movers promised to take care of it."

Reinhard rolled his eyes. "I guess we can't hope to be lucky and have them drop Lena's old piano on it."

Rosalie gave him a slap on the shoulder. "My playing's not *that* bad." But Reinhard wasn't through with her yet. He cavorted around her playing an imaginary violin, making screeching noises.

Julia directed the movers and reminded the children to keep out of the way. "Stop that horsing around. You're making me nervous. Save your energy to help unpack as soon as the movers are finished here.

"Oh, Karl, I'm so glad they came. I don't know if I could take another night on that hard floor."

"That makes two of us. But tonight we'll all sleep in comfortable beds."

"It's an old house, but I can see that it will be perfect for us," she said. "There's even room for a little garden at the back. A few potatoes would be nice."

"Potatoes belong in the cellar." He quickly added a wink.

"Now, Karl. Don't start that old song again. I'm going to have my little potato patch and that's that. You could say I need to put down roots."

"Well, if you put it that way, I'll even help you dig a little bit." Karl gave her shoulder an affectionate squeeze.

The family had decided to walk the two blocks to town and find a place to watch the Victoria Day parade. Karl had the little ones by the hand, as usual giving most of his attention to Reinhard and barely looking at Rosalie. *I suppose I can't expect anything else from him.*

As always, Julia's stomach burned with worry for her neglected daughter.

Juergen swaggered out the door with his hands in his pockets. Almost fifteen he was beginning to give orders more often and take them less. "Come on, Mutti! The parade is going to start in a few minutes."

"Yes, Juergen. Just hold on a minute. I have to find the right key to lock the door." Julia fumbled in her purse. Lena tapped her foot and waited for her mother.

"We'll go ahead and you can catch up." Juergen jumped down the four steps to the sidewalk and ran to catch up to Karl, Reinhard, and Rosalie.

A roar followed by an explosive blast shook the door and windows of the house. Julia felt the blood draining out of her face. She looked at her children. Yes, they were all right. But the bomb? What happened?

"Wow! Mutti! Did you see the jets? That must be because of the parade," Lena said. "Mutti? What's wrong? You're crying! What is it?"

Julia ran into the house and threw herself sobbing onto the couch. Lena sat down and put an arm around her mother. "What's wrong?"

"Oh...." Julia took a deep breath and choked back another sob. "For a second I was right back in the war. I thought we were getting bombed."

"Oh, Mutti." Lena gave her mother a hug. "It must have been terrible."

"You can't imagine how terrible," Julia said, "but I'm thankful that you can't. I hope you never find out how terrible war is."

"Try not to think about it now." Lena patted her back. "Let's go to the parade and everything will be fine again."

"I think I need a drink of water first." Julia clutched at her chest. "I feel like I swallowed a rock."

"You do look a bit grey. I'll get you that water."

The door flew open and Juergen stuck his head in. "Come on. Are you guys coming? Let's go. Did you see those Voodoo jets? Wow! Hey, what's wrong?"

"Nothing, Juergen. Mutti needs to catch her breath for a minute. Thought you'd gone on? You go tell the others we'll be there in a few minutes, okay?" Lena ran to get the glass of water.

Julia writhed and twisted her upper body to try to rid herself of the pain that was creeping up her chest to her throat. It would pass. It always did.

Once again music filled the Werner house. Lena was home from university for the summer. She played favourite songs from a well-worn choir book. In making those difficult decisions over what to bring to Canada, this songbook was a treasure Julia had not been able to leave behind. She and Karl had sung from it with the Koenigshofen choir group, those first years after being in the refugee camp. It contained many of the choir songs Julia had sung in the days when she had first met Michael and Lukas—a treasured thread to memories from her young life.

As Lena tinkered on the piano, Julia hummed along. "Why don't you play that song we all like, Lena? You know the one where we each have our voice. You can sing the soprano part while you play." She turned to find Karl in the living room. "Karl, come over here by the piano. You can do the bass part."

"Oh, Mutti, you know I can barely manage to hit all the right notes on the keyboard without trying to sing too. It's like trying to rub your stomach and pat your head at the same time." Lena stuck her head around the corner and hollered up the stairs. "Rosalie! Bring that screech box down here with you. We need you to drown out my playing."

"Let's just give it a try," Julia said after Rosalie had joined them. "I really like this song. It reminds me of the old days." *When Michael played his violin so beautifully and we were in love.*

"All right, here goes." Lena took a deep breath and struck the chords that took Julia back so many years.

Karl leaned over Julia's shoulder to read the words. Julia's mellow alto voice was soothing. It softened and strengthened the thin soprano of the two girls and smoothed the rough edges of Karl's gravelly bass. The harmony of their voices sent a shiver of pleasure through Julia's body. Music had always been a big part of her life, but in these past troubled years, no one had felt much like singing. How wonderful it was to have music in the house again.

When the song was over, Lena turned around and smiled at her parents and gave Rosalie's hand a squeeze. Karl hugged Julia who smiled from her heart. She always made it a policy to try to look happy no matter what troubled her, but at this moment she felt genuine contentment.

Wanting to make it last, Julia suggested two other songs that she knew her daughters could play well, and the atmosphere of the whole evening was one of love and happiness.

The next day Julia's good mood crashed. Rosalie came home from school and found her crying. "Mutti! What happened?"

"Nothing happened, Rosalie. Don't worry. I'm sorry. We had such a nice time singing yesterday and I was listening to the radio for more music. You know this song, 'I'm so lonely. I have nobody'? I think it's Bobby Vinton."

"You mean 'Mr. Lonely'?" Rosalie asked.

"Yes, I guess that's what it's called. I was listening to it and I started to feel so sad. It's silly, I know, but I felt like he was singing about me."

Rosalie hugged her mother. "Oh, no. Don't feel like that. You've got us."

"But you're at school." *And Michael isn't here.*

"You should try to go out more."

"I don't know anybody." *My English is terrible. People will laugh at me. I can't do it without Michael.*

"Vati wants to go out when people invite you."

"I don't have the right clothes for going out." Julia raised her arms and dropped them slackly at her sides.

"Mutti, come out into the garden. Show me your potatoes. You know how Vati loves potatoes. Let's see if we have enough to put in the cellar this winter ... where they belong." They laughed and went out into the warmth of the sunshine.

"I love my garden," Julia said. "Thanks for dragging me out here to remind me." She gave Rosalie a hug. "And I love you—and all my children." She sighed. *But it's not enough to fill my life.*

August 1973

Let's go, Julia." Karl carried their small overnight case out to the car.

"Yes, yes. Just wait a minute. I have to make sure the cat has enough food and water. We won't be back until late tomorrow." Wasn't it always like that? Men could just walk out the door. Women had to make sure everything was secure and the plants and animals cared for. "Just need to find my crossword puzzle to take along and then I'm all set." She knew Karl was already outside, but she didn't mind talking to herself.

"I'm so glad you're coming along." Karl opened the car door for her. "It's a long trip to Courtenay and I can't possibly fix all the appliances they have lined up for me in one day. We can make a little holiday out of it."

"Are you sure the company doesn't mind me coming along with you?"

"As long as I pay the extra expenses like your hotel bed and your meals, they don't mind. I've cleared it with them, so you don't have to worry."

As they pulled out onto the highway, Julia said, "We couldn't have done this a few years ago, but now even Reinhard and Rosalie are gone. Only the cat will miss me if I'm not home."

"It's lucky for the children that Malaspina College is open now. They don't even have to leave town to go to college like the older two did. But I don't see why they had to move out. They could have stayed at home and not had to pay rent."

"They want to be able to have their friends in and have some privacy. Don't you remember when you were young, Karl, how nice it was to be independent?"

"I was glad to be out of the house, but it was different for me. I didn't have a nice home. Why don't our kids want to be home?"

Julia sighed. She didn't want to start a discussion that would no doubt escalate into an argument, especially while Karl was driving. If only he were not so quick to put her down all the time, it would have been easier for the children to bear. She remembered mealtimes when everyone lost their appetite because of his continual sniping. The gravy wasn't spicy enough. The cake was too sweet. The cake wasn't sweet enough. Not potatoes again! The noodles were too mushy—what did she think—that he had no teeth? What did he expect from someone who grew up in a small town? And so it went, the children wincing at her pain while she kept her mouth shut to preserve some kind of peace. In the end the children got into the habit of asking her quietly if they could eat their supper early so they wouldn't have to sit through the haranguing. That spared them some stress until one day Karl snapped, "And what kind of a household are you running? We don't even eat together like a normal family anymore." She gave her head a shake to try to rid herself of those thoughts.

"Julia? Are you all right?" Karl turned to look at her. She forced herself to smile and dragged her mind back to the present.

"It's certainly busy on the roads this morning, isn't it?" She hoped to distract him and drop the subject.

"I can't even see the front of the line of cars," Karl said. "Here's my chance!" He stomped on the gas pedal and yanked the steering wheel to the left. The Corolla lurched across the double-solid line.

Julia was thrown against the passenger door. She grabbed for the dashboard and the armrest of the door and gripped them so hard her knuckles turned white. She pressed her lips together and, although she no longer believed in God, her mind formed a prayer anyway.

Karl seemed oblivious to the angry honking of car horns directed at him. He pressed his back into the seat and extended his arms on the steering wheel until his elbows locked. Looking to the right as he passed car after car, he shouted at their drivers, "Old fools! Learn to drive!" Apparently he had forgotten all about looking to the front as he sat rigidly in his seat, yelling at one car after another.

Julia closed her eyes and thought of tomorrow, or the day after tomorrow, or any time beyond the present— some time in the future when she would not be in this bizarre situation.

Karl yanked the car back into line before an approaching pickup truck whizzed by them. The cars he had passed had all made allowances for him.

"We're not in a hurry, are we?" Julia asked. "Isn't this a working holiday?"

"What's that got to do with it?" Karl gave her a sharp look. "You want me to drive like them?" He mimicked an old man hunched over the steering wheel. "I showed them. I'm not going to put up with doddery driving. Well, it looks like we're going to be stuck behind the rest of the line now anyway, so you'll be happy about that."

"Of course not, Karl. I just want to get there alive."

"So you don't like my driving? Maybe you should take over the wheel then."

"Oh, Karl! Look, let's just try to enjoy the drive." She could feel her heart racing and her chest squeezing her again. Her head hurt and she wanted so badly to lie down. "I'm just going to close my eyes for a few minutes, okay?" She had little nitroglycerine pills that the doctor had given her, but over time she had found that her counting mantra worked almost as well. She put her head back onto the headrest and slowly counted in her mind, One ... Michael, two ... Michael, three ... Michael, four ... Michael...." Gradually the pain in her chest subsided and her headache faded.

44.

Michael sat in the dark. This was the very room where he had danced with her. He remembered the herbal scent of her hair, the softness of her cheek. He had dared to put his head close to hers for a moment when Karl wasn't looking. He played the old .78 RPM record he hadn't been able to throw out and listened to Vaya Con Dios again. With the back of his hand, he wiped away tears. Why was he still thinking about her? So many times he had picked up the phone, even dialed her number, only to put the receiver down before anyone answered. Even if he'd been lucky enough to have Julia answer the phone, what could he say?

The violin case leaned neglected against the wall in a dusty corner. He had played it the last time, alone in his apartment, the day Julia left for Nanaimo. He had played all their old favourites. But even the happy tunes had sounded like a funeral dirge to him and he'd collapsed in a withering mass of misery. The violin hadn't been out of its case now for nine years.

He retired from the bakery business the year after Julia left. He had worked hard all his life. And what did he have to show for it? Car, furniture, his apartments, some investments; but for all that, now at sixty-five, his life was still empty. No one waited for him to come home each night.

"Nanaimo?" he had said. He remembered how his heart had thumped at hearing the shocking news. "No! You can't go. It's too far. I'll never see you again." He had put his arms around her, felt her quaking body, hugged her close and cried, but those tears were nothing compared to the ones he had shed over her since then.

"Dammit!" He pulled himself up from the sofa, grabbed his canes and hobbled over to the closet. "I waited too long before and Lukas got her. Why didn't I learn then? I keep making the same mistake. Where did I put that satchel?"

45.

Julia softly exhaled one long quiet breath when Karl parked the Corolla in their driveway at last. Her home seemed to smile as it waited to envelope her in safety after their overnight trip to Courtenay. The potato plants waved to her. The pear tree stretched its branches to welcome her back. Julia scooped up Molly who had run to the door to greet her. She pressed the cat's head to her chest and murmured loving words to her.

"What a fuss you make over that animal." Karl let out a snort of disgust. "Why don't you make a pot of tea for us instead?"

Julia shook her head. A small sigh escaped her. She gave the cat a kiss and set her down with one last rub between the ears. She filled Molly's water dish and topped up her food. The cat arched her back and rubbed up against Julia's legs. Karl came in, kicked in the direction of the cat, and dropped their overnight bags close enough to send Molly scrabbling out of the kitchen.

"Kettle on?"

"Yes, in a minute. I thought I'd take my jacket off first. How about if we have just a sandwich for supper? I'm not feeling that hungry." Julia wanted to lie down and sleep for the night but she knew she had to make supper for Karl. Maybe he wouldn't be so cranky on a full stomach.

"Fine with me. I'll take it in the den. Call me when it's ready. I'm tired. Need to put my feet up." The recliner made a clunk as it snapped out of the upright position and creaked back under Karl's weight.

Julia put the kettle on. Quickly she made two ham and cheese sandwiches on rye bread. She served Karl his supper, but had no appetite for her own. Moments later she excused herself. "I think I'll go to bed."

"This early? It's not even eight o'clock yet." Karl looked at her with a puzzled scowl. "Come watch some TV with me for a while."

"All right. Just for a while, but I can't promise I can keep my eyes open. I'm so tired."

46.

*A*ll my life I've waited too long and missed my chances. Michael let his mind ponder various scenarios. *Action is what is needed. Action! Starting right now. I'm going to drive down there and knock on her door and if that mean old bugger answers the door, I'll demand to see her or punch his lights out.*

Michael mused over that image for a mile or so. *Ha ha, wouldn't that be the scene. No, I don't think that will work. Besides, after two hip operations, it might be my own lights that get punched out. Okay, think, Michael. You have another seven hundred fifty miles to come up with a plan.*

At 4:00 in the morning he pulled into a rest area near Prince George. He crawled into the back—thank God he had stuck with station wagons—stuffed a pillow behind his head, lay down on the foam mattress, and pulled his sleeping bag over himself. In minutes he was asleep.

Two hours later the pain in his hips woke him and he drove on. The radio kept him alert and with a nearly empty highway he kept the gas pedal floored. Quesnel, Williams Lake, Cache Creek; the towns flew past. He stopped only long enough to gas up, check the oil in his car, and grab a snack. At Hope he found a side road and pulled over for another quick nap.

He arrived at the Horseshoe Bay ferry terminal north of Vancouver in time to catch the 7:00 p.m. ferry to Nanaimo. Exhausted, he crawled into the back of his station wagon once again. The gentle rocking of the boat lulled him to sleep.

He dreamed of Julia then. She was with him in his bed at home. He had his arms around her gentle curves. His face snuggled into her neck. The fresh scent of her hair was intoxicating. "I love you, Julia," he mumbled into her neck.

"Me too," she said.

"Oh, you love you too?" He smiled.

"You know what I mean." She nudged him with her elbow.

He loved to tease her. She was always smiling. He had loved her forever and she never assumed that she deserved it. "Julia, will you sing for me? I'll dust off that violin and give it a quick tuning. It's been so long since I've heard your nightingale voice."

"I'd love to sing if you play the violin for me."

He began to play and she sang the words to their song, Vaya Con Dios. She sang about the dark hours when the town was sleeping and lovers were parting, weeping, wishing each other well on their journey. The words seemed to have been written especially for them.

Julia's lovely melancholy voice sang straight to his heart, promising to be beside him wherever he might be, promising to say a prayer to guide him and help him through the lonely hours of every lonely day.

She sang the last words of the song and stopped to look up at him. "Michael, what do they mean, 'the dawn is breaking through a grey tomorrow'?"

"Just don't think about that part of the song, Julia."

The earth began to shake and shudder then. Julia slipped from his arms and disappeared. He woke up to find himself in bed alone. He sat up and realized he was not in bed at all.

The ferry crewman shook Michael's station wagon one more time. "Time to wake up, sir. We'll be docking in Nanaimo momentarily."

47.

The next morning Karl sat up in bed and glanced at the clock. "Good Lord, eight o'clock already. I have to be at work in half an hour." He shook Julia's shoulder. "You forgot to set the clock, Julia. Hurry up. Get my breakfast. I have to get to work. It's late."

Julia didn't move. "Julia." He shook her again, harder. "What's the matter with you? Julia? Are you all right? Julia!?" His voice became tight and high-pitched. "Julia! NO! Oh God, no. Julia, please wake up." He shook her unresponsive shoulder again in one last attempt to awaken her before collapsing on top of her, his body convulsing as primal cries of pain broke through his sobs.

48.

The phone had been ringing all morning. In spite of being numb with shock and grief, Lena took charge. She put her father to bed with a tranquilizer and he cried himself to sleep at last. Sofie and Steffie called from Dawson Creek. Juergen called from Victoria and was on his way. Rosalie was in the kitchen making tea for Lena and Reinhard. The three of them sat at the breakfast nook off the kitchen, red-eyed and shattered. In the den the phone rang again. Lena struggled to place the familiar voice.

"Uncle Michael?" she whispered.

"Is it you, Lena?"

"Yes, but what are you doing, calling here? Where are you?"

"I'm at the Tally-Ho."

"Here!? In Nanaimo?"

"I'm so glad it's you who picked up the phone. I have to see your mother. Can you help me with that?"

Oh, God! He doesn't know. "You say you're at the Tally-Ho? That's just down the street. I'll come right down. Just wait for me there." Her head was spinning. "What room?"

She hung up then. *Oh, damn!* Lena stared at the phone in disbelief. Flashes of her mother and Michael in Dawson Creek. Michael, always asking about her mother, about Rosalie. Rosalie! She still had that letter to give to Rosalie.

"Rosalie," Lena called from the den. "I need you to come with me and don't ask any questions."

"But—"

"No questions. Just trust me. Okay?"

In Lena's car Rosalie turned to face her. "All right. What's going on?"

"When Mutti first found out she had heart problems, she gave me a letter. She told me to put it in a safety deposit box in my name and to give it to you if she should die."

"Why a letter for me and not you or Reinhard?"

"I think I know, but in case I'm wrong, I don't want to say anything until you read it. After you read it, I have to go meet someone and you can decide if you want to come with me or not."

They drove in silence to the bank and retrieved the letter. As they sat in the car at the bank parking lot, Lena watched her sister open the envelope and read. Rosalie's eyes widened. Her jaw went slack, and then she pressed her lips together. She chewed the corners of her lips, tears welled, and at last she dropped the letter in her lap and cried.

"Rosalie? What is it?"

"Here. Read it."

Lena nodded knowingly as she read her mother's familiar writing. She reached for Rosalie's hand and gave it a squeeze. "It doesn't make any difference to us. We're still sisters like we've always been. Nothing will change that."

Rosalie wiped at her eyes. "I've always known there was something ... that I was different somehow. Vati always favoured you, but I didn't blame him. I just thought it was because I wasn't good enough."

Lena hugged her sister. "Rosalie, don't ever think that. Of course you're good enough. Way more than good enough. You're so special to me." Lena hesitated. "Now ... there is something more.... That phone call? That was your father. I have to go meet him—"

"He's here? In Nanaimo?"

"Yes, and he doesn't know that Mutti has died."

Rosalie clapped her hand over her mouth. "Oh my God! This can't be real."

"It's going to be a huge shock to him."

"Why? You mean he loved her that much?"

"He's loved her forever. From the time Mutti was a teenager. He was her first boyfriend." Lena handed the letter back to Rosalie. "Do you want to see him?"

"But ... what about Vati?"

"We won't tell him. What good would that do? He's hurting enough already."

"I know. *He's* my father as far as I'm concerned." There was a long pause. "Uncle Michael? My father? This is so hard to believe!" Rosalie was staring into the space in front of her.

Lena chewed her lip and patted Rosalie's leg. "You must feel pretty mixed up right now."

"You could say that." She turned to face Lena. "Know what? Give him my address and phone number. If Mutti loved him, he must be a good person, but I'm just not ready to see him right now."

"You're right. You both need some time. I don't think he'll be in any shape to meet anyone after I tell him that the love of his life has just died."

"The love of *all* our lives."

The Pontiac station wagon remained parked at the crest of the hill for over an hour after the last of the mourners left Julia's plot. Michael got out and with the help of his two canes, made his way to the new grave. He stood there for a long time, head hanging and shoulders quaking. Every few minutes he wiped his forearm across his eyes. *Oh, my poor dear nightingale. Out of my reach forever. If only you could fly back to me.*

Two weeks later Michael called Rosalie. They arranged to meet at the room she was renting just down the road from the college.

"You look just like her." Michael looked around the room. "Is that a violin in that case?"

"Yes. Do you play?"

"I did. Yes. A long time ago. When I first met your mother."

Rosalie reached for her violin and held it out to Michael. "Will you play it for me?"

"May I?"

The End

About the Author

Anneli Purchase has written two previous books, *The Wind Weeps*, and *Orion's Gift*, and her articles on British Columbia coastal life are published in Canadian magazines.

She continues to write in her home on Vancouver Island and can be reached through her blogsite: http://wordsfromanneli.wordpress.com.